LAND OF NO RETURN

A Hollow Earth Adventure

Other Books by B.L. Morgan

Blood and Rain

Blood for the Masses

Blood on Celluloid

Blood and Bones

Night Knuckles

You Play, You Pay

Red Simon: Vampire Punk

LAND OF NO RETURN

A Hollow Earth Adventure

B.L. MORGAN

NEW WORLDS PUBLISHING

SEATTLE, WASHINGTON

2011

LAND OF NO RETURN

Copyright © 2011 B.L. Morgan

ISBN: 978-0615474717

Dedication: To Judi Morgan; the love of my life. Thank God you put up with me. If you didn't, I doubt anyone would.

Special Dedication to all the Science Fiction, Mystery, Horror and Action Adventure authors I have been reading every since I was a kid. Thanks for making my life much richer.

Foreword:

An Unconventional Meeting

June 2009
Crypticon Seattle

It was an exhausting convention. The people just seemed to keep coming and coming.

I was new to the horror convention circuit so I wasn't all that accustomed to being stared at non-stop for twelve hours a day. It does take some getting used to.

Right across from us was the actors Ken Foree and Michael Berryman. They're some really cool dudes. Not the scary guys you see in the movies. Although I think I probably looked scared to death of them for at least the first four hours. That's how it is being around celebrities for the first time. You expect them to be something like the roles they play in the movies.

That couldn't be more from the truth.

Berryman was an extremely intelligent, politically and socially conscious well spoken man. I totally enjoyed the talks we had with him. Ken, well he's a barrel of laughs. He kept us laughing the entire weekend.

No matter how tired all of us got from the endless stream of well-wishers and goggle-eyed fans he kept up a steady stream of jokes.

Believe me, we needed it.

These are some of the guys who keep the movie audiences on the edge of their seats their eyes glued the big screen, afraid of what they were going to see happen next and waiting eagerly for it.

Those two, along with Tom Atkins, Adrienne Barbeau, Reggie Bannister and my wife's favorite person the extremely classy Adrienne King kept us from being overwhelmed by our small touch of what it is like to be a celebrity.

It's a dirty job but somebody's gotta do it.

What, you might be asking by now, was I doing in the land of horror icons accepted as one of their own? I am an author; a guy who writes books, mostly in the horror field since it's easier to gross people out than to make them cry. This was the Crypticon Horror Convention: The largest...well to tell you the truth, the only horror convention in the state of Washington. Me and my wife Judi were there trying to get some much needed career development for the writing career as well as sell a few books.

The selling of the books had been going OK. People came out to see the celebrities and weren't afraid to slap down a few bucks to jaw for awhile and, at least in my case, get some pointers on how to get published.

Except for the exhaustion everything was going just fine and dandy. My wife was off taking in a panel on The Changing Role of Women in Horror. I was talking with a few people interested in the first two John Dark books and doing a pretty good sales pitch of it, if I must say so myself, when I caught sight of a peculiar looking guy out of the corner of my eye.

The guy was about the same height as me, around five foot ten. He was slim but he moved with a kind of quick cat-like grace that was almost like watching a ballet dancer. I would describe the age that the man was except that this man, more than anyone else who I have ever met in my life, seemed ageless. He appeared to have a natural maturity and sureness about him that was unmistakably the mark of world traveling and wide experience. But although he had the bearing of a knowledgeable middle-aged man in extremely good physical condition he had not one grey hair on his head and no lines upon his face. He appeared to be in the peak of health and judging from his body's wear and tear he could be no more than say, thirty-five years old.

This man was walking around looking at the different photos and items that the celebrities had for sale to sign on their tables. When he caught my eye this gentleman was at John Skipp and Cody Goodfellow's table checking out a few of the books they had laid out. Skipp is a legend of Splatter-Punk fiction and Goodfellow soon will be with the kind of novels he produces. I don't actually know exactly what caught my attention but I guess I went silent because suddenly one of the people conversing with me about Blood for the Masses was pulling on my sleeve and asking, "Pardon me. I was talking to you."

Snapping my mind back to my own table I think I muttered, "Oh shit, sorry."

The people at my table laughed.

I went red. "Guess you can tell I haven't slept much the last few days," I said.

Anyway, the people who I had forgotten existed were polite. They didn't slap the hell out of me for being so rude by forgetting they were there and the two people bought a copy of Blood and Rain. They walked away smiling, knowing that they had what might be the crudest and bloodiest detective horror novel in the Pacific Northwest.

And now the gentleman who evidently had been watching us the entire time locked eyes with me. With a sure step he marched directly to my table.

This was a guy who didn't waste time. He stuck his hand out and instantly said, "Call me Lin."

I shook his hand and out of habit started into my author's bookselling sales pitch.

He smiled. "That won't be necessary," He said. "I already know about your stuff and I know something else that you don't yet realize."

This, in a day of surprises, caught me by surprise. My eyes must have widened.

Lin went on. "You want to write a real adventure."

"Well, you know," I started. "I do consider my books to be adventures even though I market them primarily in the horror field. People like my graphic descriptions of the blood-letting so that's where they fit the best."

This made him smile wider. "That's not what I mean." He paused for effect, then went on when he knew he had my full attention. "You want the real thing. Stories of exotic lands, strange creatures, beautiful women, fearsome combat, dangers a plenty, and more than that you long for it to be real."

"Doesn't everybody?" I asked. I couldn't help myself. I launched into a speech that I had only recited in my head because it sounded so ridiculous that it seemed like anyone else hearing it would think that I was permanently a ten year old child or at least a brainless middle-age man wishing that he was. "I grew up reading Edgar Rice Burroughs, Robert E. Howard, Lin Carter and a whole lot of other guys that just took me to other worlds that were exciting to go to. At that age I loved reading because it was real to me. You get older and learn some stuff about the world and you find out that nothing in those books could have happened. Books kind of lose something when that happens to you. Yeah, I guess you are right. I would like to read or even write adventure stories that I could believe were real.

"But you do get older and you do find out, it just ain't possible."

4

I guess my sadness at a lost childhood that I figured could never be regained must have momentarily registered on my face because the gentleman in front of me seemed suddenly sad as well.

"What if I told you that all of the authors that you loved as a child were telling the truth," he asked me.

"As much as I'd like to believe you," I answered him. "I'd have to tell you that you are crazy, or maybe just full of shit."

His face went serious. Lin's eyes burned with a power that was beyond description. He spoke with a voice that held the authority of total belief. It was like someone tells you that the sun will come up in the morning or that the sky is overhead. He knew what he was telling me was totally true when he said, "Anything is possible and all those things happened."

Then he was gone as though he had never been there and I found myself looking forward into a blank space that I could have sworn the elegant man had occupied not one second before. I felt dizzy, disoriented, strangely out of sorts as though something had entered my world that I was not entirely ready to accept.

The man had been there and then he had not been there. Who had I been talking to?

Either I had just had a full-fledged hallucination or … or what? I didn't know what.

I looked over to Ken Foree to see if he'd seen the man that I had been talking to and where he'd gone. A woman with a short skirt had her leg up on Ken's table and he was signing her thigh.

Yeah, it's mighty tough being a celebrity.

I decided I would wait till later to ask him.

In front of me was something I had not noticed until that moment. There was a computer disc. Someone had left it there.

Through the clear plastic cover there was a hand written note:
Mr. Morgan:

Read this at your leisure. You have my permission to do with it as you wish. It's not my story. All good adventures belong to the world. See that the world receives it.

L.C.

Although I am not sure who Lin is, I do have my suspicions. I am going to try to do what Lin asked me to do.

"This story is not mine," The man had told me. "Anything is possible."

It's not mine either.

You be the judge.

Sincerely
B.L. Morgan

ON EARTH:

1.

A Few Miles East of East St. Louis Ill.

There are some people that the world can just do without.

I was one of those.

So when I vanished from the face of the Earth nobody asked why I was gone or where I'd went to.

My name is Derek Walker.

Nobody cared one way or the other about me.

That was the way I wanted it to be.

*

The man staring cross the blacktop at me was big and ugly as cancer. He weighed in at around two hundred and fifty pounds. Only a little bit of it wasn't rock hard solid muscle.

I grinned back at him.

I didn't care if he was a big ugly scarred up piece of pure meanness.

I was one hundred and eighty-five pounds of pure death. He was about to find that out.

It was a frigid pitch black sub-zero night and wind blew stinging snow in everybody's eyes. The crowd was all of one hundred strong.

On a night like this, on a deserted street in a never completed housing subdivision, that was a lot of people to have standing out in the cold in one spot.

A fat short guy wearing a parka with the hood pulled down around his face motioned me forward.

I stepped out of the shadows.

He motioned big and ugly over. He came out.

We both stood glaring at each other illuminated by the headlights of four cars pointed at us from four different directions.

The people made a ragged square between the cars.

To me they all looked like faceless blood thirsty creatures. I'd seen that look before through forty-five professional prizefights and I didn't even know how many underground no-holds-barred fights.

It was always the same. We were there to provide entertainment and someone to place bets on.

The nameless short fat man, who I'd met in a Madison bar and agreed to do this fight with, shouted his instructions. His words were more for the spectators than they were for us.

"Y'all know the rules," he yelled. "There ain't no rules here. The only weapons allowed are the ones God gave you. Y'all fight until one of you quits or one of you dies. Now back up to the front of those cars and when I shout '*Go*,' have at it."

I looked at the big guy square in the face. That was hard to do since he was as ugly as the ass-hole of a warthog with the squirts.

I decided to take a chance.

"How about you and me stick to the Marquis of Queensbury Rules?"

"Hunh?" was his answer.

"That's Professional Boxing buddy," I informed him. "You know, like no kicking, eye-gouging or biting."

It was his turn to grin now. He was missing about half his teeth and what few remained were dark green in color.

"Sure thing," he said with all the eloquence of a Bush Ape.

I put my doubled up hand out toward him and as we bumped fists my only thought was, *That won't last very long.*

One of my weaknesses is that I do like a fair fight. The problem is no one else seems to want to co-operate.

I backed up.

The other guy backed up. He kept his eyes glued on me like I was a tender filet minion and he was a lion that hadn't ate in a month.

I backed up all the way to the front grill of an old Ford Fairlane. When my ass touched it I stopped and peeled off my old olive drab Army Surplus overcoat.

I was watching ugly boy take his coat off and loosen up when someone slid out of the crowd and touched me on the arm. Glancing to the right I could only see a black hooded silhouette where the face should have been.

The black hole in the hood leaned close.

"Make it last more than four minutes," a raspy voice whispered in my ear. A hand shoved something thick in my pants pocket. "That's five hundred," he went on. "There'll be five hundred more after you go down. Just make it look good."

He moved away and before I could even protest "Go," was shouted and the fight was on.

Big and ugly rushed at me like a Rhino in heat with both hands outstretched and wide.

I wasn't in the mood for romance so I met his attempt at an embrace with two hard left jabs and a slashing straight right to the lips while sliding out to the left side.

He threw a right hand that was telegraphed all the way from Kansas City. It came wide and actually made a swooshing sound cutting the cold air as it sailed past my head. Ugly boy was off balance by his miss so I stepped in and slammed a lead right to his big misshapen right ear.

10

The thing on the side of his head was exactly what the term Cauliflower Ear was created for. That piece of meat, skin and gristle really, had been pounded on through the years so much that the ear had taken on the look of a stomped on tomato that for some strange reason had been picked up and worn as an ear muff.

My right fist didn't help the looks of that ear even one little bit.

When my punch landed, Big and Ugly staggered to the side, then slipped straight forward and fell to his knees. He instantly wrapped his arms around his head and dived forward to the pavement.

I knew why he did that.

He figured I'd be coming in with a kick to his teeth. If his head was flat to the blacktop I couldn't kick him there. Maybe I should have. It probably would have been the smart thing to do.

But that just wasn't me.

I do have my weaknesses.

I stepped back and let ugly boy catch his breath. When he was ready to stand I motioned him forward.

He stood, dusted himself off, and did a little dance cranking the kinks out of his back and neck. Then smiling his haggle-toothed smile extended his left fist toward me for another fist bump.

I should have known better. But seeing him like that kind of reminded me of an old Pug Dog and I do have a soft spot for animals and a way with dumb creatures.

I extended my fist for the friendly bump before we got back to trying to kill each other and Ugly Boy moved faster than I thought was possible. He leaped forward and dove for my legs.

This time there was no way to slip out off to the side. We were too close when he made his move and I let a momentary lapse in concentration get the better of me.

Ugly Boy took me down.

We hit the blacktop hard.

Let me correct that.

I hit the blacktop hard. Ugly Boy slammed down on top me knocking the wind out of my lungs in one explosive whoosh. The back of my head cracked the pavement and in the pitch black night stars exploded like suns going super-nova.

With me half-unconscious watching galaxies collide Ugly Boy raised himself up to rain blows down upon me.

I grabbed him around the head with the grip of a Congressman grabbing taxpayer's money. I had my fingers dug into his greasy hair. When he raised himself up I came with him.

The boy was so strong he actually picked me up off the pavement. He was trying to stand all the way up.

That wasn't good MMA strategy but this ugly bastard never did impress me as being the smartest boy in Romper Room.

The fog cleared from around my brain just as my knees cleared the pavement. I helped Ugly Boy out by pushing off and shoving forward when my shoes were flat on the blacktop.

He went over backward.

As he fell I jerked back with my left hand that was tangled in the mat at the top of his head, let go with my right and then jammed my right palm up under his chin and shoved.

To make it short, I guided the back of his skull directly into the path of the up-rushing frozen blacktop. When we landed, his skull's impact sounded like a water melon being whomped with a wooden baseball bat.

Ugly Boy went stiff. His eyes rolled up in his head.

I raised myself up over him. I lifted my fist and looked down.

Ugly Boy coughed. Red strings of blood mixed with phlegm and snot flew up in the air illuminated by the white car lights.

I should have slammed my fist down into his unprotected face. I should have. But I've said it before and I'll say it again, I do have my weaknesses.

Standing up and stepping away I said as loudly as my breathless lungs would allow, "This fight's over."

I turned my back and took one more step.

The short fat man was suddenly blocking my way. "Ain't nothing over yet," he yelled. "You got to finish him off."

My breath was coming back by then, but just barely.

"You owe me two thousand dollars for the fight," I told him. "Pay me now or I'll find you later and take two thousand out of your hide."

He backed up, eyes frightened.

Somebody else yelled, "Yo' mother-fucker! You owe me my cash." It was the same guy who'd shoved a wad of bills in my pocket and ordered me to take a fall. His hood was down now. I saw a black face sporting a full grill of gold teeth.

"I don't take dives for nobody," I told him as I pulled the bills out and flicked them at him.

I turned back to the short fat man.

"You owe me some money," I told him again.

"You don't turn your back on me boy!" was shouted from behind me by the guy with the glittery grill.

I glanced over my shoulder as the gun roared and a bullet ripped through my flesh.

2.

Into the Pit

There was a roaring in my head and intense pain lanced through my brain as I opened my eyes and the thick smoke of unconsciousness parted from around me.

It was as dark as a politician's conscience. What little light there was came from a flashlight that bounced faint illumination off black uneven rocky walls.

Two guys were dragging me by the legs and everything sounded like it was being piped into my head through long rubber hoses.

I was so weak I couldn't even lift my head as I was dragged along though dirt and crud.

So this is the way it finally ends, I thought. *It's only fitting.* I'd lived most of my life, what little I could remember of it in the filth. Dying in the filth only made sense.

They stopped and let go of my legs. My feet slapped dirty earth.

The light swung. I saw that I was laying at the edge of a black abyss. There was no way for me to know how deep the hole was. The shape I was in I couldn't even roll to take a look over the edge.

"This is fucked up," one of the guys said and shined his flashlight on a figure sprawled out on the same edge of the hole that I was next to. The guy in the light was who I'd fought, or at least what was left of him. "Jack never did shit to deserve this. He always did what he was told. Look what the hell that got him."

14

The other guy stepped to Ugly Boy's corpse.

"Jack was told to beat that son of a bitch's ass and he lost fast," he was answered. The speaker put a big work boot on Ugly Boy and shoved him over the edge.

The push to a permanent resting place for my dead recent opponent told me everything I needed to know about what was going on here. It also gave me a sudden burst of desperate energy.

I surged up from the cave floor like one of the zombies in Night of the Living Dead and attacked.

I left jabbed one of the guys between the eyes. He grabbed his nose, stepped to the side and vanished.

The flashlight went over the edge with him.

Complete inky blackness descended over us the moment the flashlight vanished.

I leaped at the last spot where I'd seen the other guy with my hands outstretched grabbing at anything I made contact with and collided right into him.

Instantly I felt his flesh beneath my fingers and clutched onto him like we'd just jumped out of an airplane and he had the only parachute.

As we grappled I was hoping these guys weren't packing pistols. Just like all the rest of my hopes and dreams I got the exact opposite of what I was hoping for.

As I fought in the darkness to get my arm around the throat of an opponent whose face I'd never see two shots rang out and my left side felt like it was on fire.

Pain, unbelievable white hot pain flashed from my kidneys to my left shoulder.

It was at that same moment when both of my hands found his face. With the last bit of strength that I had as my life drained out of me I jerked his face toward me smashing my forehead into his nose and felt it crunch.

Hot blood spurted into my face.

15

He fell backward.

I fell forward.

We pitched into the blackness of the abyss.

*

How far we fell is impossible to tell.

It was almost peaceful for those few seconds floating down through open air like that. Maybe the sense of peace was from feeling that at the end of the drop would be instant death.

After the life I'd lived, at least what I could remember of it, being constantly on the run all the time; dying would be a relief.

I guess my instinct for survival over-ruled my need for peace because unconsciously I maneuvered the man who'd shot me so that he was on the bottom.

With no warning we slammed down into something that was like landing on sliding wet chunks of foam padding. As we smashed blindly into this moving mass a stink of rotten eggs and putrid neat rose up around me. Many things snapped beneath us like thin tree branches wrapped in Jell-O and I realized the snapping were bones breaking.

I landed with one of my knees on the guy's chest and the other one on his neck. As we smashed down his throat crunched and he instantly gurgled.

We had landed on the side of what seemed in the blackness to be a mound of rotting corpses.

The question flashed through my mind: *Just how many people had they thrown down here anyway?*

There wasn't time for me to mull that over when within seconds the corpses began to shift, move, and then the whole mass started sliding sideways and downward.

In the total blackness of the pitch black pit I sought to steady myself but wherever I reached out, my hands sank into decaying liquefying human flesh. Sliding down farther into the inky abyss nothing was visible ahead or behind.

I have no idea how long the slippery cliff of corpses slid downward. It could have been five minutes. It could have been five hours. In the darkness, in the midst of extreme terror, choking on the putrefying gasses of dead bodies, feeling the urge to heave but too weak to do so, time was distorted, elongated, stretched.

An instant went on forever.

Then I went airborne again.

I must have slid over the edge of another subterranean cliff because all at once there was nothing beneath me.

I fell.

The falling went on and on until I had no sense of what was up and what was down. With the total absence of light there was nothing above and nothing below.

I fell.

I floated, disembodied, separate from the world, alone in the nothingness of endless time and space.

The World, the Earth, Space, Time, the Universe ceased to exist.

I fell into a void, into nothingness, into endless pitch blackness.

The falling, the floating, the no-up, the no-down was pleasant.

Water hit me full force in the face like I had done a belly flop from the highest diving board in the Universe.

Coughing and sputtering I wasn't sure my head was above water until I realized you can't be hacking your lungs out unless you are sucking in air.

Things started splashing down into the water around me.

My feet found a loose pebble covered bottom. I stood and realized the water was only chest deep.

Moving away from the splashes so a falling corpse wouldn't land on top of me I moved through frigid water with my hands stretched out in front of me to detect any walls before I ran into them.

My side burned like fire, just like I'd been poked with a hot branding iron. My head throbbed so bad I didn't dare raise my hands to check that wound. For all I knew my skull might be gaping open like a sliced Christmas Ham or I might have just been grazed.

I'd have to wait till later to find out.

I waded forward through the pitch black of the pit. The splashes behind me grew fainter and the water grew shallower.

Now that the adrenalin of the moment of battle died away weakness started coming back. By the time I was in water that was knee deep I'd moved from trudging forward to staggering forward.

My head buzzed like I was in the middle of an enormous bee hive. Blue streamers, phantom lights swam in the air, danced in front of me. My throat was parched so I squatted down and drank. Just the thought of drinking water that those corpses had fallen into made me feel like vomiting but I didn't have any choice.

The water was cool going down my throat. I drank deeply until I wasn't thirsty any more.

I was tempted to just sit down in the water, lean back into the coolness and let myself fall into the deep slumber of death. I resisted that temptation. The words popped into my head, *I still live!* Self preservation is a powerful instinct.

Lurching forward, ever forward, the water grew shallower until I walked slowly into the inky blackness with hands stretched in front of me and came out of the water entirely. The phantom lights continued dancing before my eyes and those were joined after a time by phantom noises.

Echoing drips smacking down onto rock seemed as loud as the drumming of a rock band. Sounds, noises, sometimes sounding like screeches, sometimes sounding like voices, seemed to be behind and in front of me.

Some of the sounds I identified.

The old intro to Pink Floyd's Dark Side of the Moon seemed like it erupted from all around me: The tick-ticking of the clock, then the striking of alarms of all kinds.

Sounds were coming from inside my head and I was traveling though a place so devoid of sound I couldn't tell what was inside or out.

I walked on staggering forward.

After what seemed to be forever I found a rocky wall with my left hand and followed that blindly.

My throat grew parched again.

This time there was no water to drink.

The spots, dancing phantom lights, were my only companions in this world of darkness, my world of eternal night.

Up ahead there seemed to be a small pin prick of light, but no, it could have been just more of the ghost lights visiting me once more.

I trembled in the cold. My body shook. My teeth chattered together. My body was weakening probably from loss of blood and dehydration.

The water dried from my clothes everywhere except where there were two holes through my shirt and two holes through my skin.

There, it was sticky and stayed wet.

My body shook uncontrollably. I shivered like I was standing outside naked in sub-zero temperatures. I couldn't feel anything. I was numb. So for all I knew it might be twenty degrees below zero.

Stumbling forward, shivering like I was afflicted with palsy I stepped into a small depression in the uneven floor of this cavern and fell to my knees.

I sat there on hands and knees, considered struggling up to my feet to move forward once again; but to move further on into…what? For what reason?

To hell with it, I thought and fell forward onto my face and gave in to the sleep of death.

Inside The Earth:_____

3.

Nursing

I'm not even sure I wanted to wake up until I felt soft hands caressing my face and a sweet voice humming a tune I'd never heard before. Even then I kept my eyes closed. The darkness was so pleasant I didn't want to leave.

Coming back to full consciousness was a gradual process.

I kept my eyes closed and just let myself feel the soft sensation of the gentle fingers on my cheeks and brow. I also opened myself to the soothing notes of a pleasant light feminine voice creating the melody of a song unknown to me.

The touch on my face was withdrawn and the humming stopped. I waited a moment or two then opened my eyes.

At least I tried.

My eyelids appeared to be crusted over, the lids glued shut. I reached up with my hands and rubbed my eyes with the heel of my palms. Hard crusty material like dried mud came loose and my eyelids fluttered open.

My vision was blurry.

The first thing I was able to see was my palms. The dark red material I'd rubbed loose was dried blood.

I sat propping myself up with my left hand.

I figured I must be in a hospital somewhere around St. Louis. Someone must have found me and taken me there.

The bed I was lying in wasn't a bed at all. It was really no more than a very thick mat of woven grass.

This wasn't like any hospital in the U.S. that I'd ever heard of. At least they usually have beds that are above the floor.

This floor was dirt.

I looked around and saw a bare room that had walls made of thatched grasses and vines. Looking down I saw the bullet holes on my left side were dressed with a bandage made of really large flat leaves held in place by thin wire-like vines running all the way around my body. Feeling of my scalp, I found that my head was bandaged with something similar.

My shirt was gone but I still had my pants on.

I thought. *If this is a U.S. hospital I'm going to get transferred to somewhere, anywhere else.* To tell you the truth, I knew I had to get out of there as fast as I could.

A creaking sound made me look up. The door was made of the same woven grass as the walls. It swung open with a whoosh and into the room walked an attractive brown haired woman with one of the most innocent faces, and since she was bare-breasted, some of the perkiest tits I'd ever seen.

Things are looking up, I thought and smiled at her.

She positively beamed a smile back.

The young woman wore a loose animal skin skirt and nothing else.

"Where am I?" I asked.

She giggled and spoke words back at me that sounded more like bird chirps than anything else. The words were rhythmic and musical in nature.

The girl stepped forward. Leaning with her hand upon my shoulder she laid the back of her hand on my brow.

With her leaning forward like that her breasts swayed dangerously in front of my face.

I couldn't help myself. No red-blooded American male could have. Reaching up I took one of the breasts in my right hand massaging the nipple with my thumb.

"Thank God the natives are friendly," I told her.

She stepped straight back, went red in the face, then stepped forward and slapped me across the lips. It wasn't a hard slap, more a friendly tap than anything else.

Stepping away again with her hands on her hips the woman shook her finger in my face. Like she was telling a pet not to do something she spoke some words that although I didn't have a clue what they meant specifically, I knew the meaning was, "Don't do that again."

"What can I say?" I told her. "You put those in my face and you're going to have to expect me to take a feel."

She turned and left the room swinging the door closed behind her. Although the door banged shut I didn't get the impression it was an angry slamming of the door.

"Well, that was interesting," I said out loud speaking to myself. "The nurses here are always ready with cream for your coffee. But the one question I need answered is: Where the hell am I?"

I dragged myself to my feet, swayed for a moment on weak legs and spotted my shirt crumpled up in a corner.

I walked to it. Bending over to pick up the shirt was a bad idea. As soon as my head leaned forward a bout of vertigo hit me and I tumbled onto my head.

The dirt floor seemed to be a good place for the moment to be, so I sat there as I put my shirt back on. I had just finished buttoning up when the door swung open once again.

Into the room strode another woman.

This one was no less attractive although she wore a type of bikini top to go along with the leather skirt. Actually, with her long black hair and serious green eyes I found her much more attractive than the first woman who'd come into the room.

This woman had an air about her like she was on a mission and knew how to get it accomplished.

She seemed just a few years older than the other woman although I eventually learned to totally disregard any notions of age in this place.

"Ah, no bare breasts," I told her confident in the knowledge that she wouldn't understand a single word I said. "I guess that means the titty-show is over."

"You shouldn't be up yet," she answered, surprising the hell out of me. "And as far as I am concerned, the titty show never will begin for you."

My jaw must have fallen open because she followed that with, "Yes, I speak your tongue. The Man of the Mountain has taught me. He also has taught me some of his healing arts. For that I am grateful."

The woman's pronunciation and phrasing were stiff and strange sounding. It sounded kind of like listening to a well educated Scottish woman talk. Whether she had an accent or not didn't matter to me. What did was that she spoke English.

I recovered enough from my surprise to ask, "Who are you and where the hell am I?"

"I am Kalina, the one who gives care for my people the Amura. If Hell is a place, you are not there. You are in the land of Amura."

"My name is Derek Walker," I told Kalina. "Happy to meet you."

"DerrraWaakkaahh," my doctor drawled out obviously having a hard time getting her tongue around the syllables.

"Derek will do."

"Derek," she repeated.

Trying to stand again I swayed badly.

Kalina caught my arm to steady me. "You should eat. Then rest more. You are not fully healed."

25

I waved that off and stumbled toward the door. The air was warm and balmy. It had the kind of baked feeling like southern Florida in the summer. I was noticing how warm it was more every moment, so I asked, "Did somebody shanghai me or something like that and this is a South Sea Island or maybe the coast of Africa?"

"Africa?" Kalina repeated the word. It was stiff in her mouth but the word sounded nice none the less. "I do not know of that place."

"Africa, land of the Ubangi," I said.

"Ubangi?" Kalina asked.

"You bet I would," I told her grinned, winked and threw the door open.

Extreme strangeness met my eyes.

Sitting around a central fire roasting game on rotating spits several bare breasted women all turned and looked at me. Some of the women had brown or black lines and stripes painted on their bodies. All of them had skin that was coppery or reddish in color.

Some men and children were wandering around the fire as well. One man smiling touched a woman on her shoulder then leaned out, and reaching over the fire, pulled a piece of meat loose from a carcass that was still roasting. He popped the morsel in his mouth and nodded his head that the meat was good.

I held my hand up and waved hello.

The women giggled. The man ignored me.

There was a line of huts around the central fire just like the one I'd came out of. All were made of woven vines, grasses and leaves.

Over the tops of the huts at the edge of the camp I could see the tops of lush trees. Birds flew in abundance in the air and among the branches.

Above the trees appeared to be rolling green hills, then mountains in the distance. That's when it got really strange.

There was no horizon.

Past the mountain, or actually over the top of the mountain where you'd expect to see a blue sky or clouds or something other than more land, what I saw was vague greenery. The land seemed to go right on up and up until it was lost in a weird rusty mist overhead.

And what was overhead was totally alien to any landscape I'd ever experienced in my life or even heard of.

The sun overhead, *if that's what it was*, was a glowing pulsating reddish ball giving off a scarlet tinged glow that tinted tops of clouds a light crimson color.

I stumbled out of the hut staring upward into a sky I could never have even imagined before.

Kalina followed me out of the hut.

For some unknown reason, although sweat ran down my forehead into my eyes from the heat, goose bumps popped up all over my arms, neck and back.

"Where on Earth are we?" I asked her. I was full of questions and was getting no answers.

Kalina didn't change that one bit when she answered my question with a question.

"Earth?" she said shaking her head. "What is Earth?"

4.

Back to School

The effect of looking at a skyline that had no real sky was dizzying to say the least. I gazed to the left and right, in front and behind me. I got a strange sense of what an ant must feel like if he is inside an extremely large bowl, a bowl maybe the size of Texas. On all sides if I looked at the distant scenery it seemed to be receding upward away from me. But everything was of such a size that you only noticed it if you looked at distant objects.

I must have been standing there like a total idiot with my mouth hanging open because everybody stopped what they were doing and stared at me. They couldn't see that what I was looking at was strange at all.

I turned to Kalina.

She was tapping me on the shoulder and asking, "What is this Earth you speak of? I know there are many lands I know nothing about. Where is Earth?"

"Earth is my world," I told her. Jerking my gaze away from what was to me at least, the weird scenery in the distance, I looked at Kalina and got another surprise. Her skin was coppery in hue just like all the rest of the people outside. Then I looked at my arms and saw that my own skin had taken on the reddish tint.

It was the sun, or whatever that thing overhead was. It was making us all look red.

At this time a serious looking man, with a scar running from his right eye to his chin walked up and eyed me up and down. His voice rumbled as he spoke some words to Kalina all the while keeping his attention focused on me.

"This is Stian, leader of our people. He asks if you are a friend of the Amura or an enemy," Kalina translated.

"I'm a friend," I told her.

"Good," Kalina said. "It would have been bad for me to dress your wounds and then watch over you only to see you killed."

She translated my answer and Stian gave a tight mouthed smile. He said something back to Kalina then walked away as though he had something important to do.

I knew whatever Stian said was about me so I asked Kalina what it had been. She answered instantly. "Stian said that only time would tell if you are going to be one of us. He will withhold judgment about whether or not you are a friend. You will have to prove your worth eventually. For now you can stay."

"He said all that in those few words?"

"Stian is a man of few words," Kalina told me. "He says what needs to be said and that is all."

It was at that moment when something screeched incredibly loud. The sound was like fingernails being dragged across a chalkboard only magnified about a hundred times. That sound was followed by a huge shadow and then something big, I mean *really* big, around 50 feet from nose to tail coming out from over the trees that bordered the camp and soaring straight overhead.   I was startled to say the least. The thing looked like a huge screaming lizard. I had seen these things in museums, books and sci-fi movies. These flying lizards were called pterodactyls.

Right at that moment I was wondering if I was in a movie theater and had fallen asleep. But that wasn't the case.

No one else in the village even batted an eye at the flying lizard. I guess they see those things all the time. I instantly tuned in to all the strange animal noises that were filtering in from out of the countryside around the village: Primitive sounds like howls, bird caws and distant roars. These were sounds that I'd never heard before outside of a Tarzan film. The roars sounded worse than anything Tarzan ever went up against.

"What in the hell was that?" I asked about the flying lizard not even knowing if I wanted to know the answer.

"Claw-Wing." Then Kalina paused for a moment. "You will need to know our names for everything or you'll have to follow me around all the time. Now I think it would be a good time to start teaching you our words."

I glanced down at Kalina's well shaped behind. "If I did have to follow you around, at least the view's nice," I told her. She didn't get the joke and just looked at me with a blank expression. So I went on with, "That sounds like a plan."

*

My dizziness seemed to be completely gone. Kalina and me sat beside a fire and as other women went about their daily duties cooking or caring for children or whatever they did Kalina would point at things and recite a word.

She pointed at the fire and said, "Stiss."

I repeated the word.

She pointed at a hut and said, "Muah."

I repeated that word.

This went on for a long time. When I got the word right Kalina smiled and nodded. When I got the word wrong she would frown and shake her head no.

I guess nods for yes and head shakes for no are universal language for the human race.

I paid attention and learned fast.

Soon I was answering Kalina with her own words almost as smoothly as if they were my native language.

We took to strolling around the village, Kalina teaching and me learning. She pointed out hundreds of objects giving me the word for each.

Her patience seemed endless.

It may have been my imagination but I could have sworn I saw a party of hunters carrying spears lead by Stian come and go from the jungle twice before we even paused in our language lesson.

How long our teaching session lasted I have no idea. The sun, which I found was called Ra, never moved. Clouds swirled past. More Claw-Wing's flew overhead. People came and went from the fire going into and coming out of huts. People ate a few times.

Ra looked down on us with his never-ending light.

I never knew I had a knack for picking up a foreign tongue but from the way I learned Kalina's language I must have always have had that trait. Maybe it was the strange familiarity that the names held for me that helped me retain them instantly. Maybe it was the beauty and enthusiasm of my teacher that made me pick up the language fast. Whatever it was by the time my stomach started rumbling I was talking in somewhat broken sentences to Kalina.

Although I am getting a bit ahead of myself I do want to point out that through my wanderings I've found that the tongue Kalina spoke is a universal language in the world she lives. There are local variations. Like there are differences between the English spoken in upper Main and lower Alabama, but when I learned the language of the Amura I could speak and be understood anywhere in this world.

For the sake of clarity for whoever might happen to read this account I will use English terms to refer to things in this world whenever possible. I doubt anybody reading this account will be patient enough to learn an entire language to know what I went through. And as to the name of this world in which I found myself, finding that out was a story in itself.

While strolling the village and learning the names of things I got the idea that the village held roughly around a hundred people. My estimation proved correct.

For perhaps no reason at all, other than I might have seen this happen in a movie on Mystery Science Theatre 3000 I asked Kalina what the name of her world was. When I'd mentioned the name *"World,"* before she'd gotten a blank look on her face. At that time I'd just put it down to a lack of communication, but now I knew it was something much deeper.

I started by picking up some soil, showing it to Kalina then moving my hands around to indicate everything all around us and saying, "What is all?"

She looked dumbfounded then pointed to my hand and gave me their word for dirt.

"No," I said. "That's not what I was asking." Trying again I pointed at a distant mountain. I pointed at the ground beneath my feet. Then I pointed at distant greenery to the opposite of where the village was and said, "All of this, what is the name for all of this?"

Kalina contemplated for a moment. Her brow wrinkled in thought, and then she answered. "Everything we know. All the trees, mountains, lands, all of this," she swirled her hands around herself to indicate a very large area. "This is Inagi."

"So your world's name is Inagi," I told her and she got that blank look again like she didn't have a clue what I was talking about.

I wanted to make certain I had this one fact right so I did something that totally confused the issue.

Squatting on the ground I motioned Kalina down beside me. While she watched I drew a diagram showing a sun and a planet going around it.

When I explained this to Kalina by saying, "Inagi travels around Ra," she laughed.

"Inagi is everything," Kalina said. "Everything cannot move. Ra is forever. Ra gives life."

Then I started to ask what about Ra setting in the evening and rising in the morning and realized once again that the sun overhead had never moved.

It was one of those moments when you get a sudden insight that should have been apparent to you all along and feel like an idiot. I don't consider myself a genius but I don't usually consider myself mentally deficient either.

But this truth that had been staring down at me every since I'd stepped out of the hut made me feel like I was on par with a monkey as far as understanding the universe.

The sun, what they called Ra had never moved.

It never would.

Ra, the unmoving forever giver of light and life was all that these people knew and all they had ever known. Inagi is their universe. Ra is forever and the truth that was unmistakable hit me like a brick dropped out of the sky, or in this case a brick dropped from Ra.

I had been asking Kalina what the name of her world was when I had never left the Earth.

I had been thrown down into a hole.

It had been a *very, very* deep hole.

I was now *inside* the Earth.

*

Kalina could tell from the expression on my face that I was pretty much in shock about the revelation that just came to me. Why it should have been more of a surprise that I wasn't on another planet but was inside the Earth instead I'm not quite sure. Maybe it's because of strange dreams, *flashes of memories?* That I've had for as long as I can remember. Maybe it's because it turns upside down most of the concepts of how I thought the universe should be set up.

To me, gravity keeps us on the Earth because it's a large object and it's pulling us toward it. I had always been told that the Earth was solid with a core of molten lava. But here I was with a glowing sun overhead, Ra; which is at the center of a hollow sphere. That means that the Earth was a hollow ball and I was standing on the inside of that hollow ball.

That was why I had gotten that weird sense of being inside a huge bowl. To the people on the outside of the Earth the landscape gradually falls away. We see it recede downward as we look out into the distance. To the people on the inside of the Earth, the people of Inagi, they see the landscape curve gradually upward until it is lost in the atmospheric haze or distant clouds.

It just boggled my mind.

My universe had now been turned upside down.

Like any good teacher, even though she didn't understand why, Kalina saw that I was overwhelmed by the information I just gained. She decided it was time to take a break and get something to eat.

This was fine with me. My stomach seemed to be far past the point of making growls and was in the territory of making pleas for mercy to be saved from starvation.

Kalina told me to sit on a log. First, she said she wanted to check the bandage on my head. As I impatiently waited she unwound the vines from around my skull and removed the leaves that served as bandages. Taking a good look at the bullet wound on the side of my head with one eyebrow arched up Kalina appraised the damage.

She gave me a nice slow in-depth examination just like the most experienced medical doctors back home would. After a few minutes of poking and prodding and asking me where it hurts and where it doesn't Kalina was satisfied. She took the bandages away and threw them in the fire.

When she came back I asked her, "Will your patient live?"

She smiled. "As long as he doesn't cause me too much trouble," she said.

Kalina then announced it was time to eat.

I was more than ready. She turned and went into a large hut. Kalina came back out a few moments later cradling in her arms several different kinds of fruits and vegetables. I was in the mood for some meat but at the point I was taking whatever was offered.

I didn't know exactly what the food was but it did look vaguely familiar and I'm not sure I ever tasted anything better. One of the fruits looked something like an apple but was the size of a cantaloupe. When I tore a chunk off with my teeth it had a tougher skin but was very sweet and moist. The texture was something like an apple. One of the other things was just like a cabbage. When I bit in that I found it was leathery and sweet. It was strange fruit but it was good. When you are hungry just about everything will taste good.

As I was digging into the food in front of me Stian came out of another hut. He stretched like he had just awakened from a nap. From his door he looked directly across to me then ducked back inside his hut.

When Stian came out next he held in each hand some primitive weapons. In one he held the spear and a stone knife. In the other he held just a spear.

He walked directly toward me.

5.

The Hunt

I just finished taking a bite of the big apple thing when Stian stood in front of us.

He looked at Kalina. Addressing her Stian said, "Is he ready to prove himself worthy of a place among the Amura?"

Kalina started to answer but being the kind of guy that I am, a guy whose mouth has gotten him in trouble more than just a few times, I had to let Stian know that I always speak for myself.

"Whatever tests you need to run me through don't worry about it," I told him. "I can take care of myself."

Stian raised an eyebrow at me speaking his tongue.

"He learns quickly," Kalina told him.

Stian thrust the hand out that held the spear and stone knife. "You will hunt with us," he stated.

I took what he offered.

Stian turned and walked away leaving me staring at the stone-age weapons I held in both my hands.

"Have you ever been on a hunt before?" Kalina asked seeing the perplexed expression on my face.

I almost answered, *Of course,* but caught the words before they were out. "I'm not sure," is what I said. I slid the stone knife into my back pants pocket with the grip sticking out for a quick draw. I had a sudden vision of being on horseback and using a rifle but I couldn't remember

36

when or where. I also got a flash of memory of hunting with some type of long steel-tipped spear with some men who were green in color, had four arms and tusks sticking out of their faces. But I couldn't remember the details of that hunt either.

It was strange.

"You had better just try to do as the others do," Kalina told me. "Try to be of help or Stian may make you leave the tribe."

"Would you care if I left," I asked Kalina before I even knew the words were out of my mouth.

She flushed. It was a perfectly girlish blush like a high school girl asked to the prom by a boy who she never thought would ask her.

Before she even recovered her composure Stian was marching back to us accompanied by three other strong looking men and one slim youth that I would estimate was around sixteen years old.

"You will come with us," he said immediately in a commanding tone and motioned me to follow him and the others as they walked past us toward the woods.

I followed but a glance back over my shoulder showed me that Kalina's eyes were on me as we entered the dark of the jungle.

*

We entered the tree line and almost instantly were in a deep shadowy rainforest type of gloom. The bright reddish glow that Ra showered down unimpeded upon us in the middle of the village only filtered down through thick tree branches and leaves to bath us all in a greenish haze.

We walked in single file into the thick vegetation on a foot trail that was obviously well known to everyone except me. That is except for myself and the slim youth whose eyes continuously darted from side to side as though he was terrified of whatever might be just out of sight.

After maybe ten minutes of moving forward into steadily heavier woods Stian had us stop. With hand signals he told us to come to him and squat down around him. On a bare patch of dirt he drew a half-circle that faced forward, toward the direction we were going. Then he pointed to himself and put his finger to the far point indicating that's where his position would be. After that he pointed out each of the others and told them their positions in this half circle formation that we were to use.

The plan was that we were to spread out and kill any animals that we flushed out of hiding places. In the formation we were moving in unless an animal retreated exactly in the opposite of us he would more than likely run into another one of us while trying to flee.

The last two in this half circle were me and the slim youth. The two of us being the most untested hunters Stian must have figured we should be the last to have a chance at bringing any animal down.

All of these instructions were given in near silence and mostly in hand-signals. My guess was that Stian wanted to keep our presence unknown to our prey for as long as possible. The meat of our dinners may depend upon how soon we were detected. We definitely didn't want to be seen early.

We spread out and moved forward.

As the youth walked past me I whispered to him, "I am Derek."

He glanced my way, pointed at his own chest and whispered, "Jorn." He moved off and took his position.

All of us crept forward as silently as possible with our spears pointed forward and our ears and eyes straining for any sign whatsoever of any animal in hiding or maybe another predator who might be stalking us.

It seemed like this went on for hours. Really, it could have. For all I knew the actual passage of time could have been days in the outer world. Down here where the sun never sets what you are doing seems to have a direct connection to how fast time passes.

While we were stalking the jungle, creeping forward crouched over like prowling predators time seemed to have stopped. Each and every snap of a branch, each and every rustle of leaves was a heart-stopper.

We were spread out enough so that for each of us the man on either side was barely visible through the foliage. The breeze flowed slowly through and between the trees as we moved among huge tropical rainforest vegetation. Birds cawed at each other overhead. Strange animals shrieked at each other in the distance.

We moved forward, slowly, carefully. Time seemed to move in slow motion if it moved at all. We were entirely concentrated on the moment we lived in. Nothing else mattered but seeing and hearing every-little-thing that happened around us.

I felt like my senses had never been as alive as they were at that moment.

From off to my right I heard a heavy cry and the sound of multiple pounding feet. Then there was a terrific roar that instantly reminded me of a moose trumpeting.

I glanced sideways at Jorn. He was some distance away from me but still close enough to see. He shook his head, "*No*," as though he wasn't certain of what was going on either. It was at that moment when the trumpeting turned into a roar.

Moving in the direction of the roar I was met head on by the author of that angry bellow. Leaping straight over the top of a bush and charging directly at me was a bear that must have been all of seven feet tall if it stood on its hind legs. The bear was in a panic and was moving so fast that he almost bowled me over before he even knew I was there.

I leaped to the side and threw my spear at it in the best imitation of a javelin throw that I could manage. I'd never had any instruction on spear throwing so I had no idea if I did it right or not. My weapon buried itself into the beast's right shoulder. The spear made him roar louder as he ran past. He slapped the spear loose and kept right on going like an out of control Mack Truck.

Shouting a warning to Jorn to just get the hell out of the way, I retrieved my spear and saw that Jorn was nowhere to be seen.

Catching sight of the bear as he ran away I saw that his back was marked by at least two other nasty looking wounds. So I hadn't been the only one who'd gotten a piece of this big boy.

I saw the other hunters running in this direction in a measured pace after the bear and I took up the same kind of pace. The plan now obviously was that we would trail the animal until he became weak from loss of blood, and then finish him off. The other hunters didn't want to lose sight of the beast but they moved as though they were in no great hurry either.

Stian came up beside me as I trotted after the bear. All of us jogged in a loose spread out group through the woods following our quarry.

Now was when Jorn reappeared. Before when he'd disappeared I figured he'd just found a good hiding place and would keep his head down. Rabbits and moles seemed to be the kind of game that Jorn was built for tackling. He was still pretty much a kid.

Bears were a man's work.

I guess Jorn didn't share my opinion. Just as the bear was running past a large tree with a gnarly trunk about three feet around, timing his leap perfectly Jorn leaped out and grabbing onto a large knot of hair with his left hand swung himself onto the bear's back in one fluid motion that any cowboy would have admired. My mouth probably dropped open in astonishment at seeing this skinny kid attempt a bronco bucking ride on a pissed off panicked bear.

But getting a Rodeo Prize wasn't on Jorn's mind as he drew back and thrusting forward buried his stone knife all the way to the handle deep into the bear's neck. The beast reared back on its haunches and screamed out a bellow of pure rage and pain. It swiped blindly at the youth riding on his back.

One swipe of those massive claws could have disemboweled a large man but Jorn was smart enough to not give the bear any chance at delivering a blow like that. He gripped the brute's hair and pulled himself down as close to the bear's back as he could. Pulling the stone blade free he stabbed down into the bear's neck again and again. The beast stopped and spun in a circle trying to get at and dislodge the youth from his back.

This gave the rest of us time to catch up and form a circle around the grim struggle.

I wanted to jump in and stab the bear with my spear but with the way it was spinning around there was no way to do it without possibly spearing the youth. Stian and the other two hunters had their spears at the ready so they had the same thing on their minds but all we could do was watch as this drama of life and death played itself out.

Blood flew in a spray as Jorn, now wearing a death's mask with his face covered in crimson stabbed over and over again into the only vulnerable part of the bear's anatomy he could get at.

The battle seemed like it went on forever but the truth was it probably only lasted at most two minutes.

Jorn's blade must have found a vital artery because with a huge sighing squeal the bear collapsed down to the ground onto his side and shuddered all over. He rolled to his back as Jorn leaped free to keep from being crushed. The huge beast then expelled a final death rattle and died.

For a moment the youth stood there just a few feet away from the hair covered monster waiting and making certain that the brute was really dead. We all stood silently. It was a great moment for the boy. I had no doubt it was his first kill and what a kill it was.

The boy had taken down a huge cave bear. I guess now, no matter what, I should refer to him as a man because with that display of pure guts, timing, and unbelievable nerve he deserved to be called nothing less.

6.

Triumph and Tragedy

Jorn stood with his foot upon of the torso of the bear he killed and with his stone knife raised in his left hand beat upon his chest like a movie Tarzan. He gave out a great shout of triumph. How right Edgar Rice Burroughs had gotten it when he'd written those old Lord of the Jungle books I had never known until that moment. This boy had just triumphed in a battle to the death over a great savage beast. Giving a howl of victory was the only way to express the primitive joy he felt.

When he was done with his victory celebration Jorn looking straight into the eyes of his chief now stated, "Am I not now one of the hunters to be respected like all the rest of your hunters? Am I not now to be considered a man among men?"

Stian's face broke into a wide grin. "I misjudged you. I learn more as I live that appearances are not always correct. I had thought you weak and frail. I could not have been more wrong. Jorn, you have earned the right to be one of the hunters." He clapped the youth on the shoulder in what could only be called a fatherly touch of proud admiration. "You have proved your courage. But next time when we wound a large beast we trail him until he is weak and there is not so much risk in the kill. We could have lost you to the bear's claw. It would not have been only you losing your life but the entire tribe would have lost a good hunter and provider for the women and children. Remember, we always hunt as a group."

Now Stian turned to me. "You did well," he spoke simply and turned back to the youth and the other hunters who were already falling to the task of skinning and cutting the massive animal that lay dead at their feet.

*

When the cleaning and cutting was done we loaded up sacks made from the bear's hide with large chunks of bear meat and started back toward the village.

The creatures of the jungle fell silent as we moved in the direction toward the village of Amura. A new hunter was in the wood that day and all the animals understood that he was someone to be feared. As for Jorn, he seemed to be having the time of his life bragging about what he had just done.

"Now everyone will recognize me as a great hunter," he told the rest of us. "Today, I fed the village with the meat of a killer of men. I killed the killer of men. I slew the slayer of great beasts. I ..."

He went on like this as we marched back through a tropical steamy jungle loaded down with our burdens of slabs of bear meat. Stian and all the rest of us just let him talk. The youth had a reason to feel good and Stian recognized that he needed to let everyone know that he now felt the equal of any man.

Sometime during the walk back the other two members of this hunting party told me their names and I told them and Stian mine. Since everybody here seemed to only have one name I gave mine simply as Derek. The hunters were Kalar and Tond. Both of them had loosened up since we were heading back and seemed to be friendly enough now that the task that needed to be done was accomplished.

When we came up over a rise in the land and just out of a clearing Tond announced that he needed to relieve himself among the bushes. I knew there was a need to stop and wait for him but I was a bit surprised that primitive people such as these would even bother to go into the bushes to do their business. I figured they'd just drop and squat where they

43

were. Maybe a type of modesty is built into the basic make-up of the human race.

I was ready for a break myself, so stopping was alright by me.

When that hunter was doing his thing Jorn headed to the opposite side of the trail to take care of the same business. I figured I'd take the opportunity to relieve myself as well. Leaving the bear meat I'd been carrying back with the others I set out to find a relatively private spot on the same side of the trail as Jorn.

Not wanting to be staring at Jorn squatting and dropping I turned my back to him, undid my pants and commenced to letting loose with a stream of steaming urine. I hadn't realized I'd been holding myself as long as I had. The relief was incredible.

I had just finished and was shaking off the last few drops when a cry of pure terror came from behind me. Putting my equipment away as I spun in the direction the cry came from I saw a sight that would freeze the blood in any man. It made goose bumps jump up all over my body.

A grey shaggy thing with eight legs had knocked Jorn from his feet. The thing was standing over the top of him waving its front four legs at the youth as Jorn screeched out in unholy fright. I can think of nothing else that the thing reminded me of other than saying it was a huge spider the size of a small horse.

There is some kind of primitive fear of large spiders that resides in most men. Why this is I do not know. Maybe it's a racial memory of something from our primitive past that makes us wary of creatures that resemble an ancient enemy. Maybe it's just recognition of another predator that operates with so alien a method and intent as to make their motivations totally beyond human understanding. Whatever it is just about everyone's immediate reaction to large spiders is to have a moment of hesitation before we stomp the ugly bugs into crushed ruin.

This spider induced more than just a moment of hesitation. Because of the size of it, this arachnid created a desire to run screaming in the opposite direction.

After my one moment of hesitation, I wanted to grab my spear and attack. I realized immediately that I'd left that lying in the dirt back where the other hunters were waiting. Instead I grabbed for my stone knife.

It was at that moment when Jorn stabbed the thing that stood over him in the side with the same stone knife he'd used on the bear. The huge spider hissed at him like a steam hose ripped loose. Its head dipped. Jorn's arms and legs shot out to the sides of him like he had been electrocuted. He went as stiff as a plank of wood.

The spider then grabbed Jorn up in its front two arms and taking two incredibly fast scuttling steps backward vanished down into the ground taking the youth with him. The thing that had Jorn was a trap door spider but of a size that as far as I knew had never existed on the outer Earth.

All this had happened in a matter of maybe ten seconds.

I stood there stunned as the other hunters ran up beside me alerted by Jorn's cry. I told them what happened. All three of the fearless hunters now surprised the hell out of me. At my description of Jorn's attacker they all blanched and went as pale as was possible in the strange overcast reddish light of Inagi. They were clearly terrified.

It was as though I had told them that a demon or maybe Satan himself had come up out of the ground and grabbed Jorn. As they stared in mute terror at the point in the ground where Jorn disappeared I quickly retrieved my spear and turned to Stian. The trap door that the spider waited underneath for passing prey was barely visible even now that we all knew what to look for and where to look.

"You've seen these things before?" I questioned him.

Yes, he nodded and looked at the ground. The graveness of his expression was not lost on me.

"How do we go in and get him back?" I asked.

Stian's gaze dropped to the ground. "We don't. No one ever returns when taken by a Nysek. Jorn is lost."

I looked to the other hunters.

Both Kalar and Tond's stares were cast to the ground as well. These strong men, hunters of great beasts and protectors of their village were already in mourning for the loss of one of their own.

"You mean you're not even going to try to get him back?" I shouted at the three of them.

It was only Stian who raised his gaze up from the ground. All three of them looked like they were ashamed but Stian showed his shame all the more because he was the leader among these people.

"He is gone," Stian answered. "There is nothing to be done. Nyseks cannot be killed. They are not of Inagi. Jorn will be missed by all the tribe."

I looked once more at all three of these strong men with their eyes cast to the ground, giving up, letting one of their own, a young man on his first hunt, being carried off to a terrible nightmarish death.

"To hell with this," I told all three of them and none too gently either. "I'm going after Jorn. If you're not going to help me, I'll get him back myself." The last words spoken were in English because I was so angry that I couldn't think straight and all my recent language lessons were immediately forgotten. I knew they didn't know what I was saying but that didn't matter. All three of them knew what I meant even if the exact words were foreign.

I went to the flap of the trap door and reaching forward with my spear point flipped it upward and all the way back. The door was made of a collection of leaves, sticks and grasses woven together with a silky, webbing material. There was a dark hole underneath, a hole that led down into the ground. I went to the back of the trapdoor, grabbed it and dragged it all the way open. The top pealed back and revealed that the sloping tunnel underneath the trap door was large enough for a man to stand up and walk down into a sloping passageway.

The idea of going down into an underground lair of horse-sized spiders, things named Nyseks that scared the shit out of these guys did not appeal to me at all. I could understand why all of them were scared, frightened to death to do it.

That was exactly why I had to.

With my spear clutched in my right hand and my stone knife in my left I headed down into the Nyseks' lair.

7.

Into the Spider's Home

The floor of the tunnel was covered with the same silky webbing that was used to weave the trapdoor together. It wasn't sticky but was more like a very thin cloth carpet. I was guessing when it dried out the webbing lost its adhesive properties, at least I hoped so. I sure didn't want to step onto a section of it and be fastened to the ground like a bug stuck on flypaper.

The ground sloped downward gradually. I ducked my head entering the tunnel and after only a few steps descending I found I could stand straight up again. It was only a few more steps into the sloping tunnel that the floor stopped leading downward and leveled off.

I was taken aback to find that I wasn't in total darkness. I had thought that as soon as I got just a few feet below ground I'd be in pitch blackness but that wasn't true. After my eyes grew accustomed to the lesser light, darker than even the gloom of the jungle above, I found that light filtered in from overhead through places where the ceiling was so thin that there really was no more to support it other than the network of roots from all the growing plants of the jungle floor.

I moved forward as quickly as was possible but also being careful as well. While I did want to get the boy back I also didn't want to run full head-on into a nest of hundreds of these spider-Nysek-things.

I crept forward as quietly as I could, while rays of light-beams made visible by heavy floating dust shone through to the floor in strange patterns. At least half of the roof of the tunnel that I was traveling in had a covering so thin that I was surprised that at least a few of the larger animals hadn't fallen through.

In several places there were short side tunnels that led up to clearly visible dead-ends. At those dead-ends I could see the outlines of the trap doors that Nyseks would wait behind for unsuspecting prey.

Then I came upon a sight that showed me why the tunnel had been built the way it was. In the middle of the tunnel there was the shriveled carcass of a large deer-like creature. The animal was now wrapped in a type of silk cocoon but even through the thick wrapping I could clearly see that a rear leg had been broken in a fall. Overhead the roof was particularly thin at the point directly above the deer. The very fragility of the roof was also a type of trap. This animal had fallen through, broken a leg and been wrapped up and left for one of them to come back and collect later. Any creature large enough to fall through this roof probably never managed to get back out alive.

I moved forward past the deer and the tunnel turned sharply to the right hand side. As I came around the bend I stepped to the side of the tunnel to get a look before barging straight ahead. Four or five paces past where the bend was the floor of the tunnel dropped straight down about six feet.

In the thick grey dust filled light I could dimly see that what lay ahead was a type of hollowed out pit. The pit was maybe fifty feet across. In its center a large tree grew up through a false roof made of the same material as the flap of the trap doors.

Hanging from the trunk of the tree like strange fruit I could see several large animals. Among them were deer, a bear, and a tiger, even something that looked like a crocodile. All were wrapped in that gauzy, filmy, spider-silk. Some of them were already desiccated, dried out, drained of blood, dead. But a few of them though wrapped up in the cocoons were still alive.

The ones that were still alive were struggling to get free but the webbing held them in place. The spider that had carried Jorn off was all the way across the pit from the tunnel opening where I was. The trunk of the tree was almost in a straight line between him and where I crouched down. The thing was slowly spinning out silk from its own body and was wrapping Jorn in the fabric.

Jorn's eyes were open but he had the glassy-eyed look of someone who wasn't actually seeing anything.

Two other big-ass spiders or Nyseks were also sitting on the other side of the pit from where I was. One of the spiders was immobile and appeared to be breathing rhythmically. If a Nysek sleeps, I was guessing that it was nap time for that guy.

The other Nysek was up and on all eight of its legs. It appeared to be agitated. It swayed and made weird slithery chirping sounds. Then it scuttled over to the tree moving in that strange almost stomach churning way arachnids do that makes your skin crawl. With the size of this boy, my skin wanted to run screaming in the other direction.

I watched as the Nysek approached the tree trunk appearing to study it for a moment then moved directly to where the bear hung suspended glued to the side of the tree. He stopped in front of the large animal. The bear bellowed out a roar of warning because I guess he knew what was coming next.

The Nysek raised itself up on its four rear legs and waving its front four arms in the air in almost hypnotic gestures it speared straight forward with its ugly bulbous head and drove two dagger-like fangs deep into the bear's torso.

The bear roared out a cry of anger and pain. Then the animal squealed like a frightened child. That squeal was cut off suddenly in mid-stream. The bear stiffened and was still.

The Nysek took no notice at all of the theatrics of the large carnivore it had in its grasp. Next, it fed. And the way the Nysek fed was nauseating to watch.

The spider thing stayed connected by its fangs to the bear's chest and slowly, like someone drinking a strawberry flavored milkshake through a straw, sucked the lifeblood, the very juices of the bear into its stomach. I thought I could actually hear sucking noises coming from where the massive spider was suctioning the liquids from the bear's body.

The bear appeared to deflate as I saw the spider-Nysek's belly grow bigger and rounder. After a time, I have no way of knowing how long, the bear's eyes rolled up into its head and it expelled a final breath.

The Nysek now disconnected itself from the dead carcass hanging from the tree trunk. Its belly was so full and swollen that it dragged the ground as it slowly wobbled back to where the other sleeping Nysek sat. Plopping itself down heavily upon the silky carpet this big spider-thing immediately began breathing in the deep rhythm of slumber just like the other Nysek sitting beside it.

Peering around intently, taking stock of what lay ahead of me as thoroughly as possible I looked for and saw no other Nyseks in the immediate area. There was no way of telling if there were hundreds more of these spider things or if this was it for their eight-legged family. I knew that I didn't want to just wait around to get a count of all the rest if there were more. Whatever I was going to do I needed to get done fast.

At the tree one of the creatures awake and struggling in his silk cocoon was something that resembled a yellow and white striped tiger. He was hissing and growling out threats at his captors and was just generally really pissed off about the situation he found himself in. Not counting the tail this boy was about eight feet long and must have weighed at least eight hundred pounds. He didn't appear to have any broken limbs but he was wrapped up so tight that all he could do was hiss and spit. That wasn't doing him any good but like any ticked off cat he felt the need to do it anyway.

The Nyseks ignored him. They knew he couldn't get loose so the two of them slept on and the other continued with his cocoon weaving.

A plan came to me. It was far-fetched and probably a stupid plan, but since I knew I stood no chance whatsoever of straight ahead fighting and winning against the three Nyseks in the pit, even if two of them appeared to be in a dream state, any plan was better than none at all.

*

The Nysek wrapping Jorn was diligently at work. He seemed to be absorbed in what he was doing as I slowly and as quietly as possible dropped over the edge and down into the pit. I crept silently to the side putting the tree trunk between myself, Jorn and the laboring Nysek.

I held in my left hand my spear and in my right gripped the stone knife that Stian had given me. Crouching down, I crept closer to the trunk of the tree. The eyes of the yellow and white striped tiger locked to mine. He growled and spit out a challenge even though he could not move at all. I could only admire the fighting spirit of the great feline caught in this nightmarish trap. If he could, this creature was not going to go down without a fight. I couldn't but help thinking that it would be some kind of a cosmic crime if this great cat didn't get his chance to at least die a warrior's death.

Wondering if he suspected that he was a part of my plan, actually the most important part of the plan, I worked my way silently over to the base of the tree. With the tree trunk between me and the three Nyseks I stood up to my full height beside where the tiger fought against his bonds.

I set my spear down against the tree trunk and reaching my left hand out slowly toward the enormous feline I whispered soft soothing words to him. "Come on now big boy," I spoke. "We don't have to be enemies. We can work together. I bet you want to be anywhere else than here even more than I do. I know buddy. This is really messed up." With my fingers I scratched the top of the bowling ball sized head as gently as I could manage.

For a moment I thought the teeth were going to dart forward and he was going to take my hand off at the wrist. But to my surprise an astonishing thing happened.

The big cat purred.

It was unmistakable. I had heard the same thing back in the outer world when a household pet was happily getting its back scratched.

This huge beast, this engine of feline destruction that could easily take my head off with one swipe of his mighty talons, was purring like a tame house-tabby.

Leaning even closer I whispered more words of comfort. "Alright, my friend," I told him. "Now that it seems like you don't want to tear me to pieces lets see just how much like buddies we can be." I began sawing at the webbing that held the huge cat in place.

To his credit the yellow and white tiger seemed to understand exactly what I was doing. He looked directly into my eyes the entire time that I worked at the cocoon he was encased in. I got a section about three feet weakened and that fell away.

The tiger ripped loose with his front paws the remaining webbing that held him prisoner and tore itself away from the silk bag and fell forward to the dirt. He eyed me for just one moment. Did I see gratitude in those strange eyes with vertical pupils that he surveyed me with? I'm not sure. All I really wanted him to do was to not leap upon me and shred my face with his claws. That would have been gratitude enough.

In that instant it was one of those moments when they say it is a moment of truth. If this big cat had no intelligence whatsoever, if he did not understand that I had released him and meant him no harm then I was probably going to be his first choice for a meal.

The great cat growled once, hissed, then amazingly its gaze softened and it purred once again. *He understood.* Then the tiger turned away and did what I was hoping beyond hopes that he would do. The tiger stalked around the trunk of the tree and shouting out a savage cry charged and attacked the Nysek wrapping Jorn in the cocoon.

The tiger pounced and slashed and knocked the Nysek clear away from Jorn and ripped it open from head to the green steaming guts that spilled out onto the floor of the pit.

This commotion woke up the other two Nyseks but they were slow to react.

I jumped forward and ran one of them through with my spear where it sat pinning the thing to the ground.

The other Nysek turned toward me. But the tiger being already done with his first kill pounced on it from the side leaping onto its back and burying its claws and fangs into the ugly things hide. There was a confusing flurry of legs, squeals and roars as the tiger attacked and the two savage creatures rolled in the dust.

But as fast as the battle had begun it was over and the tiger was standing over the Nysek he had killed. He stood over the top of the spider-thing and roared out a savage tiger snarl that clearly said, "I am the strongest here."

I wasn't going to argue with him about that.

I picked up Jorn and hoisting him across my shoulder headed up and out of the spider pit and went out into the open air through one of the Nysek's trap doors.

8.

Stalked

It felt really good to be back into the open clean air and out of the dusty gloom of the Nysek's nest. The steamy jungle with all of its hundreds of predators and unknown perils now seemed to be a welcoming place.

I wouldn't have any problem with meeting my end in a battle to the death and could even respect the animal that brought me down if we fight it out to the end. But to be wrapped up and hung to the side of a tree and slowly drained of blood while I was wide awake, that was a death I could not stomach. Dying like that was something unholy, dirty even foul.

That was not the kind of death that a fighting man would ever accept for himself.

The words *I still live!* Thundered like lightning through my mind like a primordial memory that I could not account for. I wasn't sure what it meant. I wasn't sure if it meant anything at all.

It was a mystery that I really had no reason to pursue. I let it drop.

Since I didn't even know what direction the village was in I carried Jorn away from the Nysek's trap door that I came out of in as straight a line as I could manage. Keeping my eyes to the ground to avoid stepping onto one of the weak spots over the Nysek's tunnels I trotted with the youth slung over my shoulder. After about what I would estimate was maybe fifteen minutes, although I come again to that problem of there really being no actual time here, I stopped and laid Jorn down upon the loose grass of the jungle floor.

I still wasn't entirely sure that the boy was alive and if he was that he would survive very long. Whatever was in that spider's bite I knew it wasn't good for any warm-blooded creature. I'd seen Jorn stiffen immediately when he was bit. Then I'd seen that bear stiffen the same way. If the poison in the Nysek's bite was more than just a paralyzing agent then this kid was not going to make it back to the camp of the Amura. But there was nothing that I could do about it. I'd take care of him as well as I knew how and leave it in the hands of fate.

Setting down beside the boy I laid my finger against the carotid artery on the side of his throat. After a moment or so I felt the beat of blood being forced through the youth's body by his strong young heart. He was lying on his back and his mouth was shut. I turned Jorn on his side and instantly mucus and slobber bubbled out from the side of his mouth.

He was so paralyzed that this kid didn't even have control of his throat muscles. I'd have to make sure that until Jorn came out of this, if he came out of it, his mouth, nose and airways to his lungs were unobstructed. I didn't want to save the kid only to have him drown on his own spit.

The thick jungle was all around us.

I stood up and looked about me in all directions trying to see if I could recognize through the trees any familiar landmarks. What I wanted to spot was that mountain that seemed to almost hang in the sky because of the unending rise in the landscape. That was the mountain that I'd seen from Kalina's hut when I took my first look at this strange inner-world. If I could spot that mountain it seemed I might be able to figure out what general direction leads back to the camp. But the trees blocked the sight of anything in the distance.

I looked straight up.

Ra was there looking straight down at me. He had never moved.

Just how do you figure directions when there is no way to see stars or the moon and the sun never rises or sets? In this place there was no North, South, East or West. I didn't have a clue as to what direction I was supposed to go.

In Inagi I guess you just better never get your ass lost or you'd be in the same situation that I was in; Lost in Inner-Space.

There was a rustling in the brush just a little way behind us from where I'd carried Jorn out of the Nysek's tunnels. I saw movement through the tall grass and bushes, a large yellow and white figure. The coloring told me instantly that it was the big cat from the spider's pit.

Is that boy still hungry? I asked myself knowing full well that I didn't want him to give me the answer to that question.

Not waiting for the answer I picked Jorn up and again slung him over my shoulder and headed in as straight a line as I could away from the lair of the Nysek.

*

Still not wanting to blindly run through the jungle because with a teenage boy over my shoulder even one as small as Jorn, we were an easy target for any predator that wanted a slow moving meal, I moved as swiftly as possible through the thick foliage.

The ground moved under my feet as I hurried through the jungle stepping over fallen tree trunks, going around bushes and weaving my way through the lush vegetation. If there was a trail in this part of the jungle then I must have missed it entirely. I didn't see any evidence of man at all. This untouched land was beautiful in its savageness. It was wild and untamed, teeming with thousands of species of plants and animals. In a way this innocent untouched land, untainted by the hand of man was like a Garden of Eden. Here wild animals ruled and man was just one predator among many predators.

This was the kind of place that was swiftly vanishing back on the Outer-Earth. It was sad really. But that's how mankind is, at least on the outside of this planet anyway. Mankind for the most part uses up the land he occupies and then moves on to somewhere else to use that up.

That's how it has always been and how it always will be.

The problem was, in the Outer-Earth mankind was running out of places to use up. Soon, I guess he would start thinking about moving on to another planet to settle there and start using up that planet. As strange as it may sound, as long as they left Inagi alone, that was alright by me.

For some reason I felt no kinship or sense of belonging to the Outer-Earth. As far as my memory went back I never had. I never felt a sense of being at home on the surface of the Earth.

This is what my mind mulled over as I carried Jorn on my shoulder through the primeval jungle with countless threats to our lives all around us. This kind of life, this kind of living constantly on the edge, is where I felt at home. Inagi with sudden death waiting behind every tree, over every hill, or even hiding in holes beneath our feet, was the kind of place I was built to live in.

I heard a weak cough from over my shoulder and stopped. Jorn made a small groan.

Just a few steps ahead there was another clearing where the ground was covered with a thick carpet of grass. I went there and stopping laid Jorn upon the grass again making sure his head was turned to the side so none of his airways were restricted.

Jorn's eyes were open. He looked at me as I laid him down and now he seemed to at least be in control of where his gaze went. He groaned again.

"You just take it easy," I told him peering intently around us, taking a survey of our surroundings.

We were still in the same kind of jungle that we'd been in when we'd come up out of the Nysek's lair. In fact, if I didn't know better I might have thought that I had circled back around and wound up in the same place. I couldn't tell one tree in this jungle from another one. All of this looked the same to me.

That's probably the result of spending too many years of living a city life in the USA. If I ever had known how to live in the woods it was all lost to me now.

I heard a rustling in the brush off to my left hand side. Something big seemed to be moving around out there. The only weapon that I had on me now was the stone knife. The spear that I'd driven through the Nysek and staked him to the ground with I'd left right there.

I regretted that now.

Something moved again among the weeds making the light sound of grass rubbing on grass and now I heard a low rumbling like a deep snarl. The sound was like a cat's growl only much deeper and somehow it carried with it the sound of unbelievable strength.

A flash of yellow and white streaked by us among the waving grass and I knew that the tiger I'd released had been trailing us and was not even ten feet away.

Jorn groaned again. He moved one of his legs and moaned louder.

"Shhhhh," I told him and looking his way put a finger to my lips.

He cut his moan off in the middle but kept moving that leg like he was working the blood back into it. Jorn slowly sat up propping himself up with shaky arms.

He looked at me and I leaned close to his ear.

"I let something loose that attacked the Nyseks," I whispered. "But I think it tracked us and …"

I didn't get to finish my statement as a loud agonizing squeal broke loose and there was a roar like the entire wild kingdom had gone to battle pretty much right in front of us. The sound of crashing and loud thuds and pain-filled desperate sounding howls filled the air.

Squatting down in the tall grass I couldn't see anything but knew there was some kind of titanic struggle being fought but a few feet away from us.

I gripped the stone knife in my fist and placed myself between Jorn and the origin of the sounds of battle. I prepared myself to be attacked at any moment even though I wasn't sure what was going to be coming out of that deep vegetation. The roars sounded like the tiger I'd let loose but the other sounds were vaguely canine even though I couldn't be sure what they were.

If the tiger was fighting some kind of dogs then from the sound of the barks, snarls and yips they made they were some incredibly large dogs.

Then it all stopped suddenly.

There was a frenzy of roaring snarls, squeals of pain and the sound of grass being pounded down like one side of this struggle had decided they had enough and got the hell out of there.

I looked at Jorn. He was standing in a half crouch now massaging the feeling back into his legs. But it looked like he could carry his own weight if he needed to.

The sound of a great roar cascaded all around us then. I recognized it as the same roar that the tiger had made back in the pit after he'd attacked and killed the Nysek. I now had no doubt about who won the battle.

I'm not quite sure why but I breathed out a sigh of relief.

That didn't last for long when I heard the sound of rustling once again with grasses being folded back as the great cat approached us.

I tensed taking a crouched fighting stance with the puny stone knife held out in front of me. I would sell my life dearly before I'd let the tiger make a meal of Jorn.

The great cat came striding forward out of the grasses parting them with his huge strong head. He stepped forward with a growl in his throat and fire in his eyes. But as surprising as it was his intension was clear.

He carried in his mouth the largest wolf that I would ever even imagine seeing. A wolf this size had not existed on the surface of the Earth for at least a half a million years if it had ever existed even then. The large grey and brown wolf was all of at least five feet long not counting his tail and he must have weighed in at around two hundred pounds. This was the daddy of all dogs as far as I was concerned.

The tiger I had saved, calmly and confidently strode up to us making that deep rumbling sound from within his throat. He padded right up in front of me and dropped the massive primitive canine at my feet. Then he made that sound again that although it was deeper and infinitely louder was unmistakable.

It was the deep throated purr of a friendly cat.

Without even thinking, it was more instinct than anything else, I reached out and patted the huge beast on the top of his flat head and scratched behind his ear.

He made a contented yawning sound that went something like, "Yaaaawwwaaaahhh," then turned and took one running bounding leap back into the jungle and was gone.

I looked at Jorn.

He looked at me with an expression on his face that showed complete disbelief.

I just shook my head.

"You have made a brother of the beast," Jorn told me in hushed tones of awe. "You are a special man."

"I just wish I knew how I did it," I told him.

*

There was no way I was going to leave the gift that the tiger had given us behind. No way had I wanted to insult that boy. As Jorn loosened up by doing a type of caveman's calisthenics to help the effects of the spider's poison wear off faster, I attempted to skin and dress the wolf that the tiger killed.

61

The Nysek's poison must have just had a paralyzing effect but did nothing else. Jorn was recovering fast. I had heard that some spiders on the Outer-Earth possessed venoms that dissolved its victims from the inside out. We were both glad this species didn't have that trait.

I cut and hacked at the huge wolf and after some time had reduced him to a bag of dog skin, chopped up doggie steaks and not a whole lot else. *That'll teach him to mess with a friend of Derek Walker;* I thought as I wrapped the meat I'd cleaned in the hide. *We don't play that.*

I didn't really know what I was doing but what I ended up with was edible and nobody was judging my butcher skills anyway.

Jorn recovered control of his own body swiftly. Youngsters do seem to heal very fast especially here in Inagi. Except for a few scrapes and bruises from being dragged through the Nysek's tunnel Jorn was almost back to normal. As soon as he was ready I asked him if he had any idea what direction we should head in to get back to the Amura village.

He gave me a strange look when I asked him that and said, "You mean you don't know?"

"If I did I wouldn't ask," I told him.

"We just go this way," he answered eying me curiously and pointed forward to the area where we had heard the big cat battle it out with the wolves. "I thought you knew what way to go because you were going in the right direction already. We are almost all the way back to the village."

I picked up the bundle of wrapped wolf and said, "Let's get back then."

As I took my first step Jorn reached out and touched my arm to stop me.

"How can you not know the way to go?" he asked. There was genuine puzzlement in his voice as though this was something that was far beyond what his mind could grasp.

62

"I come from another...," I searched for the word for world but could not find any in his language so I said, "... another place."

"I have met people from other lands in Inagi, lands far away." Jorn said. "They always know where they are and the way to where they want to be. How can you not?"

I thought for a moment of some way to explain this to him but only came up with, "I come from somewhere other than Inagi."

Jorn rolled his eyes. "There is nowhere but Inagi," he said. "Inagi is everything. Inagi is ..."

"Just drop it," I told him. I'd heard the same thing already from Kalina. I marched forward into the tall grass with my bag of wolf meat.

*

The journey back was actually very uneventful.

Maybe what we encountered right off the bat when we entered the tall grass was what scared off all the rest of the predators in the immediate area.

We found the sight of the tiger VS wolves' battle because we had to walk right through the middle of it. The grass was knocked over and crushed down in about a ten foot square area. Blood was all over the place. There were two more extremely large wolves lying dead in the middle of the smashed grass. Both of them had been disemboweled like they had been attacked by someone wielding a straight razor.

Actually I guess they had met someone far more destructive than any person with a straight razor. That eight hundred pound, eight foot long prehistoric tiger had talons that were razor sharp and I'm sure he was an expert at using them.

As we passed just outside of the area where the wolves had been decimated I caught the faint sight of a tawny yellow and white hide passing close by out among the tall grass. I hoped he would not forget whose side he was on.

*

It didn't seem as though we walked far at all before we smelled the scent of wood burning and game cooking. I was actually surprised at how quick I was adapting to this primitive world. When I'd been in the US I didn't seem to smell anything unless it was forced under my nose and had an overpowering odor. Now, my senses seemed to be keying up and coming alive like long dormant capabilities being awakened.

I loved every minute of it. It was like I was waking up and becoming more alive, like I was becoming more a part of everything around me. I was a part of this strange new world, experiencing it on a deep level, even though to Inagi I was a wide-eyed child and had a whole lot to learn.

It was only a few more steps before we caught sight of the back of some of the grass huts that made up the border of the Amura village. It was also at that moment when someone else stepped out from behind the trunk of a tree.

It was that same big tiger.

He calmly stepped out and leisurely looked in our direction. Then he sat down on his haunches and waited for our next move.

I heard Jorn suck in his breath.

"I don't think we have a thing to worry about," I told Jorn and turning with a half-smile on my face stepped toward the tiger. "He was watching over us to make sure we got back OK."

I spoke to the big cat as I approached, "Since we are going to be meeting again, I'll need to think of a name for you."

He did that yawning thing again. He must have been bored with the idea.

"It's necessary," I told him. "People have to have a name for everything. I'm sure not going to call you something like Fluffy or some kind of little girl's pet name because I don't think you're ever going to be anyone's pet."

I reached out and scratched the tiger's ear.

He turned his head to the side to let me get at it easier.

I always like Frosted Flakes so off the top of my head I said, "How does Tony sound to you? Tony the Tiger kind of explains everything doesn't it?"

He stretched his neck up in the air and let me scratch him under his chin.

"So come on give me an answer," I asked. "How does Tony sound?"

He lowered his head, looked me straight in the eyes and gave a, "Yaaawwwwaaaaaahhh."

"That sounds like a yes to me."

He purred loudly. Then turned and bounded away into the jungle.

For some reason I knew this was a friendship that would never end.

9.

Welcome Back

We walked into the Amura village like conquering heroes and were treated to a heroes welcome.

At the first sight of us a tremendous shout went up among the women who were tending the fires. A moment later a woman, who only looked a little older than Jorn herself, came running out of a hut throwing the door aside and with a scream of happiness charged at him. She smothered Jorn's face with kisses, and then hugging his head to her bare breasts with tears running down her face shouted up to Ra thanks that he had given her son back to her.

Seeing her pressing his face to her breasts like that made me think, *Hey, I could use some of that kind of treatment.*

A group of women gathered around us and we were fairly mobbed.

Kalina showed up shoving her way through the group using her status as the medicine woman of the tribe to get through to us.

"Back, back, give them room," she told the others pushing them aside. "Give them air. They have come back from the dead. I must examine them."

I had to grin at the way this reminded me of the way doctors acted in the outer world as though they had knowledge that no one else would ever understand. It didn't bother me though so I played along.

When Kalina was standing right in front of me I half expected her to tell me to stick out my tongue and say ahhh. Instead she looked in my eyes and said, "I am happy you returned. When we heard Jorn was taken by the Nyseks and you went to rescue him we knew you were both lost forever."

"Well we're back and better than ever," I told her grinning. I glanced to the side where Jorn's mother seemingly had his head in a vice grip to her chest as she wailed out long sobs.

I cocked my head in their direction. "You could welcome me back like that," I said.

"You're well enough," she said and stepping forward punched me in the chest.

*

I only had a moment to catch my breath before Stian and a hunting party came in out of the jungle from the opposite side of the village that we entered from. Evidently they came back and left again without even a second thought about us. We were just put down as a loss to the tribe.

Jorn's family mourned but I was just written off.

I was going to have to show these people to never write off Derek Walker. Unless you see him dead, always figure he's coming back for more.

I still live!

Get used to it.

When Stian saw me he paled a little then recovered his composure and approached us.

For a moment he stood in front of me with a serious expression. The group of hunters he came back with followed him over to me. The entire tribe gathered around us. They all stood silently as Stian eyed me up and down. Then he smiled a half smile and spoke.

"Never before has anyone returned when taken by a Nysek," he said loud enough for everyone to hear. "Ra surely smiles upon us. We welcome this newcomer among the Amura and welcome new ways to our people."

67

I didn't know what the hell he meant by that but it sounded good to me.

While Kalar and Tond, the other two guys who were on the hunt that I'd went on, came up and congratulated me and Jorn for our return Stian marched over to the central fire and called everyone out of their huts to listen to an announcement.

"Hear me now people of the Amura," he shouted as soon as the majority of the tribe was gathered before him. "We celebrate the return of Jorn and Derek from the place of death by having a great feast."

And so it was announced!

10.

Feast

Stian gave quick orders organizing the celebration. He moved around the fire telling different women where to set up spits, what was to be roasted and where. The women went to work immediately setting several different animal carcasses to sizzling over the flames.

Several times as he did this Stian walked past me and each time he did he clapped me on the shoulder and called me friend. I guess the ice was broke between the two of us.

Next Stian had hunters drag out logs from behind huts and align them around the fire like a huge square. The logs were placed roughly about ten feet away from the blaze.

Children ran around playing. Women continued preparing the roasting animals and some of the hunters took seats upon the logs.

After he was done giving orders and everything was in motion, going the way he wanted it to Stian took a seat upon a log. He called me and Kalina over then bid us sit down at his side.

As we walked toward him Kalina told me, "Today you are the honored man. You will sit beside our chief. Remember always, now that you have the trust of the Amura each one of us would give our lives for you so long as you would do the same for us."

I liked the sound of her words. Back in the USA I was used to trusting no one and having no one trust me. I always felt strange being that way as though something was missing from life. This would be a new experience. It was something I was looking forward to getting used to.

We sat down beside Stian and he turned to me with a large toothy smile that was as unguarded and innocent as any look I had ever seen in my life.

"We are a good people," Stian told me obviously proud of being the leader of this tribe. "Stay with us as long as you like. We hope you will find a home among us." With that he glanced at Kalina and for some reason a bright pink blush rose to her cheeks.

I was really curious about the way these people measured the passage of time here where there was no rising or setting of the sun, so to give Kalina a way out of her strange embarrassment I asked, "When you took me in and kept me in the hut while I was asleep from my injury when I was first here how many things did you do?" I had to express the question this way because I was at a loss as to how to ask how much time had passed. The Amura didn't seem to have any words that expressed the passage of time.

Stian jumped in with an answer before Kalina spoke. "I hunted many times, brought home much strong meat."

Kalina spoke, "I slept and ate many times and tended many of my peoples injuries while you slept. You slept the deep sleep. It is good that you did. It is what you needed."

I wasn't really sure I knew any more than I did before. I was unconscious a long time. That was for certain.

Now is when we were interrupted by a cute looking girl with pert breasts, (they all had pert breasts) who brought her chief a large stone bottle filled with a liquid.

Drums now started up. While I hadn't been looking someone dragged them out and started pounding out a primitive rhythm that was hard not to clap your hands or stomp your feet to. It kind of reminded me of good old rock and roll.

Now I found out why the logs had been placed as far from the fire as they were. For me the real entertainment began.

The women of the tribe, and I now noticed something I thought peculiar, *there were no old people at all*, began dancing around the fire shaking everything that they had for the entire world to see. And there was a whole lot of really tasty flesh to be seen at that barbecue.

I was admiring the dancing women, probably ogling them so much my eyes were in danger of falling out of my head when Stian elbowed me. For a moment I thought he was angry at the way I was looking at his women-folk but a glance at his good natured smile snuffed that idea.

Stian was passing me the stone bottle.

I took the bottle.

"We are a healthy people," Stian said laughing and making a bottoms-up motion for me to drink.

"From what I can see you sure are," I told him and putting the bottle to my lips upended it.

It was like drinking liquid fire. White lightning had never been this strong. The drink burned as it went down and a pleasant numbness spread at once throughout my body.

Before I had even handed the bottle off to Kalina my face, head and neck was completely void of sensation.

Kalina passed the bottle over to a man sitting on the other side of her without taking a drink.

"Don't be a party pooper." I said to her. "Go ahead and down some."

"I do not think that would be a good idea," Kalina told me.

"Why? Are you afraid you won't be able to control yourself around me?" I asked. "Go ahead, let yourself go."

"No," she said. "Somebody will have to take care of you when the Boog wears off. I'll probably be the only one with a clear head."

Everything was getting extremely hazy really fast. I could definitely tell what she was talking about. Wherever the bottle went and

71

was drank from that person, be it man or woman instantly wore a stupid expression on their face.

I probably looked really stupid myself. I didn't care. I was having fun.

This was the first time since I'd started my pro boxing career that I even went to a party. The truth was I didn't trust anyone enough so I would ever let my guard down. Of the life I remembered I had lived alone never really allowing myself to get close to anyone.

These people, The Amura, had instantly accepted me. For some strange reason I felt like I had the one thing I'd never felt I had when living on the Outer-Earth … a family.

What did I care that they were mostly naked savages. I was a guy who had stood before crowds of thousands howling for blood. It doesn't get any more savage than that.

Food, mostly roasting meat was taken off the fire and passed around.

Standing up I stretched and rubbed my stomach, saw that one of the women handing out pieces of meat was walking by us. I tapped her on the arm and said, "I sure could use some of that food. Slide some of it my way."

Stian spoke, "Get him a Squack. He deserves to eat the best of the feast."

The girl turned and hurried away to the far side of the fire.

"A Squack?" I asked.

"You will like it," Stian answered. "In this part of the valley we trap excellent Squack."

What the hell, I thought and sat back down on the log awaiting my dinner.

A lot of the women were still dancing and the drummers were still drumming so I occupied my time by studying local dance moves. Studying nature in the middle of the Amura village was a total pleasure except that

Kalina kept elbowing me every time it seemed I took too long a look at one of the local attractions.

At one point I had to lean over and tell her, "Girl, take it easy alright. You didn't nurse me back to health just to break my bones now did you?"

"I should break a bone of yours," she said annoyed.

That made both Stian and me laugh, which made Kalina even madder. So I told her, "I do have a bone you could go to work on."

She slapped me and walked off in a huff.

Stian looked at me with a stupid grin on his face that was mirrored by my own. "I think Kalina likes you," he said. "If she doesn't, you will know it very soon."

"How's that?"

"She'll come back and run you through with a spear like my wife tried before she realized how much she loves me."

Primitive romance, I thought. *Not too much different than the club scene in the Outer-Earth.*

The girl with my Squack on a stick came back. My eyes almost fell out of my head when I saw what Squack was.

The thing they'd been roasting on the fire was the biggest Goddam cockroach I'd ever seen in my life. It was a roach as long as my arm and about six inches wide.

"You expect me to eat that thing?" I asked Stian as the woman handed me the stick with the skewered roach on it.

"It is the very best food we have," Stian said to me.

I hadn't seen Kalina come back because she snuck up behind me. She now whispered in my ear. "It would be a great insult if you did not crack the shell of the Squack and partake of its meat. It really is the best tasting of everything the Amura has. That is why Stian offered it to you."

I took the huge roach-on-a-stick from the girl and sat back down on the log.

"Fuck-it," I said. "Somebody give me a God-dam rock. We gonna crack some Squack."

11.

Party Crashers

I laid the giant cockroach down on the ground in front of me. Standing on my knees I raised a fist-sized stone over my head. I glanced at Stian.

"Is this what I'm supposed to do to eat this thing?" I asked.

He laughed. "Do whatever gets you the meat."

"OK," I said and smashed the stone down upon the back of the Squack.

There was a loud crunch, like the breaking of a walnut shell only five times louder. The back of the giant roach was caved in and its shell was now broken into finger sized shards of black ceramic looking chips.

From behind me Kalina applauded.

"It was a good fight by he lost," I told her and started picking the pieces of broken shell out of the caved in back and dropping them beside my feast.

What I uncovered was a white milky filmed-over white covered meat. I swallowed involuntarily.

Glancing at Stian I saw he was staring at me waiting for me to dig in. *What the hell*, I thought. *I ate some snails one time that looked like thickened snot and they actually tasted pretty good. This can't be too much worse.*

I thrust my right hand down into the back of the roach. The slimy feel of the milky film made goose bumps jump up on my arms and my stomach involuntary shuddered. Jamming my fingers down into something that felt rubbery and warm I grasped a piece of the meat and ripped it out.

The fistful of meat I tore loose was gooey and slippery. Before I had a chance to even think about what I was doing and before my belly had the chance to heave at the thought of what was headed its way, I took a big bite of the roach meat ripping it off with my teeth like a hungry pit bull.

The Squack/Roach tasted really good. It had the texture of tender beef and a taste that was slightly sweet almost like a fresh orange had been squeezed over grilled chicken.

I chewed that first bite, swallowed, then dove in for some more.

"I told you it would be good," Stian laughed and clapped me on the back.

Between bites I answered, "You were telling the truth bro."

I dug in and ate that big bug enjoying each bite more than the one before it.

The drummers kept on drumming. The women kept on dancing. The Boog bottle made its way around the fire at least twice more. Each time the Boog passed me and Stian took huge guzzles from it. Everything was swaying and misty.

The haze must have been from my eyes refusing to focus.

The colors of everything seemed to be brighter than I had ever noticed them before. The greens of the trees swaying in the breeze seemed greener. The flames of the fire were yellower. The skin of the people down here seemed vibrant and wildly alive.

Everything down here seemed to be more alive than it had been in the world I had left.

It was about this time that I turned to Stian and told him I was very grateful for the way they had taken me in and was treating me like one of their own. I guess I was feeling that type of drunken camaraderie thing that I'd heard some other guys talk about.

He listened solemnly to what I said. When I was finished Stian told me, "I am a different man from my father. When he was still the leader of this tribe he would not have given you the chance to prove yourself. You would never have been allowed in the tribe. When you were found in the cave we would have killed you on sight.

"We are but one small tribe of many who live in the valley of Amura. When my father was alive the different tribes fought each other. All the tribes raided each other for whatever they could steal or take by force. I grew up seeing friends and family fight and die and never knowing why the tribes fought when there was enough game and lands for us all.

"When my father was killed I took his place and decided I would be different. I went to every tribe of Amura, one at a time, each time expecting to be killed. I asked every chief for us all to be allowed to live in peace. Every one of them agreed to end the killing.

"We have lived in peace in this valley every since."

I shook Stian's hand and told him, "Living in peace and not in war is a noble idea. I came from a place where some people have had the same thought."

"Were they able to make peace in this land you come from?" Stian asked.

"No, I think they killed every single one of them."

That was when the ground began to shake.

At first I thought they'd brought out the extra-large drums and were pounding on those. But when everyone froze, the dancers, the playing children, even the hunters enjoying the feast froze with expressions of pure terror written on their faces. I knew something was very wrong.

Then a horrible trumpeting was heard. It was like the sound of five hundred cornets blown all at once and all of them hitting a sour note. The sound was so loud it was impossible to tell where it was coming from. The incredible rolling rumble and the trumpeting seemed to be emanating from all sides of the village, all around us.

Everyone sitting on the logs jumped to their feet. I did the same.

"What the hell is going on?" I yelled to Stian and Kalina. Kalina stood beside me clutching my arm. She looked like she wanted to find somewhere to hide.

With my question she muttered a fear choked answer.

"Bollards," Kalina whispered.

That was one of the words I hadn't learned yet but I found out what it meant instantly when the huts I was facing exploded forward and were trampled down by a massive wall of rampaging charging flesh. I had only seen these creatures on display in a natural history museum and these were far larger than the ones represented there.

What crashed through the dwellings were large wild elephants with huge mops of hair swinging back and forth on their heads as they trumpeted and charged.

It was a herd of Wooly Mammoths that stomped through the line of huts on that side of the village. They seemed crazed, incensed by something driving them from behind. I didn't have time to study what was forcing them forward. I only knew we had to get the hell out of their way.

Some members of the tribe froze where they were by the sudden appearance of the huge beasts and were trampled flat. I wasn't going to be one of them.

Grabbing Kalina by the arm I yelled, "Come on," and ran sideways across the path of the mammoths. Kalina was quick on her feet and she was right with me as we dodged between two of the stomping giants and raced for the safety of the trees.

The ground trembled as the enormous animals trampled huts, fires, and people into crushed bloody ruin.

We'd almost made the edge of the village and the shelter of the trees beyond when a long snake-like trunk reached out and batted the both of us to the side.

We flew through the air at least twenty feet like a slapped bean bag. I landed hard against the trunk of a tree seeing stars, dizzy as hell.

Climbing to my feet I saw that Kalina had at least missed the trees and landed on a thick patch of grass. She rolled over and moaned.

Most of the rampaging mammoths were already through the village and out the other side leaving a trail of broken bodies behind. A few stragglers were still trailing the herd. Among them wandered what was left of this village's Amura, a few stunned confused survivors.

I now saw what had caused the stampede.

Coming behind the last of the mammoths was a line of men wearing leather helmets carrying wooden shields in one hand and torches in the other.

Behind them was another group of men carrying swords with white blades, battle axes with white axe-heads and wooden shields. They wore a mixture of animal skins and crudely woven cloth garments.

I'd seen pictures of guys just like these in history books and I'd seen one movie with guys dressed just like this. I could be wrong but these boys looked a whole lot like Vikings to me.

12.

Viking Raid

The warriors' intentions were obvious. They swarmed into the village tackling the surviving women and children and clubbing the stunned hunters into submission with well practiced efficiency.

They didn't use the white bladed swords or battle axes that I'd mentioned. After these blond and red-headed warriors saw there was no organized resistance they put away their bladed weapons and armed themselves with what looked like small wooden baseball bats and started rounding up everyone who was not a crushed corpse.

It's amazing how fast a man will sober up when he's completely wasted drunk and a Wooly Mammoth stampede followed by a Viking attack takes place.

In an instant I was clear eyed and ready to defend Kalina to the death.

Three of the club wielding warriors detached themselves from the main body of their force and came at me.

I yelled to Kalina, "Stay behind me!"

One of the guys had long red hair, a full beard and a crazed look in his eyes. He was a bit fat and looked slow but strong.

The other two were blond headed, tall, lean and mean as hell.

The fat red head came in laughing. Maybe he figured he was Conan or something and that his grim smile and love of combat would scare the shit out of me. He was in for a surprise.

Red Beard swung his club from up over his head like he'd forgot it wasn't a battle ax. When he went to step in and deliver a down-stroke to the top of my head I surprised him by stepping forward into him. I deflected the club swing with my left forearm and slammed a powerful right cross to the point of Red Beard's chin.

He stiffened on impact and it was almost comical the way his eyes rolled up into his head before he fell stiff as a board flat to his back.

"Step right up mother-fuckers," I shouted at the other two guys. They hesitated so I leaped over Red Beard and charged them.

In close quarter combat those clubs of theirs would be nearly useless. So I wanted to get as close to them as possible. I jumped right between them and backhand-chopped the guy on my right across the throat.

He partially blocked it but he backed off a good five steps.

The other guy caught me a glancing blow on my shoulder with his club. It hurt like hell but so what. I didn't expect that they were patting for a dance.

I ducked down bending at the knees and as this Viking maniac reared back to brain me I side thrust kicked him in the nuts.

Seeing him go to his knees choking, gagging and vomiting was one of the most welcome sights I'd ever seen.

The next thing I saw was one of the most unwelcome sights I'd ever witnessed. A net was descending over me. One of the other warriors snuck up behind me and threw the dam thing over my head.

As soon as the net hit me I was struggling to pull it off and two of them jumped forward and tackled me.

I went down on my face, cursing and spitting.

Those two sat on me.

Through the net I managed to get hold of one of their ankles. I twisted it rolling him off to the side and managed to roll over to a facing up position.

81

Now another warrior stepped forward. He held a spear in his hands. He jabbed its point straight at my chest.

"Surrender now!" He shouted at me. "Or I'll run you through where you lay."

I had no choice so I surrendered.

*

As three warriors that I fought held weapons on me ready to chop off a limb if I made a move to struggle I was hauled to my feet by two other blond headed Vikings and had my hands bound behind me.

Red Beard stared at me with pure hate radiating from his eyes as I was bound. As soon as my hands were secured behind my back he stepped forward, yelled, "You dick sucker!" and threw an uppercut to my stomach.

I saw it coming and tightened my solar plexus muscles before impact so all the blow did was make me expel a loud lungful of air and stumble back a step. It really wasn't all that big a deal. I'm a guy who's been doing three hundred plus sit-ups everyday for over the last ten years. Getting punched in the gut doesn't mean shit to a guy like me.

Red Beard must have thought I'd collapse right away.

I grinned at him and laughed.

"Is that the best you can do?" I said. "Little girls hit harder than that."

He stepped toward me again this time raising his right hand to back-hand me.

Red Beard's wrist was caught from behind. It was the same guy who I'd kicked in the nuts. He was done vomiting but still looked green in the face.

Red Beard turned on him in a rage and was met with a stern gaze and a stone knife pointed at his throat.

"Never forget Loknar, we are the Nords, the Masters of Land and Sea in Inagi," he said. "We fight and conquer and take whatever we want but always with honor."

Red Beard who I now figured was named Loknar, looked for a moment like he was going to say something back. Then he thought better of it and, mumbled something under his breath. He turned and walked away.

I started to thank the tall blond warrior for stopping Loknar but as I opened my mouth he was already speaking.

"Do what you are told and give us no problems," he said. "I am Svengar and you are now my property. If you fail to obey, to make the others more obedient I will have your head cut off and we will carry it with us on a pole as a reminder.

Owned!

13.

Kalina's Tale:
Fair Weather Friends

As I squared off to bust knuckles with the three Vikings that came at me Kalina looked around to see if there were any weapons available so she could help out in the fight.

Kalina wore a knife strapped to her hip that she used in her everyday duties as a medicine woman. She knew that was next to useless against the heavily armed warriors. She saw small stones scattered about on the ground but had no sling. All the hunter's spears were in the middle of where the one-sided battle was taking place.

In front of her, there were a whole lot of strangely armed warriors kicking the shit out of everybody from her tribe who hadn't been smashed flat by the charging mammoths. To the back of Kalina was a thick lush jungle with a thousand hiding places and beyond that was literally dozens of encampments of Amura.

The land of Amura was a wide low depression similar to the Mississippi River Valley down around St. Louis. It was a large stretch of land that housed many tribes, lakes and forests.

A decision about what had to be done needed to be made in a split second. Kalina, being of a quick mind, highly attuned to taking fast decisive action, saw that I could not possibly fight off all the strange looking warriors attacking her tribe.

She was a woman accustomed to all the dangers of living in a primitive world. This was not a Charlie's Angels Fantasy. This was her life and she knew how to deal realistically with all its problems. It was a grim fact that Kalina could not be of much use in a fight to the death against vicious armed warriors.

Although it pained her heart to do so, Kalina turned and fled into the thick dark jungle.

After heading straight forward for what we would call roughly a mile, although people in Inagi seem to have no set way of measuring distance, Kalina turned in the direction that she knew the closest camp of Amura to be.

She ran fast but was ever vigilant for the countless dangers that lurked in this primeval jungle.

In this jungle and in fact just about everywhere upon the face of Inagi the deadliest predators that had ever stalked every time period of the Outer-Earth, and some that never existed anywhere else except in this inner-world, thrived. Here, in the land of Ra: The Eternal Sun, time had seemingly stopped. If a species was effective at survival, in Inagi they would survive.

Inagi was the place where the dinosaurs had retreated to when their kind were removed from the outer-world by the great meteorite impact, then the Great Ice Age. Species survival is the strongest survival instinct and somehow when a species was threatened with permanent erasure members of their kind found their way far underground to this hidden world.

That was the kind of jungle that Kalina fled through. It was a steaming hot jungle that housed gargantuan reptiles, huge cave bears and savage long-toothed tigers.

Kalina was well aware of these dangers. She moved with the sure footed swiftness of a child of the jungle and sped toward the closest encampment of Amura.

The journey was long and hard. Foot travel through the jungle always is.

At length she broke through a line of trees coming out into a clearing and before her stood a cluster of huts.

Kalina entered the Amura village.

"Where is Melar?" she shouted to a woman who was busy cleaning the carcass of a large game animal. "I have need to speak to your head man."

The woman looked up from the animal she was just beginning to skin and pointed with her knife to a large hut. The dwelling she pointed at was similar to the huts in her own village except that it was at least three times the size of the largest hut anyone in her tribe had ever built.

Without preamble Kalina marched to the door of the dwelling and rapped sharply upon the wood.

When there was no immediate answer she knocked again.

"Go away. We are resting," was shouted from inside by a crusty man's voice. That was followed by a light giggle and the gruff voice saying, "Shut up and come here."

Kalina swung the door open and stepped inside into the filtered dim light of the large dark room.

Her eyes adjusted in a moment to the gloom and she saw sprawled on a huge grass bed three naked figures. Two of them were young women and one of them was a man with a pot belly.

The man had an arm around one woman's shoulder fondling her breast as he reached for the other with his free hand.

He froze as Kalina entered. Then he roared, "How dare you enter my home uninvited. Unless you want a good beating you will leave now!" Melar's eyes took in the shapely figure of the medicine woman outlined by the light of the open door.

The head man smiled.

"You may stay," he told her his tone softening. "Disrobe and come here. My two hands are occupied but I have other parts of my body that needs tending to."

"I think not," was Kalina's answer. Her chin went up in the air. "When I choose a man to lay with I am the only one for him."

"Then leave," Melar said dipping his head toward the closest women's breast, kissing a nipple.

"I come to warn you that our people have been attacked. We need you to assemble your men to go and fight and ..."

"You are from Stian's village?" Melar interrupted looking up from the breast that he worked at.

"Yes," Kalina confirmed.

"I never liked him," Melar stated. "Him and his talk of peace never set well with me. He also would not do an exchange of women that I proposed. No, I never liked him one bit."

"But we are all Amura," Kalina told him. "We must stand together against this threat to our people."

"Get out," Melar said. "Or I will drag you over here and you will know the pleasures of a King."

Kalina could see that it was useless appealing to this pig for assistance for her people. He was already mounting one of the women by the time she slammed the door behind her.

Kalina quickly explained the situation to the woman cleaning the carcass who said she would warn the rest of the tribe.

"Men say they rule," the woman told Kalina. "But we know it is really the women who get done what is important."

Then after snatching a spear leaning against a hut Kalina trotted out of that village in the direction of the next closest village she knew of.

Kalina hoped her luck would be better there.

14.

Transportation

The rope that the Nordic warriors tied my hands behind my back with had a feel like it was made of silk. I tested it and found that the rope was extremely strong.

They used this same kind of cord to tie each of the surviving Amura tribe members together by a loop in the rope roughly every four feet and that was thrown over our heads.

Running was out of the question.

Being bound together at the neck, with our hands tied behind our back, forced forward down a narrow trail toward only God knows what did not make for a pleasant stroll. The Vikings were not concerned about our comfort. These were definitely not employees of the Viking Cruise Lines.

They prodded us forward with sword points whenever we slowed and made like they were going to chop off a limb whenever we tried to talk.

We made a dismal procession as we marched along.

Stian had somehow ended up just ahead of me.

I would have passed some whispered words with him but he seemed like he didn't want to speak with anyone. His face was set in an intense scowl.

I didn't really blame him either.

During one afternoon of partying he'd went from being the proud chief of his tribe to a down and out lowdown dirty slave. The change would take some getting used to.

After we marched for what seemed like miles the Vikings had us stop and sit in the dirt of the trail so they could take a rest.

It was then that I turned to Stian. "How are you doing?" I asked him.

His reply was a surprise.

"All of this is my fault," he said.

"This isn't anybody's fault," I told Stian.

"I should have had you killed when you came back with Jorn."

My jaw dropped. "You're going to have to explain this to me," I told him. "I save one of your lives. Now you say you should have killed me, what the hell are you talking about?"

"The Nyseks are not of Inagi," Stian said. "They took Jorn. He was theirs. You killed a Nysek and now we are all cursed because I did not make you pay for it. I should have had you killed when you returned. I turned my back on the ways of our fathers and now all my people are paying for my weakness."

"You're full of shit," I said and started to follow that up with a speech about the ignorance of superstition but one of the Vikings rapped me sharply on the back with the flat of his sword.

"No speaking!" he shouted. "We tell you when to talk."

I wanted to bash his teeth in, break his nose and crush his skull, but with my hands tied behind my back at the moment I wasn't going to be kicking anybody's ass. So I shut up.

The rest period was far too short. Sooner than I wanted we were being ushered down the trail again with sword points prodding us along.

It wasn't long after that when a sight came to my eyes that I never thought I would see. There were three lengthy wooden ships; I would estimate them as being around fifty feet long and ten feet wide in the center that had been run aground upon a sandy shore. The ships had central masts for sails and somewhere around twenty oars stood straight up in the air.

Hanging from the central mast, dangling by rope were several decomposing heads, their faces forever locked in the grimace of an ugly death.

At the front of each of these ships standing out proudly were the carved heads of fierce looking Gods. I didn't know the names of any of these Gods but I bet none of them were Buddha.

15.

The Viking Way

The scene on the sandy beach was idyllic.

Calm waves rolled in to the shore from a deep blue sea. As I faced the water, to my right the beach was bordered by thick jungle that ran off upward into the distance until it was lost in a misty haze. To the left the shore continued on for roughly a hundred yards then rocky cliffs sprang up out of the ground and ocean to stretch upward into the air two or three hundred feet. Over the top of it all was that strange upward lean of the general landscape that I don't think I will ever get fully accustomed to. Of course Ra looked down on everything with his radiant light illuminating and heating the entire inner world.

It was a beautiful scene. It was a scene where children should have been playing among the waves and women should be strolling peacefully in bikinis enjoying the sun and the gazes of admiring men.

I wasn't in a position to enjoy it.

The Vikings were met by a party of warriors that had been left behind to guard the ships. The two bands of warriors exchanged greetings and immediately we were ushered into the water.

We were forced to wade out to the ships that were wedged on the sand where it was waist deep.

It was here that I got a good idea of just how devastating the attack upon Stian's village had been. As the captives were maneuvered toward the ships for boarding I got a view of all the village survivors and there weren't many.

Formerly I had estimated that there were about a hundred people in Stian's village. Now there were only around thirty left alive.

I guess I could understand the way that Stian felt. Doom had come to his village and it had arrived right after me. Cause and effect, along with a superstitious fear of the Nyseks would make Stian connect his village's raid with me killing that big-ass spider-thing. Stian thought I was the bringer of his entire village's bad luck. But right then I couldn't do anything about changing what Stian thought.

The Vikings marched us out into the water positioning us on both sides of their ships. Then they took that rope that was looped around our heads off. We could now move but with warriors on all sides with swords in their hands to run or fight meant only to die.

Over the sides of each of the ships nets were draped that hung all the way down into the water. The women and children were made to climb those nets and get into the ships. Once they were aboard with swords pointed at our guts the men were directed to position ourselves against the hulls. There the ropes that bound our hands behind us were untied.

Now we were made to push the ships outward toward deeper water. It was slow going. There were probably fifteen grown men left in Stian's village. We were divided up into parties of five for each of the three ships. With only five guys shoving something that large it wasn't a small task.

With the water lapping against our waists we strained against the barnacled wood as hard as we could to get the big boats sliding. It was slow work but we were motivated by swords jabbing us in the ass. After much grunting and groaning and straining against the sliding sands beneath our feet we got the ships moving.

That was when they ordered us to climb the nets and get in ourselves.

We did.

*

In the ship was a grim sight.

I was just one more slave in a group of slaves when I stuck my head over the edge of the railing of the Viking ship. Inside, there were rows of thick wooden benches that other slaves with their hands tied in front of them sat upon. A quick estimate of how many slaves were already there would have been around a hundred. But there really was no way to actually tell how many people were on that ship as I was prodded upward none too gently by sword point.

A quick glance showed me that a large percentage of these people sitting on the benches were women and children. The majority of them looked very sick. In fact they looked like they could fall over dead at any moment.

I climbed up and over the railing and was forced forward down the length of the ship until I was directed to take a seat beside a woman and a girl of maybe ten years old. The child looked deathly ill, like she'd been having an extremely bad bout of sea sickness. The woman appeared to be her mother and even in her helplessness looked like she was attempting to be protective of her child.

My heart went out to them even if there was nothing I could do at the moment.

I tried to give the both of them a hopeful smile but probably failed as I wasn't in all that hopeful of a mood myself.

As soon as everyone climbing aboard was at their positions I turned to the woman and spoke simply, "Everything is going to be all right. We will get out of this."

A stinging blow that made a loud whap landed upon my back.

I turned my head and stared into the blazing eyes of Loknar, that fat red-bearded idiot whose ass I'd already kicked once before.

He was grinning. "You have been told to be silent," he growled leaning forward into my face. "For some reason Svengar thinks you are valuable as a pit fighter. I don't. But I will keep you alive so long as the

King's Son orders it. Pit fighters do not need their tongues. You will either do as you are told silently or I will personally cut your tongue out."

That didn't seem to be an appealing option. As meekly as possible I nodded my head and averted my eyes. I wanted to appear as though these warriors and this guy in particular had already broken my spirit. Nothing could be further from the truth. But since these Vikings seemed to have a love for removing body parts I would save my anger for later.

The first order of business was staying alive if I was going to do anything for any of these people and myself.

*

The twenty oars that were standing straight up were stuck into wooden rings. These we were made to hoist out and shove through holes in the sides of the ship keeping the oars held out above the water. The wind was right so the Vikings got their ships moving by lowering a sail positioned between two horizontal posts. When the sail was lowered I got another surprise.

Painted black upon white in the center of the sail was the image of an enormous spider. This spider was a bit different than your typical garden variety arachnid in that it sported the head of an evil looking man with intense red eyes that seemed to stare down at us and me in particular, with malignant intent.

Maybe there was something to what Stian had said after all, I thought just as the wind caught the sails and the ship began gliding out into deeper water. Then the order was given for us to row.

*

Being a galley slave on a Viking ship is just about the worst job that you can ever imagine. The pay is low. Hell, you're paid nothing. The conditions are horrible. Sweaty stinking sea-sick people were all around me vomiting and suffering from diarrhea. Nobody came to clean it up. A lot of people were throwing up and had the drizzling shits. If somebody fell over exhausted or dead they were just left where they were until one of the Vikings got tired of smelling them and tossed them overboard.

As for the work itself; you rowed, rowed some more, then for a change, you rowed some more.

Some idiot pounded on a drum to make us keep a rhythm to pulling these enormous oars through the water. I don't think it helped. We just tried to keep going mainly because there was a guy wandering around with a whip that loved the hell out of cracking it across your back whenever you missed a stroke.

I didn't miss very many strokes. One crack of the whip was all I needed to learn that lesson fast.

What I did do was try to take up all the strain off the woman and little girl that sat beside me on the bench. They weren't in any condition to do physical labor and I tried to lessen their load as much as I could.

On the benches around me they had the division of labor set up pretty much the same way. It was one man, on the outside and two weaker slaves toward the middle.

The sails seemed to be doing most of the work so I wondered why they had us rowing at all. But to answer my own question, I figure it was just to keep the men, busy and tired. After we rowed for hours without a break, there just wasn't enough energy left in your body to attempt an escape and fighting was out of the question. Your back was burning, aching to the breaking point. Your arms felt like they were on fire and your ass was stuck full of splinters from sitting on those rough benches. It was not a good day and down here, the day never ends.

In short, after spending a session of rowing that huge boat, I sure could have used a month at a health spa with Victoria Secrets Models to massage the kinks out of my muscles. Such are the dreams of a galley slave.

We sure as hell weren't going to get the royal treatment on this boat. Massages by models were never going to be anything more than exhausted fever dreams.

We rowed until we thought we couldn't go on, and then we went on and rowed some more. The drum never seemed to stop pounding and since Ra refused to ever stop shining down I have no idea how long that hell of endlessly pulling the oar through the water went on. The sounds of wood slapping water, exhausted slaves moaning and groaning under the strain of the oars, the creaking of the ship's timbers rubbing against each other as they flexed in the waves and that insane never-ending beat of the drum threatened to drive me insane before it came to an end.

But in time it did come to an end.

Land was sighted. Even though I knew it meant even more slave labor after that eternity of rowing I welcomed it.

16.
Viking Settlement

The sighting of land was definitely welcome. I didn't really see it. It was shouted by one of the crew members. The picture popped up in my mind immediately of how Gilligan's Island looked from a distance.

We were ordered to slow our rhythm with the oars to near stopping altogether. Soon after they had us withdraw the oars entirely from the water and stand them up using the wooden rings we'd gotten them from in the first place.

As we, the slaves sat on the benches with our arms hanging by our sides like lead weights the three ships were guided in using wind power and a rudder controlled by two men. It was slower going gliding along like that. If I didn't have a life of enforced servitude or a quick painful death to look forward to I might have thought it was peaceful. But as we glided toward a shore that I could not see and one by one each slaves hands were bound together, this time in front of us, this was not a scene that I was capable of enjoying.

All of us galley slaves were exhausted.

After what seemed like far too short a time the ship bumped into something that felt heavy and solid. Our forward momentum was stopped dead. I could feel more than see when the ship was secured.

Then they began unloading the slaves.

They treated us like the cattle that we were, ordering us out of the benches and down the narrow walkway that made up the middle of the ship. We were marched up and out of the ship onto a dock that was roughly the same height as the side of the ship.

The warriors who shoved and guided us along were dirty and sweaty and looked like they were far past due for a shower. All of us galley slaves looked like we were ready to drop dead at any moment.

We were marched down a long wide wooden dock toward a cluster of rough low wooden buildings.

In single file we were forced from the dock onto a well worn trail where we were met by a pack of laughing, dancing children. These kids were like a pack of dirty little wild animals. As we were shoved and prodded by sword point toward the cluster of wooden buildings that I was guessing made up the Viking's village the kids started pelting us with rocks and dirt clods all the while shouting curses at us.

The little bastards were the best examples of bad inner breeding that I'd ever encountered or even wanted to. I wish I could have taken a picture and sent that back to the Outer-Earth as proof that sometimes abortion should be mandatory.

The sun was hot but one thing I noticed was that despite the hellishly long bout of rowing I felt no sunburn upon my face. It was just one more curiosity of this strange underground world that I'd have to file away and investigate later. The curiosities of Inagi were piling up. Probably like the world outside, most of the mysteries I never would understand.

We were marched along a trail that led up a hill to the cluster of buildings. As we got closer I realized they were larger than I originally thought they were although all of them were single story structures.

One other thing that I could make out as we got closer was that the buildings were not entirely made of wood. They were also made of mud or a type of red clay that was used to seal the cracks between the logs that made up the walls. The tops of these buildings looked like thatched grass. Where the roofs of the huts in the village of Amura were flat almost all of these roofs were rounded off. In fact these dwellings looked vaguely like what I had seen in museums illustrating Bronze Age England.

As we approached the village the warriors that were guarding us ran off the children tormenting us. I guess they didn't allow rock throwing in town. They sure didn't stop them because of any concern for any of the slaves. A few of the children that numbered among the slaves had been knocked to the ground by some stone throws.

The warriors guarding us had just laughed and shouted at the kids to get up and get moving or get a swift kick to the head.

We entered the village and were treated to the sight of an open town square that measured roughly fifty yards across. That town square could have been mistaken for an open air flea or farmers market if it wasn't for something very large in the center of it.

There was a massive cage in the center of the plaza. The cage was made of poles driven into the ground, arranged in a square with side bars tied tightly together to make sure nobody could easily climb out. The poles were roughly fifteen feet tall and the cage had no roof. There was no need for a roof since whatever anyone did in that cage was easily visible for everyone to see.

There would be no secret midnight attempts at escape from this open air prison even if Inagi had night.

There was only one door in and one door out. We were shoved inside and the entrance was locked behind us with a heavy wooden latch.

*

Now at least I had a moment to stop and think and maybe plot some course of action.

Until this moment every since the attack on Stian's village I had just been reacting to the situation rather than trying to make some kind of a plan to do something about it.

The first thing was to take stock of just who was here and who wasn't. Knowing who we had with us would tell us what kind of a fighting force we would have at our disposal if we had any kind of a chance at planning an escape.

Looking around at the broken exhausted slaves the first thing I noticed with relief was that Kalina was not with us. I told her to run before turning to bust knuckles with the Vikings but hadn't seen if she'd listened or not. It was good to know that she wouldn't be under the control of these animals. I wasn't a very attentive student of history but something deep inside me told me that somewhere before I had personal experience with slaves. I knew that unless the master was exceptionally kind hearted, women slaves, especially attractive women slaves, had one main purpose to the men who owned them and it wasn't doing the dishes or picking up around the house.

Jorn was also nowhere to be seen. I was hoping that meant he escaped into the jungle like Kalina and wasn't lying dead back at the village. It would be a long time before I'd know what happened to either of them.

The two hunters Kalar and Tond, were among the warriors that were now sitting in the dirt catching their breath. I was glad to see them.

There were around two hundred people in that cage. We had enough room to move around but if everybody decided to lie down and take a nap we'd run short of space.

Villagers walked around the outside of the cage looking in at us, checking us out, no doubt estimating the value of each one of us. The men stared at the attractive women and made crude comments about what they wanted to do to them. I wanted to bust those guy's teeth out: *Maybe later?*

Stian was sitting in a crouched over position against the wooden bars of our prison. He was staring at the Vikings that walked past outside. He still had that dour expression of total doom upon his face like his world had come to an end and there was nothing he could do about it. He looked like he was past the point of giving up. If we were going to have any chance of getting the hell out of this I was going to need him whether he wanted to have anything to do with me or not.

I went to Stian and sat down beside him in the dirt. My leg and back muscles thanked me for giving them a moments rest after all the time pulling that dam oar.

I leaned over and whispered, "We have to talk. You need to start acting like the leader of your people. They need you."

"I am no one's leader anymore," Stian said and the devastation on his face told me he was entirely serious. What he said he felt all the way through down to his core. He felt like he failed his people.

"They need you," I repeated.

He just shook his head and looked down.

"What the hell is wrong with you?" I asked him. My voice was getting louder even though I didn't mean for it to. To see this man reduced suddenly to having no guts drove me to the point of wanting to bash his head in. "You can't just give up when things go wrong. You've got to fight."

He spoke softly almost apologetically, "I went against the warnings of my fathers and brought this down upon us all. There is nothing that I can do to change what must be."

"That's bullshit!" I told him.

"The ways of the fathers are all we have," Stian said as though he was reciting scripture from the Bible. "When we go against them everything falls apart."

"You want to blame yourself and me for these assholes destroying your village?" I shouted at him. "You're totally fucking nuts."

"I went against the ways of my fathers," he repeated like a broken record. "I should have known better. What have we got if we do not follow the ways of our fathers?"

I opened my mouth and began to shout something back but the words caught in my throat. I had no answer for his question. The ways of my fathers were completely unknown to me.

It had been a long time since I had thought of my own life, what I could remember of it anyway.

*   *   *

My Mysterious Origins:

As far as I can tell I've always been roughly around the age of thirty. I have no memories of any family at all. I do not know my Father. I do not know my Mother.

My origin is a complete mystery to me.

The first thing I can remember is being on a dark icy road somewhere outside of a city. The pavement is coal black. The sky is coal black.

The year is lost to me even now. All I know is that it was sometime in the middle of the winter. I was walking.

The cold was deep inside me, down all the way to my bones.

My head ached. My feet ached. My legs ached. Everything hurt.

I was one big walking wound.

Lights, unbelievably bright, shone straight into my eyes, tearing through the retinas all the way back into the center of my skull, blinding me, frying my brain.

I put my hand up to shield my eyes and a horn like the roar of some kind of prehistoric creature blasts my ears so loud I feel my skull vibrate all the way through.

Icy cold arctic wind blasts my skin, scraping from head to foot like frozen sandpaper. A huge thing, a tractor-trailer screams by almost smashing into me. It misses me by a bare two inches. The wind in its wake pulls the oxygen from my lungs.

I suck in gasps of air.

The truck drives off into the distance and I am again alone in the darkness.

Time passes as I stumble forward in the blackness toward a destination that is totally unknown. The cold cuts deep into me, burrows beneath my skin, settles inside my body. I become one with the cold of this place, the absence of heat and warmth is what I am.

Another pair of headlights appears in the distance. This time the two white lights are accompanied by flashing red and blue lights over the top of them.

The vehicle slows as it approaches until it stops ten feet from where I stand. The lights bath me in a colorless pallid glow. It is now that I realize I am standing out in the middle of the open paved road in the freezing weather with not a stitch of clothing on.

Over a loud speaker came the words. "Put your hands up over your head."

I do as they ask.

From both doors uniformed men come out. Both have guns drawn.

I wonder why. It's not like I could have any concealed weapons.

They order me into their vehicle and I comply welcoming the warmth.

When they question me and ask who I am I have no answer.

I don't know who I am. I don't know how I came to be on the road where they found me. The blackboard that holds the story of my life has been wiped clean.

On the way to the police department when they call their dispatcher to make their report the policeman states into his radio, "We have a Walker, in the Dark, on US47, totally unclothed, alone, no ID. I repeat, on US Highway Forty-Seven, in the dark, a walker. Please run a check of local hospitals for patients with head injuries who may have wandered off. He appears to be a total amnesiac. We're bringing him in."

The next few days are a blur of questions, no answers, and being placed into a mental asylum until someone, anyone would come forward with information about who I am.

At the asylum the interns are friendly enough. They immediately took to calling me Dark Walker as a nick-name for obvious reasons. That evolved into Derek Walker.

After six months of tests and questions, endless questions, I am informed that as far as the doctors know there is nothing wrong with me. I am in perfect physical and mental health. There is no evidence of brain trauma.

I just do not remember anything at all.

I probably would have lived out my existence in the asylum as a quiet inmate, reading in my room if it wasn't for the government's budget cuts that made them discharge me into the streets of Chicago. The staff got together and bought me a suit of clothes. They took up a collection and gave me five hundred dollars to make a new start in a life with my new name Derek Walker.

It wasn't much but it was better than nothing.

Now is where I get one of those blurs again of memories running together.

The five hundred didn't last long. That dwindled down from living in a hotel and the basic necessities of eating.

With no memory of a past life or what I could do, I could not land a job. I didn't even know how to apply for one.

When the five hundred dollars was exhausted and I had to leave the hotel I spent my time begging upon the streets and most of the time going hungry. I lived in a makeshift home in a wood packing crate in an alley behind a dumpster.

That was until one night when the peace of my solitary existence in the middle of a city of millions was shattered.

I came home from a day of holding my hand out and three men were outside my packing crate. They were laughing making wise cracks and passing back and forth a cigarette that smelled like burning rotten socks. I went to slide past them to retreat into the sanctuary of the only place upon this Earth that I could call my own. All I had inside the crate was some discarded blankets.

One of the guys was a tall thin Hispanic. One of them was a short stocky Caucasian. The other guy was a muscular Black.

As I went to slide past them the Black stepped in my way.

"Yo' mother-fucker," he said. "You got to pay a toll to pass. Slap a dollar out there and I'll let you by." He held out his palm that shined white against the black of the rest of his hand in the dim light of the back alley.

I went to step around him to get home. I must have pushed him because he shouted, "Hey!" and slammed a punch hard to the side of my head.

Lights spun. The world tilted crazily. I hit the gravel of the alley hard.

Feet wearing expensive tennis shoes struck me on my back, arms, legs, ribs, and head from all three of them as they laughed, called me names and tried to kick my guts out.

I curled up into a ball, figuring they would soon tire of their game and accepted the punishment.

With my arms wrapped around my head and my knees up to my face I heard something shouted louder than their laughter.

"Stop that!" The words cut through the night. They cut through the blows and dizziness in my head.

My three attackers now turned their attention to someone else.

I looked up from the ground as a short skinny Black man with grey hair stepped out of the light of the street and into the darkness of the alley. "Just leave him alone boys," the man told them. He walked over to where they were kicking me "This guy's been living here for months. He ain't done nothing to you."

The white guy giggled nervously. He stammered, "M-m-m-m-maybe you'll pay his toll. You got some m-m-money old man?"

"I ain't paying you shit." He answered.

"Goooooood," the Hispanic said. He spoke smoothly stretching out the single word making that one utterance suggest something of the reptile. "I been wanting to beat me an old man's ass all day."

"Tyrone is that you?" The old guy said to the Black. "Boy you need to stop playing these stupid games. If you'd start acting like you got some brains I'd take you back in at the gym. This is the kind of bull I threw your ass out for. You got some talent but you act like you got shit for brains."

"Hey fuck you!" The Black answered.

Without warning the Hispanic stepped forward and shot a straight right cross to the old guy's jaw.

The old man flew from his feet.

I was now standing. I don't even know how I got up. I was just standing.

Grabbing the Hispanic by the hair of the head I jerked him sideways and threw him face first into the dumpster.

The white guy lunged at me. One side thrust kick to the gut folded him up like an accordion. He went to the ground gagging and spitting up his dinner in rancid smelling chunks.

"Oh, you think you a bad mother-fucker hunh?" The man who the old guy had called Tyrone yelled at me. "I'm gonna bust your head wide open."

He put his hands up and took an orthodox stance with his left hand a bit low tapping himself on his left rib with his right hand up by his ear. He made head feints and shuffled in toward me.

I put my hands up, chin down, right fist partially open touching the right side of my cheek, left hand open in front of my lips waiting for Tyrone's next move.

Tyrone laughed, "So you think you know what the fuck you doing hunh? What, you been watching the Friday Night Fights?"

I said, "Are you going to bore me to death or do something?"

Tyrone stepped in with a left jab, right cross, left hook combo designed to send me back to the gravel.

The way that last punch whistled over my head it probably would have if it had landed.

I slapped the left jab off over to my left shoulder, leaned under the right cross and weaved back around as the left hook passed over my head. With my knees bent I came out of my crouch and whipped a left hook of my own straight through Tyrone's non-existent guard.

The hook landed with a loud hand-clap POP!

Tyrone's head was snapped back. His knees buckled. He went straight down to the gravel busting both his knees on the rocks.

I stepped in with a right uppercut, wound up and ready to throw, but Tyrone was out colder than a slab of beef that's been on ice for a month. I let him fall forward onto the ground.

"God-dam boy, where'd you learn to fight like that?" the skinny old Black man asked me. He was now climbing up to his feet, dusting himself off.

I turned to him and didn't have an answer. I guess the expression on my face gave away the fact that I was tired of answering questions I had no answers for.

"It don't matter anyway," he continued. "Let me get you off the street son. With a little polishing you could really be something."

Then my career as a prizefighter began.

17.

A Decision

For a time our existence was pretty routine. We ate, slept, and relieved ourselves as close to the bars as was possible so we didn't have to sleep in our own crap. We repeated that routine.

There's no way of knowing how long this went on. I wasn't keeping count and I didn't ask if anybody else was.

Life is different in a land where the sun always shines. You don't worry about the time because there are no clocks. Things happen when they happen. That's just how it is.

One thing that happened continuously was that the Viking idiots stared at us non-stop. I imagine that they took turns making faces at us but since they all blended together after awhile I could never really be sure. They all kind of looked alike to me. That might be politically incorrect to say but then I imagine to monkeys in the zoo most of the people staring at them look alike too.

At first it was a bit uncomfortable taking a dump with them pointing and making remarks about what we were doing. But after a while I took to fantasizing about a few of them wandering a bit too close so I could grab a handful of crap and throw it at them.

It didn't happen but it did give me something cheerful to think about.

I needed something cheerful to think about.

Time went on, or at least what passed for time down here.

We ate, shit, slept, ate, shit, slept. We got stared at. It got to be a habit, a routine.

I tried to talk with Stian a few more times but that was a "No Go" situation. He would see me coming and either walked in the other direction or acted as though he didn't hear me when I spoke to him.

To hell with him, I thought. You can't force someone to come out of a shell. If he didn't want to do something for himself or his people there wasn't any way for me to force him to.

I found Tond and Kalar and spoke with them about it. They said Stian was the same way with them and everybody else. The boy was falling into a deep depression. My attitude was, he had better shake himself out of it pretty dam quick or he'd find himself dead.

When things don't go your way you can't just crawl into a hole and the problem just goes away. You try that, usually the problem gets worse.

As I was contemplating this bit of philosophy worse stuck its ugly head right in my face.

After one more failed attempt at getting Stian to at least act half-way like a leader of men I walked over to the bars to make faces at the people staring in making faces at us.

We were in the center of town, in what looked like an open air market and now was when I found out just why we were here.

From the same direction we had originally come, marching up the hill was something that just the sight of it made the hair on the back of my head want to stand on end. Accompanying one man dressed all in fine white and red robes and four soldiers who appeared to be his body guards was another of those God awful huge furry spiders that the natives of Inagi called Nyseks. This one was completely cold snowy white.

The Nysek walked beside a large barrel-chested Viking who when he talked gesticulated with his hands in wide full bodied gestures as though he was trying his best to make himself understood. The man in fine robes walked humbly behind the mega-spider and the soldiers marched stiffly behind them.

I was too far away from them to hear what they were saying but what I was seeing (even if seeing a horse-sized spider was not enough to keep my interest) was fascinating to say the least.

The Viking would say something, gesticulating with his big hand gestures all around his head. Then the Nysek would wave two of its arms in front of its face in a complicated pattern. The man walking behind him would say something.

It appeared to me, even from a distance that the man who walked behind the Nysek was translating for him to the Viking. It was weird to say the least.

I watched them do this all the way up the hill. Then I watched them do this as they approached the cage that all of us captives were in.

Also all the way up the hill the pack of little animals that passed for children yelled curses and shook stones at the Nysek, the guy with him and the soldiers guarding them.

I have no doubt if they weren't being guarded those little bastards would have pelted those guys with rocks just like they'd done us.

Unsupervised kids are known for their displays of kindness. These children were no exception.

As it was about three quarters up the hill the big Viking leading this party had enough of what the kids were yelling and shouted back at them that he'd bash their heads in if they didn't go somewhere else to play.

That was advanced child psychology as far as the Vikings were concerned.

Most of the kids took off out of there and headed off to find someone else to torment.

The party of visitors, led by the big Viking, continued on up the hill, straight up to our cage.

They stopped on the other side of the bars and looked in. After walking back and forth a few times to get a complete view of everyone inside, the big Viking spoke. "You can see we have a good selection this time. Several of the women are good breeding stock and all the men will be strong workers. We deserve a better price than usual."

The Nysek waved its two arms in the air.

"We'll decide individually what each is worth at the auction block." The man in robes answered for his spider master.

"I could give you a special price if you were to buy them all at once," the Viking spoke. "Buying individual is more expensive. Buy in bulk and you will get some free."

The Nysek waved its arms.

"This is exactly why we will bid on the slaves individually. We do not want problem slaves at any price."

As I said before they were marching back and forth in front of the bars as they took stock of all of us inside. They continued to do this as they bartered about the method of purchase.

While the parties attention was directed at the livestock in front of them they didn't notice one little brat sneaking closer to them, at least not until he gave a banshee wail, yelled, "Nysek!" and hurled a stone with all the strength that his young arm could wield.

The baseball-sized piece of rock flew straight, between two of the soldier-guards, past the man in robes doing the translating, and smashed into the back of the huge chalk white Nysek with a resounding thud.

The Nysek stumbled to the side one step and gave a little squeak like a mouse stepped on. It pivoted to the side and locked all of its eight eyes on the boy.

The boy jumped up and down clapping his hands in glee. He was laughing and giggling while saying, "I got you one! I got you! Ha-ha!"

Silence descended over the Viking camp.

Spitting out a sound that was somewhere between a bull's snort and a cat hissing, the Nysek launched itself sideways knocking the large Viking and two guards sprawling.

It went straight for the boy, who was frozen in place in stark wide-eyed terror. The huge spider raced at the kid who suddenly came out of his funk and squealed out an unholy cry of terror that turned my stomach.

The child was bowled over and knocked from his feet by the eight legged monster. The Nysek climbed up on top of the boy and hissed out an ugly snarl that was pure hate and rage.

The boy screamed, "Help me, please!"

The huge spider dipped his head and sank his ungodly venom-filled fangs into the child.

The boy's cry ended in mid-stream. He stiffened. His eyes sank into his head.

The monster fed, sucking the juice of life out of the child right before our eyes.

I should say, before my eyes only.

When I could rip my gaze away from the atrocity taking place before me, the murder of a child, I saw that everyone else; all the Vikings, the four guards, the robed man, even all my fellow prisoners, every single one of them had their eyes glued to the ground in meek surrender to the will of this ugly abomination of nature.

As the Nysek fed and the child died, I decided right then I could not allow this to continue.

18.

The Auction Block

The auction block consisted of a large platform that really looked like nothing more than a huge picnic table.

I knew what it was the first moment four big burley Viking warriors dragged it out from behind one of the buildings and positioned it directly in front of the door to our cage.

The Amura observed this with disinterest.

The captives taken from lands other than Amura paid no attention at all.

I put it down to them not understanding what slavery was and what was going to happen to all of us.

Since it made no sense approaching Stian about any plan for an escape I went directly to Tond and Kalar.

They were standing staring blankly through the bars when I approached them

Keeping my voice low, barely above a whisper I stuck my head between the two of them and said, "The best chance we have of ever getting away and getting back to your home will be when they open that cage door to drag some of us out to sell. If we do it right, since the doorway is too narrow for them to be able to use swords effectively we have a good chance at surprising them and getting hold of some weapons. Then …"

I stopped cold. They were both looking at me but not with interest and hope. It was a gaze that someone would give you if you told them that you can make it by rowboat from Seattle to China if you keep a steady pace and just keep rowing."

This apathy completely caught me off balance.

"What's the matter?" I asked them. "Don't you want to get out of this and get your own lives back? I don't know about you but I don't want to have anybody telling me what to do every moment of my life. I won't let anybody own me."

Tond turned dull eyes on me, eyes that were sympathetic and somehow dead inside. "If it is the will of Ra," Tond said. "Then I will serve whoever owns me."

"The will of Ra, just when was the last time either of you talked to Ra anyway?" I asked.

Kalar spoke. "Ra lets his well be known."

"So you figure the will of Ra is for all of us to just go along with whatever happens, to accept it when someone, like these ass-holes take away your homes, your families, your lives. We are supposed to say, 'It's the will of Ra,' smile and take what's thrown at us?"

They both looked at me with their dull, beaten eyes. They looked to the ground at their feet.

"Then fuck Ra!" I told the both of them as the crowd of bidders gathered in front of us.

*

The cage door was opened.

Since there was no one who was on my side I was going to have to do this alone.

It was a pretty informal arrangement.

People came out in pairs or in threes from a short squat building. One from each group was obviously the man with the money. It was

115

obvious because that guy was dressed in finer clothes than the man or men with him.

The rest of the men, judging by the swords on their hips or the battle axes in their hands, were the body guards for the rich guys.

They all made a wide half circle around the open door to our cage.

The Nysek, with the man in red and white robes and his four body guards was the largest group of bidders among this gathering.

There was a wide mixture of races among these purchasers of people. I saw a few pairs of slant eyed Orientals and three pairs of pitch black Negroes scattered among the predominantly Caucasian bidders.

There was one race here that when I caught sight of them seemed for some reason to make my heart stop in my chest. Although they were different from any race of people spawned on the outer surface of the Earth still I felt a kinship with this pair more than even the whites that were sharing the cage with me.

It was a single pair of four-armed green men that stood among the others appearing to be as much at home in this Inner Earth as all the rest.

Of this pair it was hard to tell who the bidder and who the guard was. Both were armed and wore expressions of such seriousness on their faces that both looked capable of dealing out sudden painful death.

The Viking who led the Nysek's party up the hill now came forward. Six heavily armed warriors were with him.

There was as space wide enough for two men to walk shoulder to shoulder between the auction block and the wood bars of our cage.

The big Viking walked to that space, stopped and pivoted to face the crowd before him. He held his hands out to quiet the throng.

"Today we have a superior selection for you," He spoke loudly in commanding tones. "My son, Svengar has traveled far collecting the best from wide spread lands. He has proven himself an excellent leader and will make a fine king when I am gone."

116

He motioned with his hand and indicated the young warrior standing off to his right who commanded the raiding force that captured us and destroyed Stian's village.

"Pay him back for his efforts by bidding high and there will be even better stock when next we summon all of you together. Today he will conduct the auction."

The son came forward and his father clapped him affectionately on the back.

"My father King Fafnir is only flattering his son," Svengar told the cluster in front of them. "He's had far better hunts than I and Fafnir will reign as king until Ra goes cold and dark. But enough of this backslapping let us get on with the business each of you traveled here for, the buying of slaves."

Yeah, I do got to say all that family, father-son affection being shown by these murderous kidnapping bastards was about to make me puke. I was happy to hear they were getting on with it.

With two other warriors guarding the door with white swords out and ready to inflict damage and pain a third slipped inside the cage. He grabbed a woman by the arm and dragged her out. The door was slammed shut behind them.

It was simple.

It was fast.

But in that moment was born the seeds of a plan.

19.
The Break for It

They took that first woman, shoved her up the one stair, then onto the auction platform.

Svengar jumped up beside the female and eyed her up and down. She was well built with long blond hair. The hair was dingy and matted since she hadn't had access to a bath for quite a long while. She had a strong body just like most of these primitive people. The only garment she wore was a one piece animal skin tunic that covered her from neck to mid-thigh and was tied at the waist.

She shrank back away from Svengar's hot gaze.

"What do I hear for her?" The Viking Prince bellowed over the heads of the crowd. "This female is fine breeding stock. She'll make many more strong slaves for your household or," he leaned down and slapped the woman hard on the ass. "She can satisfy all your manly needs."

The woman shrank back from the touch of the leering Viking Prince as the crowd of onlookers hooted. She looked like she wanted to turn into smoke and evaporate.

Unfortunately, that option was not available.

"Show us more of the goods," one of the bidders shouted.

"Why not," Svengar answered. "I wouldn't mind seeing what she's hiding." With that he reached out with both hands grasping the woman's tunic at the top on both front and back sides. Ripping both hands to the side he tore the garment into two pieces right down the middle.

The woman screamed as her only piece of clothing was torn away and her nakedness exposed.

Svengar laughed long and loud.

The bidders cackled like wild hyenas.

The woman fell to her hands and knees attempting to cover herself any way she could.

Tond and Kalar were only a few steps away from me.

"Is this the will of Ra?" I asked them. "This is what Ra would allow to happen to your women?"

Neither of them could meet my eyes. Neither of them answered.

One of the bidders, I think it was one of the Negros yelled out "Two horses for the wench. She looks as though she won't be much of a ride."

That bid was answered by two horses and a milk cow.

Somebody else made another bid that this time included a barrel of a type of beer.

I'm using the English words for the items bid so as not to confuse anyone who might read this account, words that I learned as I lived in Inagi.

Back to the bidding: the Black man upped the bid by offering four horses.

That brought a collective gasp from all the rest. Evidently among these people horses were a valuable commodity.

Seeing that there was no immediate answering offer Svengar raised his right hand in the air and shouted, "Calunda of Wampa has bid four horses. Do I hear more than that?"

From off to the side I saw the Nysek wave its two front arms in the air in a complicated pattern.

"Do I hear a higher bid than four horses?" Svengar shouted.

There was no answer.

"Then the girl is sold to ..."

119

"One horse," the man in the red and white robes shouted for his Nysek master interrupting Svengar and cutting him off in mid-sentence.

"My master bids one horse," the man repeated.

Silence descended over the gathering like a blanket thrown over a corpse.

Svengar looking confused with his arm still raised in the air looked to his father for guidance.

King Fafnir, the proud ruler of his blood-thirsty slave stealing people nodded his head then looked to the ground meekly.

Svengar glanced at the man in red and white robes, and then averted his eyes as quickly as he could. His voice was harsh as he spoke words that it seemed he choked on, "The girl is sold to Sist, merchant-buyer from the kingdom of Nysek, masters of all Inagi."

No one, including the Black disputed this as the girl was lead away to be kept in a separate holding cell inside a building on the other side of the square.

All of their eyes looked to the dirt at their feet.

*

After a few moments the guards entered the cage to grab the next slave to be sold.

I slid away from them as unobtrusively as possible worked my way to the edge of the cage against the thick wooden bars.

Everyone's eyes were on the guard.

This time after walking forward and peering around searching through the mass of human cargo around him he reached out and grabbed a youthful boy by the arm. On the Outer-Earth I would estimate the boy as being around fourteen.

"You'll do as well as a wet wench I suppose," the guard snarled at the cringing boy dragging him forward toward the cage door, a door I noted earlier opened outward. "Whale blubber will slicken you up and some of our buyers like a bit of mud on their meat."

"No!" the boy yelled back as he drew away and fought to get free. He knew he was in for a rough ride whether he fought or not. At least this boy chose to fight.

I had worked my way, quietly and nearly invisible in back of the rest of the slaves keeping a line of them between myself and the pitiful struggle taking place.

The boy was pulling backward making sniffling protests of, "No, no. Let me go. Let me go!"

The guard giggled like he was seriously in need of some psychiatric care. He jerked the boy to him suddenly, shouted, "Shut-up!" and backhanded him.

Both were now near the door, a door that was still part of the way open.

I stepped forward, slipping between two of the captives that were attempting to look anywhere else but at the violence taking place in front of them. My hand snaked out, fingers seeking and clutching the object I needed.

It was an object that I expected to feel foreign to me, a thing strange, unfamiliar. But instead the grip of the sword that I touched, that I drew smoothly out of the rough leather sheath at the Nord guard's thigh was like a tool I had spent thousands of hours training to use.

That first touch of my hand gripping a sword was electric. This was something I knew on an instinctive level, something buried deep inside that had been waiting to be rediscovered.

With this sword in my hand I was once again the most fearsome swordsman on two planets, hell ... on any planet.

I ripped the sword free. My lips curled into a grim smile. More than likely I would die here. But it was better to die in battle that to meekly surrender.

The guard glanced at me over his shoulder. He let go of the boy.

"Hey ..." he started but that was all he got out.

I whipped the white blade in a tight left-right slash that opened his gut and sent his intestines plopping to the dirt at his feet.

Kicking the cage door open I jumped out among the Nord idiots and split one's skull before he even knew that anything was wrong. As he fell with his brains showing green up towards Ra's red another of them rushed me.

This Nord had a battle-ax. He came in swinging huge hefty strokes designed to overwhelm me with his pure strength and aggression.

The strange white blade that this sword had was lighter than any steel I'd ever felt. It also felt strangely soft almost like it could be made of a bone of some sort. I had no conscious memory of having held a long blade before but I deflected the ax-swings with practiced efficiency.

One, twice, he swung that battle-ax at me in a berserker's fury. The third time he drew back I anticipated it and a simple forward thrust sent my blade in through his jaw, upward through face muscles and bone and on deep into the middle of his brain.

He collapsed gurgling out his blood at my feet.

Moving forward I ripped apart two more Nord guards like weeds in a field.

Svengar and Fafnir like all true royalty had retreated away from the fight to let their loyal subjects spill their own blood before they'd put themselves in harm's way.

Nord warriors came at me in a wave and I cut them down left and right. I hewed a path straight forward away from the cage aiming toward a space between two of their low-slung buildings and the open country beyond.

Nords and slave buyers alike parted before me like the Red Sea and the dirt was slick with blood beneath my feet.

Four of them made a rush at me at the same time hoping to bear me down with the sheer weight of their combined attack. It almost succeeded too.

As it was their rush made me stumble sideways as I slashed one's throat with a backhand slice and ran another through the heart.

I bumped into someone who had not retreated from the fight. I was surprised to note that it was the four-armed Green Man who'd refused to even back away one step from the carnage taking place.

At this point I had already accounted for eight Nord warriors lying dead in the dirt.

Glancing at the Green Man I saw he wore a strange grim smile upon his face.

"My people have legends of a warrior like you," he spoke. "A man who never backs away from a battle and never gives up."

"Then fight at my side with me, back to back," I answered him. "Today we will create new legends."

I turned my back to him and met a new charge of another pair of Nords. They came more carefully than the ones before them.

It mattered not.

One thrust at me extending his hand a bit too far and I sliced his arm off at the elbow. The other I nearly decapitated when he stumbled after stepping on the arm I'd cut off.

The Nords fell back away.

A path was open and clear straight ahead, between the buildings and into the open countryside beyond.

I made a motion to follow me to the Green Man guarding my back.

"To freedom!" I yelled and a glance over my shoulder showed me the descending stone in the fist of the Green Man.

The rock smashed me in the side of the head.

Ra fell down upon my skull and I knew only pain and darkness.

20.
Kalina's Tale:
Homecoming

As Kalina came up to the final line of trees that separated what remained of her village from the savage untamed primeval jungle, a sight unfolded that chilled the blood in her veins.

Lying in the lush, thick grass between the trunks of two trees was the young hunter Jorn. He was sprawled out, face turned away from her, lying on his side as quiet as death itself. But that wasn't what caused her muscles to tense, for every sinew to tighten in the sudden fight or flight response.

What made Kalina's survival instinct alarms to go completely into red alert was that a huge yellow and white jungle tiger stood over Jorn as he lay in eternal rest.

Kalina instantly surmised that Jorn, being the heroic brave youth that he had already proved himself to be by single-handedly slaying a great bear, had refused to surrender to the warriors that attacked their tribe. Jorn had been slain and the jungle tiger seeing an easy meal had dragged the boy's dead body out of the village to a spot that was more suitable to relax as he ate his fill.

The great feline lifted its head, sniffed the air then turned its cold gold-rimmed eyes full upon Kalina as she stood in a ready stance gripping the spear she'd taken from the first village of Amura she'd visited to warn of invasion.

A deep menacing rumble came from the jungle titan's throat as it took in the sight of the scantily clad medicine woman. The yellow and white cat stood and stretched, then it opened its mouth exposing huge razor sharp teeth with enormous fangs designed for ripping apart prey. The tiger hissed and its message was clear.

You had better leave me alone while I eat or you will be dessert.

Kalina knew the best thing to do, *the only thing to do*, would be to back away with the spear held out in front of her in a defensive position.

After all, Jorn was already dead.

Leaving his corpse to the jaws of the tiger would make no difference anyway.

She took one cautious step backwards, retreating away from the fearsome feline. Kalina didn't know where she was going to go next but she knew she couldn't stay here.

The great cat rumbled and hissed out a warning again as Kalina readied to take another step backward into the deep dark jungle when … Jorn moved.

The youthful hunter stretched out his arms, straightened his legs as he rolled over and sat up.

"Is something wrong?" Jorn said as he wiped the sleep from his eyes with the palms of his hands. Then he did something that totally amazed Kalina.

Jorn threw his right arm around the tiger's thick neck and hugging him scratched the enormous cat on the flat of the top of his head.

"Why did you wake me up?" he asked the feline.

Then his eyes focused and he saw Kalina with her spear at ready not fifteen feet away. "Oh," he said. "I understand now." He rubbed the tiger's neck. "She's a friend, Tony. Not a meal. Friend, not food."

Kalina was hoping the big cat understood that last command very well.

*

It did take some getting used to for Kalina to let Tony get close to her. On Jorn's word Tony did not eat her.

As Jorn stretched himself, fully waking up from his healing sleep the tiger eyed Kalina curiously. Now that Jorn evidently knew the human female and she was no threat to him the big cat acted with no malice toward her.

Kalina watched in astonishment as Jorn first yawned, stretched, scratched the tiger's ears and head then leaped on the huge beast's back and they both tumbled to the grass rolling around. She grabbed her spear up but relaxed when the youth laughed as he playfully wrestled with the tiger.

They rolled in the deep grass until the tiger got the upper-paw and sat upon Jorn's chest pinning him down. Then the tiger slowly placed his big paw upon Jorn's forehead. He raised his head and looked full into Kalina's eyes.

The tiger's eyes now seemed to somehow have softened. His face was relaxed, not tense as he opened his mouth and voiced a mild, "Yawaaa." It was like he was saying, "He's a good kid. That's why I put up with this."

"All right, all right, I give up." Jorn said from beneath the great cat. "Let me up. You're crushing me."

Tony stood and padded away from Jorn. He walked toward Kalina as Jorn shook the grass out of his hair.

Kalina stiffened as the feline approached.

"Just let him sniff you," Jorn told her. "He likes to sniff all his friends."

Kalina resisted the impulse to run or fight as Tony the tiger used his nose to fully catalogue exactly who this human was and seal her in his memory. She stood stiffly as he circled around her inhaling her scent and touching her several times on the legs and arms with his big snout.

As he did this Jorn explained how Derek had freed the tiger in the Nysek's lair and why the cat was now friends with all who were friends with Derek and him. Kalina got so caught up in Jorn's tale that she actually forgot about the tiger being a threat and found herself reaching out and scratching the huge beast behind the ears without even a second thought as to why she was doing it.

Tony the Inner-Earth Tiger sat down on his haunches and leaned his head against Kalina's thigh and purring loudly let the woman stroke him behind and under the ears. He obviously loved it.

To a woman whose people had no domesticated animals at all this was a revelation. Kalina was amazed.

"I don't think you have to worry about Tony now," Jorn told her. "Just keep scratching his ears and he's always going to be on your side."

*

Despite not really wanting to after a time they went into their village.

All the huts were knocked to the ground and before leaving the Nords had put the torch to everything. Amid the smoking ruins of both of their lives Kalina and Jorn saw the remains of friends and family scattered like so much discarded trash.

There were so many bodies strewn about that even if the Amura had had any burial rituals, which they did not, disposing of the bodies was not a task either of them were capable of accomplishing.

While on the subject of burial rituals it may be of interest to note the normal method of disposal of a loved one if they died of injury or sickness. The Amura are extreme ecologists in that they simply said their good-byes then carried the body deep into the jungle and left it.

Nature took care of the rest.

This time there were too many bodies for Jorn and Kalina to even consider carrying them into the jungle. It just wasn't practical.

If primitive people were definitely one thing, it was that they were practical.

If something needed to be done, they did it quickly and efficiently. If something wasn't essential, they didn't waste the effort or energy on that task.

American Politians could learn a lot from the Amura about getting things done.

Jorn found the bodies of his father and mother. Both were killed in the invader's attack.

Jorn had fought, and then fled into the jungle when he found it was hopeless to fight anymore.

He now mourned the loss of his father and mother.

Jorn shed his tears, said good-bye to each of them then turned away to meet whatever new challenges life threw at him.

Kalina searched the village for signs of Derek Walker. She found none.

When she asked Jorn if he had seen Derek fall in the battle Jorn answered, "Derek was captured along with many of our people. They were tied together and marched toward the great water."

"Then we will follow them," Kalina stated flatly. "We will get them free."

"I already followed them as far as I could," Jorn explained. "They were carried away in very large boats. We need to go and get help from the other tribes of Amura. We …"

That was when Kalina stopped him with an upraised hand and explained seeking help from the other tribes. After Kalina's first misadventure with the amorous Chief Melar she visited two other tribes who turned her down completely when she'd asked for warriors or assistance.

The Amura were a very loose confederation of tribes living in the same spread out valley. When Kalina asked for assistance she found out just how relaxed their alliance was.

None of the tribes were willing to fight for any of the others. They only thought of their own welfare and no one else's.

When Kalina was done explaining the situation to Jorn she again stated, "We will follow and free our people."

"But they got in the boats and went out into the great waters," Jorn told her. "We cannot follow."

Kalina smiled. It was a grim determined smile. Her eyes were steely and resolute.

"When Derek went to take you back from the Nysek I am sure the other hunters told him it could not be done because it had never been done before," Kalina said. She now pointed to Tony the Inner-Earth Tiger who Jorn was scratching behind the ear. "Has ever before a great jungle cat and an Amura been a friend?"

Jorn shook his head no.

"We will follow them and free our people," Kalina said. "Nothing is impossible. We will find a way."

21.
It's the Pits

A cold clammy feeling on my face along with the stench of rot and dirt is what I awoke to. It was not entirely unpleasant so I decided to keep my eyes shut a few moments longer and just enjoy the dark of nothingness and peace.

But there was to be no tranquility for me.

That feeling of nothingness and peace was interrupted by being doused in the face with a stream of hot rancid liquid. The fluid burned my nose and where it sneaked in around my lips to seep into my mouth tasted fowl and horrible.

I opened my eyes and the stream stung them as I rolled away and blocked it with my hands. The laughter of several men came from somewhere up above me.

I wiped the wet away and looked up.

Above me, at least twenty five feet up, that fat red-bearded Nord, Loknar was putting his dick back inside whatever the hell these guys used for underwear.

Beside him laughing was Svengar, his father King Fafnir, The Nysek and the man in red and white robes who attended the Nysek.

"I didn't tell you to piss on him," Svengar said still laughing.

"But you did tell me to wake him up," Loknar answered. "And you must admit he's a wake now."

I finished wiping the warm urine off my face while promising myself that if I ever got my hands on Loknar his end would be brutal and filled with pain. I studied the situation I found myself in.

There were red clay walls on two sides of me that were at least twenty five feet high. I was in some kind of trench with walls too high and steep to climb out of. The channel appeared to be roughly eight feet wide.

Glancing behind me the ditch curved toward what would be my right if I was facing in that direction.

It was impossible to see very far that way because the trench wasn't built in a straight line. In front of me the situation was the same. I was in some kind of deep ditch that I couldn't see the beginning or end of.

Svengar spoke again. "You are in our shit trough," he said. "Notice the smell. Breathe it in. That is the rich aroma of Nord shit. It is the shit of men, the shit of fierce warriors. Enjoy the smell. It will be one of the last things you do smell."

This boy has got some serious problems, I thought. *He doesn't even thing his own shit stinks.*

Svengar went on. "For the amusement of our guests," he waved his hands indicating all around him, and he was joined by the four-armed Green Man who'd cracked me with the rock. "We have arranged a contest. It's simple, we will send down into your ditch beasts or warriors. They will attack you until you die."

"What if I beat all the beasts and warriors you put against me?" I asked.

"You won't," Loknar shouted down.

"But what if I do, do I get my freedom?"

King Fafnir spoke this time. His voice was harsh and dour, just like the voice I would expect to come from the leader of a horde of murdering barbarians. "Yes, you will gain your freedom, the freedom of death.

"If somehow you should survive the pit we will tie you to a post in the public square where all can see. As an example for all the other slaves

131

to never attempt to escape we will cut you open and remove your guts slowly so that we keep you alive. Your screams will ring in everyone's ears for eternity."

The other Nords laughed at this. The man in red and white robes blanched going a bit paler than he already was. The Green Man's lips curled in a grim smile.

If they figured I was going to go pale and weak at the knees they were sorely mistaken.

I looked square into the eyes of the Green Man and with clenched jaw spoke the words, "I still live."

The Green Man's eyes widened in surprise. If it was possible for one of his race to pale a bit then I believe he did so.

He reached into his belt and withdrew something. He tossed it down at my feet.

I picked up the object. It was a slim dagger, the kind you would expect an aristocratic woman to carry. The blade was obsidian black. I was guessing it was made of some kind of dark volcanic rock. It wasn't much of a weapon but it was better than nothing.

The Green Man looked to King Fafnir. "That will make the show that much more interesting. He doesn't stand a chance anyway. The knife will make the death a little slower, more fun to watch."

Fafnir and Svengar both laughed.

"Release the first beast," Fafnir commanded.

I heard the creaking of wood somewhere up ahead of me. That was followed by a bellow and the sound of pounding hooves.

I tensed and took a low slung crouched fighting stance in the center of the sewage ditch. Whatever was coming at me, sounded big and angry.

A moment later I found what I guessed was true. Around the curve in the tunnel up ahead, snorting and digging up the red clay dirt as he charged forward, came the big daddy of all buffaloes.

This boy was huge. At easily over a thousand pounds, this mammoth oversized prehistoric bison was five feet wide at the shoulders and stood six feet tall while charging on all four legs.

The beast snorted, pawed the ground and came at me with a lowered head and horns driving toward me attempting to rip me open from groin to throat. I barely had a moment to jump to the side to avoid being trampled. As it was, I slammed hard into the slimy wall with my right shoulder. My feet slipped out from beneath me in the muck as I fell splashing to my knees.

Clapping came from above, but I ignored that. They could cheer all they wanted to. I didn't give a shit.

The bison slid past me in the mud as I regained my feet and turned to face my first antagonist. The thing had a hard time turning around for its second charge. A tunnel eight feet wide was tight quarters for this titan.

But he did manage to turn around after banging his head into the wall a few times. Seeing him do that, gave me an idea.

The beast pawed the mud and looked at me with little pig eyes radiating pure rage.

I didn't know why this thing was pissed off at me. We were actually both in the same boat. That didn't matter much when he charged again.

This time when the rampaging beast rushed at me I faked to my right. When the buffalo lowered its head and went to ram me into the wall to crush and snap my bones, to rip my guts out, I leaped to the left instead.

The beast hit the wall with half its head, his horns cutting a furrow in the red clay wall and slid past me again.

This time I was ready.

I ran forward and behind him then leaped onto the creatures back grabbing a handful of hair in my left fist and pulling myself up toward its neck.

133

The thing thrashed underneath me, bucking up and down like he'd been taking lessons from a rodeo bull.

I had not been taking lessons from Rodeo Cowboys so I had no idea how to ride a wild bull. I just held on for dear life because I had no doubt if I was thrown to the mud I would be stomped to mush.

Working my way up each time the beast slowed its bucking I stabbed it a few times with the dagger I clutched in my right hand.

I might as well have been patting him for the good job he was doing at shaking my teeth loose for all the good that did. While the blade did penetrate the skin it didn't dig deep into the steely muscles of the beast to puncture anything vital beneath.

So I just stabbed and kept on climbing upward toward its head.

The beast didn't have much imagination so he kept doing the same thing of jumping up and down and bumping against the walls.

By the time I'd worked my way up and grabbed a handful of hair on the top of its head pulling myself up over his skull the beast was tiring and slowing down.

That was good because I was getting exhausted too.

I had been shimmying up the beast's back clutching as tightly as I could with my one hand and my legs and then I took a single moment to catch a breath and relax.

It was a bad idea.

Maybe the beast sensed me relaxing. I'll never know. He bucked up one time out of rhythm with his other movements and I was thrown up and over his head.

Since I still did have hold with my one hand I was slung in a tight arc where I actually landed on my feet right in front of the buffalo staring straight into his dumb rage-filled eyes.

Without even thinking I jammed the blade of the dagger into the bison's left eye and savagely twisted it to the side.

The beast gave an inhuman sickly cry then collapsed straight forward into the mud. It heaved out a sigh and shivered one long last time and died.

I jerked the dagger free and staggered away.

The Green Man was looking intense as Fafnir and Svengar both clapped.

I looked up and told the pair of them, "Bring your ass down here and I'll give you both something to clap about."

"Release the next beast," Fafnir shouted.

Although I didn't have much breath to use I used it to curse at them. "You Nords are cowards," I shouted. "You sneak attack peaceful villages and send dumb animals to fight your battles for you. I might die down in this shit and mud but at least I'll die as a man. That's more than any of you can say."

There was a moment of silence. It seemed like all of the rest of the spectators looked at Fafnir.

After all, he was the King of the Nords and I had just insulted the honor of his kingdom, no matter how degenerate it was.

Fafnir's hand went up. "All right," he said "You wish to die by the hand of a Nord."

He turned and looked directly into the eyes of Loknar.

"Give him your sword," King Fafnir commanded.

Loknar looked shocked.

"But your highness, I ..."

He didn't get the next word out. Fafnir backhanded him so hard one of his teeth flew out of his mouth along with a spray of blood.

Fafnir reached to Loknar's side and withdrew his sword from the leather sheath. He tossed it down to land in the mud at my feet.

"Question me again, or even hesitate when I give you an order and I'll have your head on a pole," Fafnir told him.

Then he said to everyone else, "Call Syrinx. We'll show this slave what a real Nord is capable of."

22.

Syrinx the Insane!

Someone behind King Fafnir, who sounded suspiciously like The Town Crier from a movie that takes place in Colonial America, shouted loudly, "Send for Syrinx; Syrinx the merciless, Syrinx the vicious, Syrinx the insane!"

This should really be interesting, I thought as I caught my breath.

What I said was, "So are you sending for one guy or his entire family?"

"You'll think it was his entire family by the time he is done with you," Fafnir yelled back.

The shout for Syrinx was relayed to someone else who shouted it again.

Jesus, I thought. *These idiots sure as hell like hearing themselves yell.*

After a moment or two of near silence where the crowd above patted each other on the back and I sweated in the stink in a sewage trench while Ra burned holes in the top of my head something like a deep bass drum began thudding in the air.

Actually the sound built from the dirt since I felt it more than heard it at first. Large loud booms vibrated through the ground and built up and got louder until finally an enormous figure appeared over the rim of the trench to stare down at me.

The thing was huge. This thing was some fort of freak of nature, some sort of abomination. It was in the form of a man although I doubt a man ever grew to this size. It stood anywhere from fifteen to twenty feet tall. At that size it's impossible to judge because you can't compare an object to anything other than maybe the nearest tree.

To put it bluntly, the boy was big. He also had a head far outsized for the rest of his muscled up lean body. His head was as large as a washing machine.

The chief feature that this big boy had on his head was one that marked him as a figure out of Greek Mythology. Syrinx only had one eye that shined dumbly out of the center of his forehead. This boy looked exactly the way that I'd always thought a Cyclops would look.

Why did it not surprise me when the King of the Nords spoke to this thing as though it was family?

"This outlander, this captive, this slave has insulted the honor of The Nords, the Lords of the Land and Sea." King Fafnir spoke to the big boy who looked down at me as everyone else stepped aside. "What is it that we do to anyone who insults the honor of the Nords?"

Syrinx giggled like a gibbering idiot. He probably was mentally retarded. Due to his massive abnormal growth his brain was probably malformed.

I would have felt sorry for him except that his next words didn't bode well for forming a friendship based on mutual kindness.

Syrinx giggled and drooled and answered his king. "We tear the arms and legs and heads off them. We stomp them into nothing. We bash their skulls in and eat their brains. We kill them!" He giggled some more, picked his nose and ate it.

"Then kill him," Fafnir commanded his slobbering champion.

I got to admit that I backed up when that big boy leaped down into my trench.

Syrinx carried with him a club that could have been used as a railroad tie in the Outer-Earth. He smiled and his teeth were green with black stains. I could have sworn that I saw worms wiggling in the spaces between those teeth.

There wasn't much else to do. I turned and ran.

Syrinx bellowed out a cry of, "Hey little man, you're not getting away from me. I'm going to eat your brains for my stew," He laughed long and loud.

I half expected him to follow that with, *Fee Fi Fo Fum.* But he didn't.

It wouldn't have mattered much if he had because I ran back down the sewage trench away from Syrinx and just as I came around the bend saw maybe thirty yards up a wall of wooden bars blocking my way. The bars were made from felled trees that would be too large around to be able to grasp to climb and they were too close together to be able to squeeze between.

My retreat would be terribly short-lived.

I was hoping my life wasn't going to be.

Stopping and sliding in the mucky trench bottom I found that Syrinx was faster than I'd anticipated when he narrowly missed smashing my skull with a swing of his log. If I hadn't fallen I'm pretty sure he would have crushed me with that first swing.

His club slammed into the mud wall like an earthquake sending sludge and caked on feces flying. Some of it splashed back in his own face so I ducked and ran back past him as he wiped the muck away from his one eye.

I saw the eye was abnormally large and the lid wouldn't close all the way because of that.

On pure impulse, probably a suicidal whim, I stopped as soon as I was behind Syrinx and sank my left hand up to the wrist in the gooey sludge I was attempting to run in.

Syrinx turned toward me even as he slowly pawed at this eye with his one free hand.

Standing at my full height I only came up to about waist high to Syrinx. This was like a battle between a five year old toddler and a full grown man as far as the relative size of our bodies was concerned.

The major difference in that analogy was that in the size of our minds he was the toddler and I was the experienced fighter.

He turned still wiping the muck out of his single eye. The moment Syrinx moved his hand away from his eye I slung a fistful of mud and shit right back up into his face.

This time when he screamed it wasn't from rage. It was a cry of pain.

He'd taken the brunt of that handful of slop full force right into his eyeball.

Syrinx swung wildly with his log and even though I tried to dodge he got me across the side driving me into the trench wall.

Pawing at his eye once more the giant staggered away from me.

With ribs aching, seeing spots before my eyes from having the air knocked out of my lungs I forced myself forward chasing the wounded giant.

Syrinx' back was to me so I hacked at what was available. Using the sword more like a woodsman's ax I cut a gaping wound into the back of Syrinx' ankle.

He squealed and fell to one knee.

The one shriek told me all I needed to know. This huge warrior had never felt any real pain in his entire life. All of his battles had been one-sided. He didn't know how to handle the feeling of pain at all.

Syrinx crawled away from me bawling like an infant.

I followed him.

The muck finally washed out of his eye from massive tears and he looked at me over his shoulder.

"Please, don't," he begged. He knew it would be a simple matter for me to just run him through or start hacking pieces off him. "Please don't!" Syrinx begged more.

I wondered how much mercy Syrinx had shown his former opponents as they begged for mercy. But no matter what he had done I know what kind of man I am even if I can't remember most of my life.

I could see Syrinx was just a big, mentally deficient fool doing what he was told to do. He was really nothing more than the village idiot. Syrinx was someone now to be pitied, not feared.

"Put down the club," I told him.

Syrinx dropped his log. He crawled away and I let him go. He slowly and laboriously stood then climbed out of the sewage ditch. As he dragged himself out of the trench I saw Syrinx look back over his shoulder one last time. The look in his eyes was grateful.

The audience watched me from the top of the trench in silence.

I met King Fafnir's eyes.

"Is that the best that you've got?" I asked.

Fafnir's lips curled in a scowl.

"I tire of these games," he growled. "Flood the sewers and be done with it. Drown this vermin."

23.
Something's in the Water

A shout came from behind Fafnir and his gang of party animals, "Flood the ditch!"

Fowl smelling, rank, tainted water mixed with human excrement shot into the trench from somewhere ahead of me. In an instant the trench was ankle deep and rapidly filling.

I looked up and grinned at my audience. "Every single one of you are gutless cowards!" I yelled at them. "All of you belong down here floating with the rest of the shit."

Behind me the trench ended at that wall of wooden bars made of logs. I didn't have to study it to know that was a dead end. Since I hadn't seen how far the trench went to the front I decided to find out now. It sure wasn't going to be any worse than what was behind me.

The sewage came in hard and fast like it was being shot out of a high pressure fire hydrant. It was like a dam had been opened and all the filth that the entire Nord nation crapped and pissed was being flooded through this one small ditch.

That probably isn't far from what was happening.

By the time I rounded the bend in the trench heading forward the thick noxious smelling sludge was waist deep. The smell was so bad it burned my eyes and made it hard to breath.

Ahead of me I saw where all of the onrushing sewage was coming from. This trench stopped cold at a flat stone wall. At chest height a round hole about four feet across was cut into the wall.

All of the rank crud that poured into this ditch was flooding in from there. The hole was big enough around so that a man might be able to climb inside and maybe, I was hoping, swim his way upstream to some sort of opening at the other end.

With my luck I figured I'd probably come up in some outhouse under a Nord that had the squirts after a bad drunk. What the hell, I thought. It wouldn't be much worse than what I was already in.

It wasn't the most pleasant task that I'd ever contemplated taking on. The idea of diving into a noxious sea of filth was not the kind of relaxing swim that I'd dreamed about. But if I was going to have any chance at all of getting out of this ditch alive it looked to be my only chance.

Moving forward toward the exit hole of the spewing sewage the level of waste got even higher. As the crud reached my chest I looked up to see what my audience was doing. The thought did occur to me that Fafnir might have gotten so annoyed with me that he'd decide he wasn't just going to wait and watch me drown.

He might call for some of his spear throwers to turn me into a pin cushion.

At the top of the trench I couldn't see Fafnir or Svengar any longer. They'd probably backed off because the stench coming from the flowing crud was too much for them to stand. They probably went to get some fresh air.

Everyone else seemed to have backed off and went away as well. I guess watching someone drown in a sea of piss and shit just isn't as exciting as watching him get stomped to death by a buffalo or beat to death by the Jolly Green Giant. *Yeah, I was really sorry I'd spoiled their fun.*

143

My only observers after the others left were the Nysek, his assistant and that four-armed Green Man. The three of them looked like they were having an animated conversation with the Nysek waving its front arms in the air excitedly, the guy in red and white robes translating and the Green Man answering back. I watched them for a moment.

The sound of the spewing sewage prevented any possibility of me hearing anything they might be saying.

I reached the round opening in the stone where the filth spewed from just as the level of the sewage came up to my neck.

I didn't really want to do it but I had no choice, I sucked in as much of a lungful of the noxious rank smelling air as I could stand, grasped the edge of the sewage exit hole, I closed my eyes and dived beneath the surface.

*

It was as thick as watery partially set chocolate pudding with bits of things I didn't want to think about flowing around in the muck.

My eyes were squeezed shut tight. There was no way in hell I was opening them while my head was below the surface of this vile stew of human feces. I stuck my head inside just past the lip of the edge of the sewage exit hole and pulled myself forward. I worked my way inside swimming, actually more crawling forward through the crud.

The feeling of being trapped squeezed inside a constricting small space was overpowering.

I fought that feeling and something thick and muscular banged against the top of my head.

What the fuck? I thought and instantly asked myself, *What kind of shits did these Nord warriors take anyway?*

The thing that banged against me was alive and wiggling.

At this point I wasn't exactly doing a cold calculated study of the thing I encountered but I will tell you the thing felt thick, round and solid. I'd estimate the circumference was around a foot thick. As to its length, I never exactly found that out. Whatever it was, it wasn't going to sit still and get measured.

The creature slid down my body.

I did as quick a retreat as I could manage, shoving myself backward out of the primitive stone sewage pipe. Just as I reached the freedom of the open trench something wrapped around my left arm like a muscular fire hose coiling around it.

I jerked loose peeling some skin back and kicking from the bottom shot up to the surface of the river of muck.

My head broke the surface and I shook it hard to fling any crap that might be in my eyes away. Then I opened them.

I caught sight of only one person peering down over the edge. It was that four-armed Green Man.

Sucking in a breath of foul air I got ready to hurl a stream of obscenities at my one-man audience. Just as I opened my mouth the thing in the water jerked me back under the surface.

How I missed sucking in a mouthful of shit I'll never know. Maybe your mouth closes instinctively when something that awful approaches it.

The thing was I was at the bottom of a cesspool of ripe sewage. Something had me by the legs that was wrapping up around my torso with crushing force. I had already dropped the sword I'd hacked the Cyclops with but for some reason, definitely good luck, I'd kept the little stone bladed dagger clutched in my left hand.

Now I used that little dainty woman's weapon to stab and slash at the thing that was wrapped around my legs, stomach and chest. Fighting long and hard, spots danced before my eyes from the oxygen starvation of being beneath the muck and being squeezed so hard, so tight that my ribs threatened to break.

One of my feet hit the muddy bottom of the trench so with what was left of my waning strength I pushed upward with all I had toward the surface and whatever air I could get.

I came up and the thing came up with me wound around my torso like a huge spring.

My head broke the surface. Two sights met my eyes. Over the rim of the trench the Green Man stared at me with enraptured intensity. Breaking the surface beside my face was the head of the largest snake I'd ever seen. The snake's skull was easily the size of a bowling ball.

I now knew what had hold of me was a huge Boa Constrictor. But I doubt the Amazon River had ever seen a monster this huge. The reptile looked into my eyes like it was annoyed with me for not going easily into its stomach.

Although everything else was wrapped up tight and was being squeezed with bone-crushing force my left arm with the dagger was free.

Gritting my teeth I shouted my battle cry, "I still live!" as the snake's head waved in front of my face.

Then I stabbed the big ass snake in the top of the head driving its face toward me.

I couldn't get much leverage since the head was in the air and the blade just barely broke the scales. Jerking the blade toward me, pulling the snake's head with it I knew I needed to anchor that head somehow to drive the blade deep.

There was only one way to do it.

I dragged the snake's head to my face and sank my teeth into the muscle at its jawbone at the corner of its mouth slit.

The thing wriggled and thrashed.

We went beneath the surface again as I ground the dagger blade deeper into its brain.

But the creature had a death grip on me that wasn't loosening as we sank to the bottom of the sludge. We fell to the bottom, to the mud, the slime, the filth. Then we sank deeper down past the bottom.

Darkness closed over me.

Darkness, deep blackness, an endless void … nothing.

*

I floated in the empty nothing.

Floated … fell … flew ... it didn't make any difference. It was all the same to me.

Nothingness, pitch black nothing was all around.

It was strangely peaceful this total absence of pain or sensation of any type. I felt isolated, alone, but that was all right.

I had been alone before.

That feeling, that realization of knowing I had been alone brought a longing, a want, an ache and that brought the voices, voices out of a past I could not recall.

Many bodies, many lives, but one mind, one spirit, one soul.

Flashes of places and faces came to me: Red dead sea bottoms, a distant dim sun on a dying world and a woman, a princess of red skin and black hair so beautiful that the very sight of her takes my breath away.

New York City, the mean streets where death came swiftly in dark and dingy alleys: A woman of dark hair, strong eyes and more curves and hills than the Cascade Mountains. She was always waiting ... for me.

I should have married her a long time before I did.

Inagi, the Amura a primitive peaceful people needing to be shown the way and Kalina, the healer of her tribe, the healer of me, my mind and soul; The woman who I have always needed will always need.

Flashes of places and faces came hard and fast. Always the setting was different, but strangely the same.

The places were dangerous locations where only idiots willingly went. I went to those places and walked unafraid.

The women were strong-willed women who none the less needed a man to rescue them. And I always needed the woman to rescue me from ... myself.

Over and over again scenes of carnage and rescue were shown to me.

Memories? ...

Maybe.

My life, my lives ... who knows?

I floated or flew or fell, it didn't make any difference.

Many bodies, many lives, but one mind, one spirit, one soul. I always came back and ended over and over again with Kalina. I knew I needed her and somehow knew she needed me.

A blast of cold water hit me in the face.

24.
Back on the Slave Trail

I opened my eyes, wiped the cold water away and looked into the face of the Green Man who'd been so interested in watching my battle to the death with that big snake. He held a bucket, now empty, in his lower set of hands.

"So, as you say, you still live," he spoke with a wry half smile upon his lips. "You took so long to wake up I feared I had bought a dead man."

When I looked at the Green Man I saw him through the wooden bars of a cage I was in. The cage was on the back of a horse drawn cart. It was large enough so that I could sit but not stand up, lie down but not stretch completely out. It was cramped quarters.

"Why do you imprison me? I have done nothing wrong to you or your kind," I asked.

The Green Man considered my question with amusement. He actually laughed and when a Green Man laughs it is an ugly thing.

"You must have been dropped on your head when you were an infant," he said. "It is obvious. You are my slave. As to what you did to my people, if you are the man from our ancient legends, from the tales of our glorious past on our beautiful dying red world then you are the one who brought it all to an end."

His face darkened. For a moment I though the Green Man would draw the sword at his side, thrust it between the bars and run me through me where I sat.

He seemed to have a need, a compulsion to get rid of, to vomit upon me the words that next fell from his lips.

"Unlike the savages of your own kind that live here on the inside of this hollowed out world we The Green Men, The Bastion Thralls know the true order of the universe. Here we are few in number. Our eggs mature with dead infants inside. This place, your world will not let us build a nation to become strong because we are stronger than humans and would rule you all."

"You can't possibly blame me for that," I told him.

He went on as though he never heard a word I spoke.

"How we came here is lost to the mysteries of time but we do still have the tales of our past to help us survive this hell of enforced weakness of race. Once we numbered in the thousands. We roamed the Dead Sea Bottoms wild and free, killing, conquering and pillaging as we saw fit. We are a warrior people. For the Bastion Thralls, a nation of Green Men with the taste for shedding blood, the Red Planet was what your weak species would call heaven.

"Then you came, wearing a different name and face. Yes I do believe it was you. The names are lost to the generations. With the might of your sword you united first the Red Men, then all the tribes of the Green Men.

"We lived in peace."

The last word, PEACE, the Green Man spit out like something vile, something that was rotting inside his mouth.

"What is peace to a warrior nation other than just enslavement? Where before we fought and died in noble combat, when the tribes united in peace we sat and grew soft. Our people grew weak. The young men of our nation had no reason to train in the arts of war. They had no reason to forge the strength within themselves and keep themselves strong. We only had dreams of former times and the memories of former glory to give meaning to our lives. We were a people without purpose.

"Now, somehow my people have come to this land, this Inagi and we are enslaved here in another way. We cannot breed in sufficient numbers to be the conquerors we were meant to be.

"Yes, I blame you. You forced peace on a people meant for war. I bought you when you looked to be nothing more than a lifeless carcass so that I can take my vengeance, the long over-due retribution for my entire nation.

"I am taking you to the city of Xibalba. I will have you put into the arena. I will watch you fight and struggle over and over again, forced to kill warriors of your own kind while I make profit from the blood you spill until finally you fall.

"It will be a glorious day indeed when I see you face down in the sand bleeding out the last of your life for the amusement of soft effeminate humans. It will be wonderful to know that when you finally die it will have all been for nothing."

"I Sakar Thosis after a life spent mourning my people's lost glory will finally have a reason to rejoice."

*

With that he strode away.

The order was given and this slave caravan, a loose collection of horse drawn wagons with the dangerous slaves in cages riding, docile slaves tied together walking, moved forward down the wagon trail toward a destination I dared not contemplate.

25.
Kalina's Tale:
Infinite Possibilities

The scene that Kalina and Jorn found as they came out of the jungle beside the trail and moved onto the white sand beach where the Nord slave ships cast off was peaceful and lovely.

It was also desolate and frustrating.

What Kalina hoped to find here when she'd insisted that Jorn guide her to the last location where he saw Derek Walker she wasn't sure. But Kalina knew she hadn't wanted to only see empty sand and rolling waves.

She sat down on the beach and contemplated what to do next.

Jorn sat down beside her.

They both sat in silence.

The sounds of the waves softly rolling in to shore washed over them. In the distance a seagull called out and dove down into the waves. He came back up clutching a wiggling fish in its beak.

Here, even on this peaceful beach the eternal struggle for survival, the drama of the strong survives while the weak die was played out. They watched this in silence.

After a time of quiet consideration Jorn's head snapped up. "There," he said and pointing out to his own right he indicated a faint white object far out in the water. "That is what the warrior's carried our people away in."

The ship was farther away than we would ever be able to see it, even with a telescope, on the Outer-Earth. One of the advantages of living on the inside of a sphere is that distant objects do not vanish over a horizon created by the curvature of the Earth. Indeed, on the inside of the Earth, in Inagi distant objects as they move away, seem to move up and can be kept in sight until atmospheric haze hides them from view. Since there is no smog in Inagi to speak of, the air being clear and pure, the viewing of distant objects is enhanced. In an old song the lyrics were sung, *'I can see for miles and miles.'*

On the inside of the Earth, in Inagi, this was more than true.

Kalina silenced Jorn with a finger to her lips. Something stirred within her mind that she could not quite grasp yet. It was an idea that was not fully formed but was on the edge of her consciousness.

They watched and saw the ship move in a straight line from their right across the vast waters. It moved smoothly until it passed straight in front of them, and then continued on to the left to move upward in their line of sight and fade out into the misty distance.

Kalina contemplated this.

After a time she stood and followed by Jorn walked down the beach until she found a small piece of driftwood that washed ashore.

Kalina picked up the fist-sized piece of wood and walking with Jorn first toward, then into the water she waded out.

Jorn had no idea what was in Kalina's mind. But he knew if she had any idea of drowning herself out of despair, he would find a way to stop her. He would never allow his one remaining friend to do anything to harm herself.

But Jorn need not concern himself with the possibility of Kalina's suicide. Such an action was not a part of her nature. She was a fighter, not someone who gave up in the face of adversity.

She waded out into the waves until the water was chest deep. Then as hard as she could manage, Kalina threw the piece of driftwood out.

Jorn was puzzled. He again opened his mouth to ask why she had done this. Again Kalina silenced him with a finger to her lips.

Tony the Inner-Earth Tiger watched the human's actions with interest from the beach. He didn't like the water but he would occasionally catch fish in streams and lakes by wading in and just grabbing them. The humans were not hunting so Tony did not understand why they were in the water at all.

Humans did many strange things that he would never understand.

He just watched.

After Kalina threw the piece of driftwood out into the water she turned and marched back up out of the ocean and sat down upon the beach once more.

Jorn did the same but this time he went and sat beside Tony and threw his arm around the big cat's neck.

Tony opened his mouth and gave voice to a, "Yarraaa."

"Yeah," Jorn answered as he scratched beneath the feline's left ear. "I don't know what she's doing either."

*

The driftwood drifted.

Kalina watched.

It drifted some more.

Kalina watched some more.

Finally, the driftwood drifted so far away that it couldn't be seen.

Kalina had seen what she needed to see.

She stood, dusted off the sand that clung to her long slim legs then turned and marched up off the beach then into the jungle.

Her sudden departure caught Jorn by surprise but it was only a moment later when he was bolting after her, followed by Tony, into the thick of the jungle. He found that he had not needed to hurry.

Just inside the line of trees Kalina was already hard at work finding slim vines to cut and looking for saplings small enough to bring down but big enough for her purposes.

Jorn tapped her on the shoulder to get her attention and Kalina turned on him with a hurried, "What?"

"Well, if you will let me know what you are doing I could help," he explained.

Kalina suddenly stopped. She hadn't realized she had set off into her task with a single-mindedness that even excluded Jorn and Tony from the work that needed to be done.

Now she gave Jorn a motherly hug, wordlessly thanking him with her actions for reminding her they were a team and set about explaining her plan.

"When you pointed out the thing they used to carry off our people that put into my mind the idea that if they can build something that large we should be able to build something big enough to carry the three of us. Then I had to test to see if something thrown into the Great Waters would go where they were carried to. That's why I threw the piece of wood out beyond the waves and watched where it drifted.

"The stick followed the same path where they went. Everyone knows wood floats. So I figured if we tie many small trees together we can float on top of them. Then all we have to do is push it out past the waves, climb on top of it and we will drift to where our people were taken."

It all seemed rather simple to Jorn now that it had been explained. The both of them set to the task of cutting the trees down and finding and trimming vines to be used as rope.

The task was long and laborious but they fell to it tirelessly and without complaint.

Both Kalina and Jorn had stone knives. These they put to good use. Cutting down trees, even small ones, with only stone knives was hard, slow, and exhausting work. But it was work that had to be done so they did it.

Tony kept watch over all of their laborious cutting and hacking, comparing and carrying to the beach what they chose to use.

155

He made certain that nothing or no one disturbed his new friends in the midst of their work.

Tony did no understand the ways of humans but he would protect his friends even if he didn't know what they were doing. The Great Jungle Cats were solitary predators who hunted alone but Tony had grown fond of the young male and female.

He had grown fond of being scratched behind the ears and on the top of the head. In a strange way, on an instinctive, entirely emotional level, Tony now accepted Jorn and Kalina as being members of his family.

But there were differences between these two humans and others of his kind. Where the other Great Cats of the Jungle were strong and fierce and needed no protection these humans were not.

They needed the protection of a group of humans or in this case, they needed him.

During his short experience with Jorn and now Kalina, Tony had grown accustomed to the feeling of being needed. It was a new feeling.

It was a feeling he liked.

*

On the beach with a large pile of limbs, branches and small tree trunks Kalina and Jorn tied bundles together with lengths of slim vine. They did this until their arms ached and their stomachs growled from emptiness.

Without a word spoken, with only the message that a loud stomach can communicate Kalina and Jorn halted their labors and stood simultaneously. They nodded to each other and picking up their spears stepped toward the thick jungle.

Jorn looked about for Tony who they had left to his own devises as they worked feverously at their task. He was nowhere to be seen.

That was OK, Jorn decided. Tony knew where they were. He would come back to them when he wished.

Tony was not like a pet would be on the Outer-Earth. No one would ever own a Great Jungle Cat of Inagi. He was a friend to the humans. He was their protector.

He came and went as he wished.

Just as Kalina and Jorn was about to enter the line of trees bordering the beach they found where Tony had went off to and why.

Tony came striding out of the jungle carrying in his huge jaws a creature that looked something like a large overgrown warthog. Tony walked directly to Kalina and Jorn pausing not even one little bit until he stood in front of them.

Then he simply dropped the wild pig at their feet. Without so much as a glance at his friends Tony shifted his attention to one of the rear legs of the beast he had obviously hunted and slain.

With a sudden snapping forward of his head the Great Cat buried his teeth into the muscles of the hog's left rear leg. Jerking his head from side to side then backward, he tore the leg completely loose from the rest of the carcass.

Tony the Inner-Earth Tiger walked off then plopped himself down into the soft sand and ate.

Jorn and Kalina did not need further invitation. They normally ate their food cooked over an open flame but this time they cut slices of meat from the hog and dined on raw food so that they might return to their job as soon as possible. Time might be an unknown concept in Inagi but the need for haste was frequently not.

The meat of the pig, uncooked and still warm from being recently alive was greasy and tough to chew but to the hungry pair it tasted wonderful. They ate until their stomachs were full and no longer complaining to them.

Then it was back to work for the two of them.

Kalina and Jorn already had a large pile of bound together sticks and twigs that they now set about finding ways to bind together into a large firm flat surface, a sea-worthy mat, to ride the ocean on.

Some of the tree trunks they cut down resembled a species of bamboo on the Outer-Earth. These they used as a frame for their ungainly raft. Although neither Jorn nor Kalina had ever seen a raft before that was exactly what they constructed.

After much tying and binding and retying and rebinding Kalina and Jorn had a six foot square raft that the both of them were confident would not come apart as they drifted in the vast ocean. As they made a final inspection of their raft a great fatigue overcame the both of them.

While in the midst of their labors with a task at hand needing accomplished both Kalina and Jorn had ignored their own bodies' natural rhythms but now the need for sleep spoke its message loud and clear. On the Outer-Earth a week may have passed. But in the Land of No Return there was no way of knowing how much time had gone by if indeed a thing such as time does exist in Inagi.

In Inagi, its creatures and people rise and sleep when the need takes hold.

Kalina and Jorn had stifled this impulse.

Now they could ignore it no longer. They lay themselves down on the warm, open beach with Tony watching over them and slept.

*

They awoke simultaneously well rested.

Ra shined down upon Kalina and Jorn. A warm breeze blew from across the land making this idyllic setting just that much more peaceful and inviting. This would have been a nearly perfect place for the pair to build a hut, establish a permanent camp and live out their lives in peace and harmony.

But such is not the nature of man, or in this case, young man and woman. The best members of the human race have never taken the easy path through their lives. They suffer and strive to accomplish great things.

Kalina and Jorn had the task in front of them of finding Derek and if possible helping free the people of their tribe. They could not rest until these tasks were accomplished or they knew without a doubt that the task was impossible.

The two of them cut and ate their fill once more from what was left of the pig.

Tony napped on the warm sand.

Kalina inspected their rudimentary ocean craft once more while Jorn went and scratched behind Tony's ears to wake him up.

Going from corner to corner, one at a time, picking the raft up by that corner Kalina shook the raft. She shook it to see how solid the bindings were and just generally how solid it felt in her hands.

After she had went around the six foot square craft twice, shaking it and looking for flaws she was satisfied. The raft appeared to be bound together too tightly to come apart. Kalina dropped the raft back into the sand. The real test she knew would come when they climbed aboard and set out into deep water.

Done with her inspections Kalina patiently watched Jorn first pet, then caress, and then play with his enormous feline friend. The Amura had never domesticated dogs much less had cats for pets so the warm bond that existed between Jorn and Tony the Inner-Earth Tiger was a revelation to Kalina.

As far as Kalina had formerly known man's relationship with animals was only that of eat or be eaten, with man hoping to be the one doing the eating. She watched Jorn and Tony and realized that the world, her Universe, Inagi was an unusual wonderful place of infinite possibilities.

If a young hunter and a fierce tiger could become fast friends then anything was possible.

When Jorn and Tony were done with their play Kalina indicated the two of them needed to get back to the task at hand.

Jorn and Kalina dragged the raft to the water and pulled it in behind them.

Tony watched from the beach.

The waves were not strong so it was no problem getting out past the gentle breaking surf and into deeper water.

When the water was at Jorn's neck and the midst of Kalina's breasts they climbed aboard.

Their raft floated easily on top of the waves. It instantly caught the current and was pulled toward deeper waters.

Jorn looked with longing toward his friend on the beach. It had been an unspoken understanding between Jorn and Kalina that Tony would have to be left behind but seeing them watch each other across the distance separating them brought a pain to Kalina's heart not easily pushed aside.

Jorn raised his hand and a tear ran down his cheek. He called out, "Tony, I will see you again. I'll be back. Don't forget me."

His voice was choked with sadness and regret but he was a young man learning the practicalities of life. Sometimes there are things you have to do even if it is difficult and hurts to do them.

Jorn turned away and looked out to the deep vast ocean and whatever lay ahead of them.

That was when something unexpected happened.

Kalina spoke, "Jorn look." She was pointing back to the beach from which they came.

Jorn snapped his head up just in time to see Tony the Inner-Earth Tiger dart into the water and start paddling out toward them.

Kalina and Jorn had never seen a Great Cat in the water before, didn't know if they could swim, but as Tony made it out past he breakers, going under a few times to do it, they saw he was doing a good job of cutting the distance down between them.

Swimming with a strong ungainly but effective dog-paddling rhythm Tony surged through the water straight toward their raft and it wasn't long before he reached it.

Clutching the sides with his huge claws Tony hauled himself upward.

At first it seemed like the raft would capsize from the weight of the big feline so Kalina and Jorn rushed to the opposite side. But when Tony climbed aboard the craft flattened out in the water pushed down beneath his stabilizing weight.

Tony shook the water from his fur spraying Kalina and Jorn and stretched out all the way across the raft from corner to corner.

Jorn hugged the big cat and Tony taking Jorn's head in his big paws gave a satisfied, "Yaarawww," and licked him across the face.

The Great Cat's tongue was like sandpaper upon his forehead but that was fine with Jorn. With Tony the Inner-Earth Tiger at their side Jorn had no doubt that they could handle anything thrown at them and even conquer the world.

26.
City Life in the Inner-Earth

Through the bars of my cage as I rode imprisoned on the wagon as part of this slave caravan I watched scenery drift by. We rode over soft rolling green hills then down a narrow wagon trail cut through a lush forest.

I watched mountains drift by in the distance.

Every now and then the caravan would stop. One of the docile slaves would run up and down the line carrying a basket filled with fruits and vegetables that I couldn't identify. He distributed the food among us without a word or a glance at anyone's face.

I tried to get him to talk asking where our destination was.

The young blond headed man would only shake his head, *"No,"* and hurry away.

I tried this several times with the same result.

Green Warriors who wandered up and down the line of wagons threatened to chop off body parts when I said anything to them. They were not a talkative bunch.

There was no one else to talk to so this guy seemed to be my only link to humanity. Just when I was about to give up attempting conversation the young blond headed guy stopped at my cage as he pushed a few apple-looking things between the bars. He looked around nervously then beckoned me closer.

I leaned against the bars and whispered, "Do you have something important to tell me?"

He shook his head, "*No*," then opened his mouth, pointing for me to look inside. I now saw why he had never spoken. This man had no tongue. It had been cut out at the roots.

"I guess I better keep my mouth shut, right?" I asked him. "Or that could happen to me."

He nodded his head and moved on.

*

The land rolled underneath us and we moved forward. It's impossible to know how long we travelled or what kind of distance we covered. I got the impression that people in Inagi just kind of go until they get where they are going.

Finally, far away I saw the towers of a city reaching upward toward Ra. This was also the first time I saw anything that resembled smog since I'd been in Inagi.

A grayish film seemed to hang over the city and even in the distance I could see plumes of smoke rising from dwellings on the other side of a rough stone wall that looked to run all the way around the entirety of this town.

Viewing it from a distance, the city we approached looked run-down, dingy, decaying and gray. It gave the impression that this town was in bad decline, like nobody cared to build anything new that might be pleasant to look at or live in.

There was one thing that surprised me as we approached this crumbling metropolis. This city that looked to be barely at the level of Bronze Age technology with horse drawn wagons in common use also had airships floating in the sky above it.

When I say Airships, I mean exactly that. Platforms that looked like huge gondolas, resembling the ships the Nords transported us in, were hanging suspended by near invisible wires from massive gas bags keeping them afloat.

These airships floated majestically over the city inside the crumbling walls.

The one thing that this town reminded me of the closer we got, was what I would have figured an Ancient Roman city would have looked like after a very long siege.

Our caravan didn't slow down as it approached an enormous wooden front gate. The gate was already open. Over the top of the gate sitting on what looked to be a big silken nest was a very large black shiny Nysek. Having a gargantuan ugly spider looking down on me from overhead kind of made my skin crawl.

The Nysek seemed to be observing, supervising everything happening at the city's entrance. I half expected him to leap down, grab someone, and suck the blood out of him. But if he did that, I never saw it.

Down on the ground where our caravan was passing through the opened gate soldiers armed with those curious white swords were inspecting everything that traveled by their checkpoint. We must have passed inspection because we didn't even slow down.

One thing I noticed was that as our caravan approached the gate the swords and spears the Green Warriors carried were hastily packed away in wooden crates. As they did this they re-armed themselves with wooden clubs resembling baseball bats.

I wouldn't like getting hit by one of those bats. But getting hacked by a sword, even one of the lightweight white ones we find down here would be a whole lot more lethal.

Inside the city beyond the gate was even more crumbling decay. The worst ghettos on the Outer-Earth were not as bad as the filth and degradation that was visible as I passed into this ruin of a city.

I was looking at the distant drama of a skinny, sickly woman fighting with a child over a piece of bread when something wet and slimy hit me in the face. Wiping it away, turning my face toward where it flew from I saw a group of boys hurling rotten vegetables at me and other slaves in their cages.

This makes a whole hell of a lot of sense, I thought. *That starving woman fights for crumbs while you kids throw food at us. I guess there are idiots no matter where you go, even inside the Hollow Earth.*

The caravan moved on deeper into the city.

I ducked what was thrown at me as well as I could while making mental notes on the environment I now found myself in.

Most of the people in this city looked hungry as hell. They were emaciated and sickly.

I couldn't help asking myself, '*Why the hell didn't these people just up and leave the city if they couldn't get enough food here?*'

From what I'd seen Inagi seemed a mostly untouched wilderness with abundant plants and animals. Why anyone would willingly live in these conditions was a mystery to me.

Something else I noticed was that none of the citizens looked to be carrying any weapons.

Soldiers patrolling the streets keeping order were well armed. But I didn't spot one ordinary citizen with a sword or knife hanging at his side. In a primitive society like this one I would have expected that anybody who could carry a weapon would want to be carrying one.

We moved on into the city, on through the crowded avenues. Street vendors sold blankets, clothes, clay pots and drinking vessels all up and down the thoroughfare.

The streets seemed to have no real plan. They wound around, started and stopped and came to dead-ends with no rhyme or reason. I was completely lost although I have no doubt the man guiding this caravan knew exactly where he was going.

165

Then the caravan slowed down and we came to another archway entrance. At this archway, several Green Warriors stood guard.

They held the heavy clubs in their hands that the Green Warriors escorting us carried. I could see past them.

Inside, beyond the border of the archway, other Green Men stood. These Green Men were fully armed with swords or spears.

I realized right then that we must be entering an area of the city that was considered Green Man Town just like in the Outer-Earth most cities in the US have a section that is China Town.

The archway was not large enough to let the wagons pass within so they were unloading the slaves on this side of the arch and marching them through. Looking even farther in, into the territory of the Green Men I saw something that was very disquieting and did not bode well for my own future.

It seemed like just about every Green Man who did not have to be on guard duty was in possession of a slave. These slaves … men, women and children were being led about at the end of sticks with a rope attached at its end and looped over the slave's neck. Those stick and rope apparatus looked something like a device called an animal snatcher that I'd seen a dog catcher use.

Every single Green Man used that stick and rope system to guide their slaves around with one hand. In the other hand every single Green Man had a lash. These lashes were being used liberally to say the least.

In the few seconds that I had to observe the goings on beyond the gate I saw a woman and a boy-child individually beaten cringing to their knees.

These Green Men, who I had known as noble warriors in some former life, now lost to the dark catacombs of forgotten memories, had forfeited all of their nobility. I sensed that before there had been a rude code of conduct that although harsh and sometimes cruel was fair and even in some cases chivalrous.

That code of conduct seemed to be long gone.

Only the butcher's cruelty remained.

There was no way I would let myself enter the territory of the Green Men.

27.
Nuts and Guts

Observing closely I watched the slaves on the back of the wagons ahead of me dragged out of their cages. Then their hands were tied together in front of them and that stick with the rope was looped over their heads.

The slaves were then led past the stone arch and into Green Man territory where their new masters immediately introduced them to the lash.

They could kiss my ass if they thought I was going to willingly stroll onto that kind of life.

My cage door was opened and I was prodded from behind, through the bars at the opposite side of the cage, to get out. I slid forward and stood up.

My knees and back were tight from being cooped up in a bent over position for so long. When I straightened up my knees popped and my backbone crunched.

A tall Green Man, hell all of them are tall, who I'd never seen before stood in front of me.

He snarled like an angry pit bull.

"Stick your hands out slave." He emphasized the word *slave* like it was a curse he was hurling at me.

I smiled.

"So, you are happy," he growled. "We'll change that."

I stepped forward quickly and slammed an uppercut to this Green Man's nuts lifting him completely up off the ground. His eyes bulged out so far they looked like they would fall out of his head.

He collapsed straight down and as he fell I ripped the club from his hands. The club was almost the same length as a good maneuverable Louisville Slugger.

I spun the bat around and went for a home run on the side of the Green Man's dome. The blow landed with a sickening crunch and splat as his brain fairly flew from the side of his busted open skull to plop into the dirt beside us.

I turned to face the others.

For the moment at least, they seemed stunned, frozen by this unexpected turn of events. It had been a very long time since a slave had fought back. They were facing one now who not only was willing to fight but knew how.

I jumped forward and took another green Man down with a sharp crack across both his knees. He hit the dirt with a howl of pain. From the sickening snap when the bat landed I knew he was out of this fight.

Now the Green Men came suddenly out of their funk and surrounded me. At least eight of them charged in waving clubs just like the one I possessed.

Slipping one blow, sidestepping another I delivered a short straight thrust with the end of the bat to a Green Man's teeth.

Spitting blood and bicuspids into the air that guy went down.

Then I was slammed in the back by a club blow that made the air whoosh from my lungs and knocked me to my knees. Stars blinked in front of my eyes as darkness threatened to engulf me.

But I fought it back.

Rather than stand straight back up and present my head as a target I rolled forward while blindly swinging the bat to the side.

169

Somebody's ankles must have gotten in the way of my club because after a smack a thud landed beside me that was big and green.

I was struck again on the right shoulder. The pain made my entire arm spasm out of control. The bat flew from my grasp. Rolling to my back and looking up I knew I was in some serious trouble as four pairs of pissed off Green Men eyes stared down at me.

All four moved in for the kill.

One raised his bat up over his head to bring it down like a sledgehammer and cave in my face. Blocking the blow would only break my arms but I was going to do it anyway.

Then all at once he dropped his club and was grasping at a thin bladed knife protruding from his throat. Blood squirted in a stream as his eyes bulged and he staggered back.

A huge man stepped forward. At a glance he could have passed for the German guy that played Conan in the movies. He had a short sword made of that same white material all their bladed weapons seem made of. With a mighty yell he cleaved the skull of one of the Green Men clean in two.

One Green Man thought to surprise him by running in screaming, swinging his bat. That was a bad idea. The big guy ripped to the side with his short sword. The Green Man's stomach was torn open and his steaming guts found a new home in the dirt at his feet.

The remaining Green Men were beating a hasty retreat shouting for assistance from other Green Men inside their territory.

A smallish, but strong, wiry looking guy now bent down over me offering his hand.

"I think we'd best be going," he said as I took the hand offered. "Or do you need a written invitation?"

"There's no time to talk," the big man said as I regained my feet. "Let's go!"

170

To my surprise both of these men spoke English. It had a different accent than what I was used to hearing back in the Mid-Western United States, but it was still my language.

I didn't have time to contemplate this as my new friends took off at a run with me close behind them.

*

We ran down busy streets like the Hounds of Hell were on our heels dodging around people that got in our way.

Merchants sold all manner of goods out of storefronts with big shuttered windows. The window ledges of many of these shops served as countertops.

Beggars tried to stop us, stepping in our way with raised hands. We shoved them away. The short skinny guy seemed to take particular pleasure in tripping one beggar and roughly pushing him into a cart full of smelly, rotting fish.

Whores yelled at us to not be in such a hurry, that *real* men take their time.

We ran past.

I followed my two rescuers as closely as possible. I was already lost in this city but that didn't make any difference. I knew no one here so I had no place to go other than to follow.

The three of us zigzagged in and out of tightly packed streets until it seemed certain we had lost all our pursuers. Then they slowed their headlong flight to just a brisk walk.

I wanted to talk now. I had many questions to ask. The main one being, where did they learn to speak my language?

Just as I opened my mouth to ask that question, the small man followed by the Conan look-a-like ducked in through a door and went into a building. I followed. The door was only a hanging cloth we pushed aside. We followed him inside to a humble shop that sold bowls and mugs carved out of wood.

A man was dressed in dingy robes not much better than the ones some of the beggars wore.

"Here, quick," the man told us speaking in the native tongue of Inagi and grabbing a hide from the floor that served as a throw rug. He pulled it to the side revealing a door in the floor.

The door was thrown open and a wooden staircase led down.

We hurried down into the metropolis beneath the city of Xibalba.

28.

The Underground

A faint glow was coming from below us. I estimate that we went down that wooden flight of stairs probably about thirty feet. On both sides of us as we descended were cold clay walls.

It was dark on those stairs but not pitch black. We could barely see the walls and the steps in front of us but there was enough light so that we did not have to feel our way down.

As we descended the faint illumination increased until we came to the bottom of the stairs and the ground leveled off. Fifteen feet in front of us was a thick wooden door that had a large square cut into its upper half at roughly head height. There was no knob or rope or anything to pull the entrance open from this side.

We approached the door and the smaller man pounded on it with his fist.

A face appeared at the barred window.

"What's the entering word?" the man on the inside asked in native Inagi.

"How about you kiss my cock?" he answered.

"I should turn you away for that."

The big man breathed a heavy impatient sigh. "You know us. Just let us in."

There was the sound of wood scraping on wood, and then a clunk and creak as the thick wooden door was slid inward toward us.

Coming from the dim staircase where we'd been standing the light from the other side of the entrance was nearly blinding. It took a moment for my eyes to adjust.

"Who's he?" the guard asked as we stepped inside. The door was pulled shut behind us and latched.

"We snatched him from the Green Bastards just outside their gate as they were about to beat his head soft," the small man said.

I looked past my new friends and the guard and saw an open torch lit subterranean city stretching off into a hazy smoky distance. This appeared to be an enormous cave with natural stone supports that held everything up. While it was not as crowded as the city above there was a thriving community living down here. At a glance I could tell that anything you got in the middle of the city on the surface could be obtained down here.

The ceiling to the entire underground was lost in the vague flickering illumination of hundreds of torches from street merchants, cook-fires and shops set up right in the middle of open walkways.

The big man slapped me on the back.

"Welcome to Hades," he told me in English. "At least that's what I call it."

The guard looked at us strange. I could tell to him the words the big man spoke were pure gibberish.

"How do you know English?" I asked.

"It's what we grew up speaking," the small man told me. He held his hand out. "I'm Slickman."

"Call me Bub," the large man said as we exchanged handshakes and I told them who I was.

"How about we have some grog," Slickman said. "I'm parched."

He led the way and we followed.

*

174

We walked down a wide relatively flat footpath past merchants and craftsmen who joked and smiled. I got the general impression that most people down here were grateful to be free from the city above.

Dwellings or places of business were built of a wide variety of different materials. Some were stone or wood structures. Some of them were simply large tents. I was unsure of the need for a roof over your head when you already live in an underground chamber but I guess old habits die hard.

It wasn't long before we came to a stone structure. With Slickman leading the way we went inside. This subterranean tavern had the same look and feel that the few I'd ran past above had.

Inside, there were six heavy wooden tables with five already occupied. We went to the open table and took up three of the four chairs around it.

We were barely seated when a pretty young woman came to the table. Bub told her to bring us three mugs of something named Splotch.

Slickman said, "They call it that because if you drink this stuff too fast that's what your face does against the floor."

Before it seemed I'd even taken a deep breath three full mugs were slapped on the table before us. They were paid for with a wink and a smile.

Simultaneously both Slickman and Bub turned to me.

"Before we tell you our tales," Slickman spoke. "Since we pulled you from the fire we get to be entertained with the story of how you came to be where you were."

That seemed fair to me.

So I took a long deep gulp from the mug. Whatever that drink was, it was strong and bitter and tasted of barley and fruit. The brew started welcome stars blinking before my eyes and loosened my tongue.

***

For the sake of not repeating myself because you really don't want to be bored by hearing the same story twice I will skim over the part you've already been told.

I spoke of how I woke up on a cold lonely pitch black road completely naked just outside Chicago. My tale described having no memory at all and being placed in a mental hospital until government budget cuts sent me out unknown and alone to a cold hostile world.

I also let you know about begging on the streets of Chicago until I was attacked by three street punks, accepting the beating, until they attacked an old man who tried to stop them.

That old man was Pops Williams. After I mopped up the alley with the three punks to stop them from hurting him Pops took me in and gave me a sleeping room in the basement of his Boxing Gym on Kedzie Avenue.

I don't know why I know how to fight so well. I have no memory of ever learning the techniques that make me lethal.

The first day at Pops' Gym was interesting to say the least.

The night before Pops had been impressed with how I'd handled myself. He took me back to his place, gave me a ham and cheese sandwich and for the first time since I'd been put out of the hotel for not having the rent money, I slept in a warm bed.

The next day it was before dawn when the fighters began arriving.

I was down in a room in the basement. Even down there the rhythmic drum beat of the speed bag being slapped around drifted through the concrete walls to where I was.

After dragging myself up and out of the single bed I stumbled up the stairs and into the noise of the busy gym. The night before when we'd come through here I hadn't seen much because all the lights were out.

Now I saw three floor-level Boxing Rings where guys sparred lightly. There were three heavy bags being pounded on and three speed bags being worked at.

176

Pops was working with a mouthy Caucasian light-heavyweight when I came into the room. It seemed like the kid was more intent on telling Pops how Boxing should be done rather than taking instructions and learning anything.

Pops caught sight of me over the shoulder of his non-attentive pupil.

"Well, speak of the devil. He arises from the dead," Pops said with a big grin on his face. "Ain't you never heard the early bird catches the worm?" He went on.

"Why would I want worms?" I answered.

"Touché' boy, touché'."

"Aye man, you supposed to be talking to me," the light-heavy said with an edge to his voice.

"Oh, now you want to listen?"

"Yeah, if you know any fucking shit worth learning," the white boy snapped back his voice raising an octave. He was speaking with a mouthpiece in so his words were a bit garbled. But being a smart-ass gave him the incentive to keep right on going despite the fact that he sounded like he was chewing on a handful of rocks. "So far I ain't got nothing that a dollar-fifty Boxing Basics book wouldn't have given me."

Pops answered with, "That's because you ain't learned the basics yet boy. If you don't listen, you don't learn. When I tell you to keep your hands up, step in with a jab, I mean every single time. Not once in a while when you feel like it."

"Yo', fuck that, you old bitch! Ali didn't do that shit. Look where the fuck he got to." The young guy was fairly screaming through his mouth guard by now. Veins stuck out on the sides of his neck and he was breathing hard.

Pops turned away from the fighter.

"Yeah, look where he got to," he said glancing back over his shoulder as he walked toward me. There was a touch of sadness to his words. "The man can't tie his own shoes today. He can't wipe his own ass without help. He took far more punishment than he ever had to. Keep doing it his way. You can be just like him."

Pops ducked and stepped out through the ropes next to where I was standing.

"Do you want a job son? I could sure use someone to sweep up around here. The pay ain't much but you'll have a roof over your head, eat whatever I have in the ice box and a few dollars spending money."

"Sure," I got out just as the young fighter shoved Pops.

He yelled, "You don't turn your back on me, bitch! I will fuck you up for disrespecting me."

As Pops was saying, "You don't know what respect is boy," I was stepping between them raising my hands.

The young fighter had pulled off the sparring gloves and stood glowering at me with taped fists. Words sprang out of my mouth that I didn't realize I knew. But they were good words, words to live by.

"The warrior arts are only intended for the strong to protect the weak. Live with honor and strength like a man or die like vermin in the mud."

"Bitch, you don't raise your hands to me," he yelled. He really seemed to like the word *Bitch.*

The young fighter flew at me in a rage swinging a wild left hook that was telegraphed all the way from Cleveland.

I caught the punch with my right open palm slapping it down, snapped out a left jab, followed with a right cross and finished up with a tight left hook to the point of the mouthy fighter's chin.

All three punches landed with loud whip cracks, snapping the light-heavyweight's head in three different directions. He was on the other side of the ropes so the last punch left the young fighter draped over the top rope, glassy eyes staring straight down with slobber spilling from between his lips and snot mixed with blood flowing from his nose.

178

His mouthpiece fell out and bounced. His knees buckled, gave way and he crumpled unconscious to the mat.

"Dam boy," Pops told me. "Son, you need to get paid for knocking guys out. You can't keep doing that just for fun." He motioned me to follow him.

You could hear the clock ticking up high on the wall as we walked across the gymnasium to the stares of the other fighters. Just as we got to the door that lead into the locker room Pops yelled back to the other guy in the ring with the mouthy fighter slowly climbing to his knees, "Mike, when that idiot has enough senses back to know what you're saying, tell him to pick up his teeth and go home. He ain't welcome here no more."

After that day I became a professional prize fighter.

For me it was easy. I loved the training and the disciplined combat was second nature. Boxing and combat in general was something I seemed built to do. The only time I felt true peace was when I was totally concentrated on the opponent in front of me.

While all the rest of the world might be a blinding chaos the simplicity of combat was the one thing I truly understood.

With Pops training me I climbed the ladder slowly but surely toward a title fight. While working my way up Pops was my trainer and manager. He chose the opponents carefully to teach me how to deal with everything I might have to run into in a Boxing Ring.

I lived a Spartan life, only training and fighting with very few entertainments. In that kind of life I was relatively happy. I say relatively because my past was and is lost to me. And there has always been something nagging at the back of my mind that I just can't put my finger on.

Something seemed to always be missing from my life, something that I could not remember. The training and fighting occupied all my time, gave me no time to think.

That was good. That was the way I wanted it to be, the way I needed it to be.

Then it all changed.

I was rated just outside of the top ten of all three sanctioning bodies when Don Rump paid me a visit. Don was one of the world's top promoters of Boxing and other entertainment events. Early in my pro-career Pops warned me about guys just like Don. I found out why.

The guy had the look of an oily pimp and in a way I guess that's exactly what he was. He was tall and skinny, always sweating and wore jheri curls that slapped him in the face whenever he moved his head. He always had a smile ready and loaded just waiting to show off his two diamond-studded gold teeth.

Yeah Don Rump was really something. He showed up at the gymnasium with promises of mansions and millions, limousines and the high life.

None of that stuff really meant much to me. For some strange reason I never really thought much beyond the present moment. Maybe that's why I was always such a good fighter.

I was always in the here and now, not seeing much of maybe what's to come.

The first time he showed up I told him to get lost.

A few days later a funny thing happened.

I was doing road work jogging around the mostly deserted early morning streets of Chicago lost in my own thoughts of, jab-jab, step to the left, block, and counter with straight right, left-hook when she was there and we were colliding into one another.

She fell and I stumbled grabbing onto her with my left hand and caught the both of us with my right hand before we hit the pavement.

My palm smacked the cool early morning cement as I stopped her body a bare two inches from the sidewalk.

Both our breaths caught in mid-exhale and we froze looking into each other's eyes. She had liquid blue eyes as soft as a dream and as deep as the ocean. Her lips were soft and pouty and her hair was flame red.

I lowered her softly to the ground. She seemed like something from a forgotten memory of a far better time.

"I'm sorry," I muttered. "I didn't see you."

She laughed and it sounded like angels singing in my ears.

To a man accustomed to barked commands and the grunts from hard punches landing, a woman's laugh is like a soothing pleasant touch.

I helped her to her feet and my roadwork was done for that day.

Her name was Crystal. She also had been out jogging, she said. When I told her it was dangerous for women to be out alone in this neighborhood she said she was new in town and didn't know.

How could she have not known? Everyone knows women don't walk the backstreets of American cities alone unless they're suicidal.

How could I have not known? I was blind, choosing to be blind. Willingly I was lead astray from the path of the innocent honorable warrior.

We began seeing each other and she began whispering in my ear. The whispers were that I needed a high powered manager and promoter to get the most out of my career so that we could get married and have kids and live happily ever after.

I believed each and every lie.

When Don Rump showed up again against Pop's wishes I signed with him. Pops was kept on as my trainer but Don became my manager.

For a time after that things were still relatively fine. I beat a few contenders and the money began rolling in. I went on seeing Crystal but put off any talks of getting married. She seemed to be pushing too fast for us to be tied together for life.

Shouldn't the man be the one doing that?

181

Don Rump kept proclaiming to the press that I was the next great fighter that I was going to be the greatest of all time.

Finally the offer I'd been waiting for came: A title fight with the Undisputed World Champion.

The same day that I signed the contract to meet the champion is the same day that crystal dropped the bomb on me. She told me she was pregnant and that we needed to get married right away.

I was happy and sad at the same time as I went off to training camp. I didn't exactly agree to marry her but I did agree that since she was pregnant we did need to get married. It was the right thing to do.

For this fight Pops had set up a different location for my personal training camp in upper Michigan because it got so we couldn't get anything done with all the reporters hanging around his gym. I spent two days there banging the bags, running and sparring before I decided to grab a cab and go back and surprise Crystal with a ring I'd bought and just take her to Vegas for a quickie wedding.

We'd to the honeymoon the right way after I won the championship.

I left a note for Pops at the gym and just went.

Crystal was supposed to be at work. She told me she was a secretary for a firm but never said which one.

I had the key to her apartment. I figured I'd just wait for her there and surprise her when she got home.

It was a surprise all right.

I unlocked the door and silently walked in. Moving silently is just the natural way that I move.

I heard voices coming from the bedroom.

"Yeah, yeah girl, go ahead, that's right. Go ahead and eat this dick." I recognized the voice. It was Don Rump. "Yeah, go ahead. That's right. Suck me hard. Then I'm gonna fuck you worse than we fucking that stupid white boy."

182

I'd heard enough.

I kicked the door open. It was latched shut so it splintered and fell away from busted hinges.

Don yelled, "Oh shit!"

Crystal fell sideways off the bed. Her head immediately popped up like a jack-in-the-box. White drool spilled from the corner of her mouth.

She squealed in fright.

Crystal didn't have any reason to be afraid.

As for Don, that was a different matter.

I marched across the room and grabbed him up off the bed by the top of his jheri curled head.

"I'll sue if you hit me," he screamed as I dragged him forward.

I slung him around the room by the hair then slammed his face into a chest of drawers. Gold teeth and diamonds flew in different directions.

I punched Don Rump twice and looked into his face. His eyes were squeezed shut tight. He gurgled up bubbles of blood through smashed lips.

"You don't deserve to live," I told him. I picked Don up hoisting him up over my head. Then running I pitched him through the window out to the pavement five stories below.

*

Slickman and Bub looked at me long and hard because I stopped speaking and went totally silent.

Finally when it seemed like silence would go on forever Slickman raised his mug for cheers. "Tell me you threw her out the window too," he said. "You would have to needed to have seen how the girl bounced."

"I'm not that kind of man," I told him.

He choked on a drink of his splotch.

"I sure as hell am," Slickman said as soon as he could draw a breath. "I'm the kind of man that would have tied one end of a rope to her neck, the other end to a tree, and then had a rope to her ankles and a horse. I'd like to see her head pop off!"

183

Bub spoke. "You're also the kind of man that would fuck a cow that looked pleasantly at you."

Slickman came back with, "Don't talk about your ex-girlfriends that way. It ain't polite."

Bub asked me how I came to be in Inagi.

I explained that after killing Don Rump I had to go on the run for the next few years and began taking underground fights to make money. Then I told them all that transpired after the fight outside St. Louis up to the moment I met them.

When I was done our throats were parched so we drank what was left in our mugs in one big gulp.

I told them it was now their turn to tell me their tales.

They ordered another round of splotch and I listened with blurring eyes to the stories of their lives. I have recorded it here as well as I can.

Slickman and Bub:
At The End
Of
Time

1.
Hairy Legs and Memories

In a land forever shrouded by boiling thick gray clouds night comes suddenly and black like a blindfold drawn over the eyes of a condemned man. Only the brave or foolish venture out into nights like these, all others huddle beside fires, grateful for the walls that are between them and the black things that roam the darkness.

It is on one such pitch black night, that a man of less than average stature comes to the island of Mercy moving with practiced stealth. He moves with the agility of a monkey and easily scales the walls of The Temple of Arac.

Built thin, his small size belies the strength within his diminutive frame. The muscles on his spare body are like steel cables hardened by a life living on the streets of one of the few remaining human cities.

This is the man known by the name Slickman for his quick hands and skill at being a pick pocket. He peers down from his perch at the rim of the circular opening at the top of the dome over the sacrificial chamber of the Temple Of Arac.

Dressed in subdued colors of black, brown and gray, he is all but invisible against the roiling black sky above him. The only things he wears that are not of dark colors are the glistening silver rapier that hangs at his side he has named Stinger, and the three throwing daggers stuck in Slickman's belt.

He sees what he came here for: The treasure that could buy a long life of safe lodging, good food and willing, enthusiastic bed partners.

The Eyes of Arac!

The eight glowing green eyes of the statue of the Spider God, said to be made of magical jade, are priceless and would fetch a huge amount of gold in any marketplace.

The statue sits against a stone wall on a throne. Eight thick hairy legs hang over the arms of the throne. The bulbous round body rests on the central cushion of the chair. A jeweled gold and platinum crown sits on top of the massive spider head.

The regal black granite statue of The Spider God Arac watches over his chamber and his kingdom.

Slickman looks down at the eyes and fastens a hook to the lip of the opening and begins to climb down into the pit.

*

With a lantern held out in front of him, a massive Barbarian moves through the dark ancient sewer system tunnel beneath The Temple of Arac. Although it was not necessary he crouched as he walked. The tunnel was large enough for him to move standing at full height, but he stooped anyway.

Accustomed to being in open spaces he hated the feeling tight quarters gave him.

The lamplight illuminates every silvery breath the barbarian exhales. His garments of thick wool and animal skin only partly fight off the cold.

This is the man known as Bub. He is a barbarian warrior who makes his living sometimes as a personal guard, sometimes as a mercenary and sometimes like tonight, as a thief.

He was just now thinking that if the drunken deposed acolyte of Arac from whom he purchased the information of this secret passage into the sacrificial chamber was lying to him and this was a dead-end, he would have to go back and crush the guy's skull.

187

Wading through ancient shit was not his idea of an enjoyable night. He would rather be spending this time in the warm arms of one of the slim working girls at Mother Teresa's House of a Thousand Pleasures.

But the promise of treasure beckoned.

The Eyes of Arac would sell for enough money so Bub could continue his quest uninterrupted till the end of his days.

At least the shit left in the tunnel was so ancient that the only smell remaining was something like moldy bread.

He moved down the stone cold damp tunnel resembling in his own way a huge predator cat.

Bub came to the steel ladder that led upward to the sacrificial chamber just where the acolyte had said it would be. Raising the lantern over his head he saw the steel circular sewer cap that he had also been told would be there.

Well, he thought, *maybe I won't be crushing the poor drunkard's skull after all.*

Setting the lantern down on the cement floor so he could make use of both hands, Bub touched the heavy broadsword at his side. It was an unconscious gesture. He was never without his blade, and he always made sure it was with him.

*

By the light of flickering torches mounted on a raised platform in the center of the sacrificial chamber Slickman descended on his rope as Bub silently raised the sewer lid above him and slid it off to the side.

Strange light gray gauzy material hung in strips from the domed ceiling and Slickman noted absently that the chamber was in bad need of a good dusting.

Bub watched as Slickman touched the cement floor of the chamber and went directly to where the statue of Arac sat.

Both of them knew there would be no guards inside the chamber at night. Guards were outside the only set of doors, but no one would dare disturb the Spider God after dark. It is said that when the sun sets, the Spider God wakes.

Superstitious nonsense, Bub had called the warning when it was given to him, but as he watched Slickman go toward the black granite statue he saw stuck high up on the walls, wrapped in the same gauzy material that hung loosely down, things that looked like mummified people.

The head of one of these mummy things moved.

Pulling himself up out of the hole in the floor Bub stretched himself to his full height. He pulled his broadsword from his scabbard and pointed at Slickman.

"Hold it there little man!" He said. "It looks like you're about to be trying to take what I came for." He spoke loud and clear. Bub knew no one outside could hear anything spoken inside this chamber at night.

Slickman was reaching for the jeweled eyes when Bub's words reached him. He ripped his rapier from his scabbard and spun about facing the towering barbarian with drawn sword.

With a smile on his lips he spoke. "Well, who do we have here? Oh, don't answer. It doesn't matter. I'm here first. These are mine."

"Only if you can get past me, Bub told him. "I'd wager you'll have a hard time climbing that rope after I hack the arms from your shoulders."

Bub moved forward.

Slickman made four slashes in the air between them. "Stinger will have something to say about that! One thing's for sure, you'll not be riding any more whores after I cut the nuts from between your legs."

Bub laughed. It was a blood curdling thing to hear. The laughter of the barbarians from The Mountains of the Olde Gods is usually the last thing that rings in their opponent's ears before they come to a bloody end.

Slickman's gaze jerked upward to a point somewhere behind Bub.

"Behind you!" he yelled.

"You think I'd fall for that?" Bub shouted back as he came forward. Then he was dodging to the side a backhand thrown dagger Slickman had aimed at his face.

The dagger flew past Bub's head and from the sound of it, struck something in the air.

Greenish, slimy, sticky liquid splashed on Bub's head and shoulders as a furry eight-legged thing that had been descending on a thin string spewed out its lifeblood from the dagger wound.

All around them, descending on webs, black spiders the size of hunting dogs came down from the ceiling.

Their fight against each other was forgotten.

With the first sight of the spiders, goose bumps jumped up all over Bub's arms. The one thing he almost had a primal fear of was spiders.

But he didn't have time for fear now. With a savage yell he cut two of the descending arachnids in half in the air. Their green blood splashed across his face.

The spiders were coming down from all parts of the domed roof. There were too many of them to be counted.

Slickman's rapier flicked left, then right and sixteen legs kicked in the air from four separated halves of spider bodies. He danced around the room in a strangely graceful dance of death slashing the huge bugs as they came down.

Each time a spider was hacked in pieces the thing screeched out a loud squeal that was something like a cross between a seagulls cry and a woman's scream. The squeals were unnerving. They sounded almost human.

Bub was bellowing challenges at the descending spiders until he caught a look at the webbing high up on the ceiling and saw something that chilled his blood.

The webbing was being ripped away by a spider leg that looked to be around twenty feet long.

"We have got to get out of here!" Bub yelled and Slickman followed his gaze to the huge thing at the ceiling ripping itself loose.

The spider that stared down at them was easily twice the size of an elephant. Against it, their swords would do no more than give it a moment's annoyance before it ate them.

"By the Seven Hells of Hasper," Slickman said and stepping backward disappeared down the manhole. From down in the hole a clank followed a thud a moment later.

Bub cleared a path through the dog-sized spiders and virtually dove down into the hole he came from.

At the bottom, on the cement floor, Slickman was unconscious.

"A good time to take a nap," Bub told him. He grabbed the sword lying at Slickman's side and slid it back into the little man's scabbard.

Above them, the huge spider was trying to fit itself into the manhole. Its legs were reaching down and beating against the rungs of the steel ladder making it ring like a chime. As big as it was, Bub could tell it would still be only a matter of minutes before the huge arachnid squeezed itself down into the hole.

"Well, I wouldn't leave anyone to a death like that," Bub muttered under his breath. He picked Slickman up and hoisted him over his right shoulder. Picking up the lantern and holding it out in front of him with his left hand, Bub took off at a trot back the way he came in.

*

Slickman awoke to the sound of swishing water as oars parted the surface and pulled the rowboat he was laying in.

He was in total darkness except for a line of lanterns that were bobbing in the distance.

"Where the hell am I?" He asked almost shouting the words.

"Keep your voice down," Bub told him, "Or I'll toss you overboard. The Acolytes of Arac are searching for us. There are too many of them to fight and I don't feel like being Big Ugly's next meal."

191

"Where are we going?"

"Away from them," Bub answered and the line of lights did appear to be receding into the distance.

"Are we to the east of Mercy Island?" Slickman asked.

Bub didn't answer.

"Well?" Slickman asked again.

"No!" Bub said.

"That means we're heading in the direction of The Ghost Lands … right?"

"Tonight, there's nowhere else to go."

*

Through the chill black of night they took turns rowing toward the west. When Slickman first awoke, he heard the cawing of a few of the night ocean birds overhead.

Now, he heard nothing.

The lamps on the boats of the Acolytes of Arac were far behind them.

It was like they moved away from nothing and moved toward nothing. Blackness was behind them and ahead of them.

It was so pitch black they could not even see each other in the rowboat. The only sound that broke the silence was the rhythmic slap, splash and swooshes of the oars as they were drawn through the water.

It seemed for awhile as though nothing in the universe moved. They were alone among the stars. Except, it was so pitch black, even the stars were blotted out.

Bub spoke and his voice breaking the silence almost sounded as large as some Ancient God hurling pronouncements down upon worshippers from high on a mountain peak. "Is this how it will be, when all things come to an end?" Bub asked.

"I don't know." Slickman answered in a whisper that sounded as loud as a booming foghorn. "I doubt I'll be here when we come to the end of all things."

They glided through the thick dark. A Stygian blackness so thick its weight could be felt upon the skin like a physical touch.

Whispering sounds started gliding to them over the subdued waves.

Speech, words, cries, moans, wails, screams, begging sounds, so faint it couldn't be identified for certain. Things were out there, in the chilly blackness, things that whispered and tittered with voices too weak to be heard by human ears. But the voices could be felt.

They glided on.

Both of these men had faced death in ugly ways more times than they could count. When Death looked their way, they would stare it down and fight it to the last breath. That was their way. To fight and die when their time came. They accepted that fate.

But these voices, these crying things unnerved them. Here, there was nothing to fight. There was only the chorus of a million maddening voices crying out that they wanted to live, they needed to live, that they did not even know they were dead.

From overhead came a chopping noise such as they had never heard before. Chu-chu-chu, chu-chu-chu... and something streaked, flying through the air above them, roaring.

A boxlike thing glided in a straight line past the end of their boat. It had glowing white eyes and screamed a warning shout of anger. It was followed on its path and joined by hundreds of things that glided smoothly along at speeds that were far faster than any of the fastest racing steeds.

Some of the things were the size of ox drawn carts, while others were the size of buildings. They flashed past in a bewildering display of color and raw power.

Behind the lines of the things that flashed past, what looked like black mountains sprang up. These black mountains shot straight up into the sky. They were made entirely of sharp black cliffs so steep the two men knew no one could ever climb them. The thing that was the strangest about the sheer mountains were the unearthly lights that shown from out from the faces of the black cliffs.

Lights do not shine from the sides of cliff faces. Slickman and Bub knew this. But here, they did.

Slickman and Bub were speechless at the massive display of ghostly apparitions.

For ghosts they knew these things surely were. Their skins were translucent. One could be seen through another.

Now they started getting visions or were they memories of a way of life that was alien to the two of them. People sat inside the boxlike things and were propelled at dizzying speeds along wide flat trails built for these things.

These people were people who lived in comfort. They had joys that Slickman and Bub couldn't even dream. These people who never even knew how to harvest their own food or hunt never knew hunger. Searching for amusements from day to day was how they lived.

They lived in a self-made paradise and it was all brought to a sudden and total end. Now they screamed that they didn't know where their lives had gone and they wanted their lives back.

Slickman grabbed one oar while Bub grabbed the other and together they paddled as fast as they could away from the shoreline of The Ghost Lands.

What little they'd seen of that place told them, to land there would cost them their sanity. In such an alien land a man could not even hope to keep his mind.

*

194

They rowed heading north, although at this time they weren't sure what direction they were heading. Being in pitch blackness, on an open body of water will take away all sense of direction.

Slickman and Bub knew they were going north when the sky to the east started getting light for the morning. That was also when they came to the broken down Bridge Of Memories.

In a land always covered by thick dreary clouds, morning comes in muted shades of blue and gray. The Bridge Of Memories rose up out of the mist in front of them like a long gray many humped sea monster.

The Bridge Of Memories was a left over relic from the ancient civilization of men, who strove to become Gods and blasted their own world to hell. It was a steel and stone construction that was missing segments. Once, this bridge joined The Ghost Lands to the mainland. Now it was only a lonely reminder that men do not have the wisdom to control the power of the Gods.

Turning toward the east, they rowed until they beached their boat at a point just north of the town of Bella. It had been a long night and both of them were exhausted.

Slickman turned to walk into Bella and Bub turned to head into the forest to the east. Bub was more at home among trees than under a roof and inside confining walls.

"Where will you be?" Bub asked as Slickman started to walk away.

"What's it to you, where I will be?" Slickman said back.

"You owe me for the Eyes of Arac," Bub said. "If you wouldn't have been there, I would have taken them."

"No!" Slickman said. "It's you who owes me. I was there first, remember. I would have been out of there before the first crawly woke, if you would have kept your bellowing barbarian mouth shut."

"I saved your sorry ass," Bub told Slickman. "I could have let Big Ugly gnaw you up like a child's piece of chew gum."

"And I saved you and lost a good throwing knife in the bargain."

195

Both of them went to draw their swords, ready to spill blood. They stared in each other's eyes. Hot-blooded murder radiated in the air between them.

A growling sound came from deep in Bub's throat. The barbarians from the foot of the Mountains of the Olde Gods considered themselves more animal than man and were proud of it.

Slickman bounced lightly on his toes. Standing sideways, he readied himself to draw and slash. A sound like an, "Aaaaaaw, aaaaaaw," came out of his mouth that sounded almost like a birdcall.

Why he did this, he wasn't even sure. It just seemed like something strange to do just before a fight. So he did it.

Bub told him, "You sound like a Hoot Owl with the runs."

Slickman answered, "And you sound like the last woman that I fucked!"

"I'd hate to see that girl," Bub told him.

"Yeah, me too," Slickman answered.

After a time of cawing and growling and staring at each other, they grew bored with that and broke it off.

"I'm going to Barbara Walter's Bed'em and Bang'em Motel," Slickman told Bub. "I'm going to do it the other way round. Bang'em, then get some sleep. Where are you going to be?"

Bub pointed toward the tall trees of the emerald forest. "I sleep better underneath pines," He said. "When I awake I'll be traveling to the east. There's much out there that's not known. You could travel with me until you find a way to repay what you owe."

"Maybe, I'll consider it," Slickman answered. "I've seen what there is to see in this part of the world. And, it would be good to be around when you have the money to pay me what you owe."

Slickman turned and began walking toward Bella. As soon as he was sure he was observed by no one, he patted the side of his jacket to make sure by touch that in the inner lining was two rock hard eye-shaped items that felt very much like two of The Eyes of Arac.

***

I took a very large swallow of the Splotch as both Slickman and Bub paused in the telling of their tales. There story was obviously at a juncture in the events they were recounting that was less than memorable.

Bub seemed a bit annoyed and suddenly turned to Slickman. "You never told me you managed to make off with two of The Eyes of Arac."

"You never asked me," Slickman answered.

"And if I had?"

"I would have told you I didn't and kept the both of them myself," Slickman said.

"So you're a liar."

"I don't deny that," Slickman said. "But I'm at least an honest liar because I will admit to lying."

Bub fumed, starring daggers into Slickman.

After a long moment of hot silence Slickman said, "Well, Gods-be-dammed I'll give both The Eyes of Arac to you if you want them now."

"These people don't use coin or jewels for currency. They're worthless here and you know it," Bub said.

"Then don't take them. I'll keep them as good luck charms. At least I offered," Slickman answered.

As they took large pulls from their mugs to change their train of thought I chose that moment to ask them some questions.

"The world you talk about seems somehow to be the same one I came from when I was tossed down the hole outside St. Louis. But it also seems to be a different place too."

"We never told you we came from the same world you did," Slickman snapped. "We only know that it's far different than Inagi. We're

197

not even certain how we got here but we'll explain that later when it makes sense."

"Besides," Bub cut in. "After what you've told us you seemed to have experienced more of this world than we have. I got a few questions I'd like to ask you.'

"Fire away," I said. "If I've seen more than you and have answers I'll tell you what I know. You never know, maybe all our bits of knowledge will add up to some real facts."

Slickman was the one that spoke now. "OK," he said. "Where are all the old people? In this city, in this world, if that's what Inagi is, we've seen not even one person sporting even one gray hair. Do people not even age here or what?"

I had to admit he had me on that one. I did have to admit I had not seen one old person since I woke up in the village of Amura. I told them that.

Bub said, "And I'd like to know what has happened to all the metal here. There's got to be at least a little. I've been badly missing the feel of good solid steel in my hand. These things," he drew his white-bladed sword partially out of the scabbard. "I think they are made of a hardened bone of some sort. They dull fast and just don't have enough heft for a real man. I miss my steel."

All I could do to that question was shake my head. I had no good information for him.

"Well, what good are you then if you don't have any answers?" Slickman asked me.

"Probably none," I said.

"Then I guess there's nothing else to do but continue on drinking and telling you how we came to be here," Slickman said.

"Nothing else to do," I told him.

"Continue on," Bub said. "Tell him what happened the second time we met. And if your lies stray too far from the truth to be tolerated, I'll correct your version of the events."

"You do that," Slickman said.

They continued on.

2.

Roasting Rabbits
And
Romance

A night crow shrieked out his call to the other black birds of the dark from his perch high up in the treetops of the thick forest. He was answered by other flying creatures that were up there.

The bugs pretty much kept to their silence.

They were the prey. They didn't want to be located.

A light breeze rustled the leaves and branches of treetops Bub could not see under the cover of night.

Bub sat cross legged on the ground in front of his camp fire and turned the spitted rabbit he was roasting.

Bub liked the quiet peacefulness of the forest. The wind sounded like the Earth was whispering secrets that if he listened hard enough he would be able to hear and understand.

Bub listened hard.

He heard the crackling of his fire and the sizzling of the rabbit juices as it cooked, and he heard something else.

Just off to the right of the front of him was a rustling, shuffling noise.

Bub transferred the stick with his skewered rabbit to his left hand. He felt down beside his knee with his right hand and located a good sized rock.

The shuffling came again from behind a row of bushes next to a huge pine tree.

Bub stood up and with all the strength his muscular arm had in it, he hurled the rock directly at the location where the sound came from. The stone flew through the bush and struck something hard with a thud.

"Ow! ...Damn-it!" A cry came from the other side of the bush. "What are you trying to do, you idiot? If you would have asked who was there, I would have told you."

Slickman stepped out from behind the bush leading his horse and rubbing a growing knot on the top of his head.

"You should have announced yourself," Bub told him.

"You should have asked."

Slickman tied his horse beside Bub's, then came over and laid his carrying bag on the ground between them. He then sat down on the ground himself.

He looked at the rabbit sizzling over the fire. "That looks good," He said.

"It will be," Bub answered.

"I'll travel to the East with you," Slickman announced. "You'll need someone like me who knows his way around to keep your bumbling barbarian ass out of trouble."

"Really?" Bub asked.

"Oh yeah," Slickman said. "I'll show you the ropes real fast."

"So you have been to the lands to the East?" Bub asked.

"No," Slickman said. "But I've been so many places that nothing surprises me anymore. Are you going to share some of that rabbit?"

"There's not much," Bub said.

Slickman went into his bag and produced a bottle of wine.

This will make it go down easier," Slickman said, "If you share." Slickman uncorked the bottle and took a long drink from it. He went, "Ahhhhh," when he was done.

"Pass the wine," Bub said.

"Going to share?"

Bub pointed to the tree on the other side of the fire. Another spitted rabbit was leaning against it. "Yours," He said.

"There's more than enough to go around," Slickman said. "You're a greedy bastard aren't you?"

Bub laughed and took the bottle from Slickman's hands.

Rabbits were roasted. Rabbits were eaten.

Wine was drunk.

And in the dark of the night beside a glowing campfire, Slickman and Bub began telling each other tales from their lives.

*

Love on the Wing

(A Bub Tale)

So, you want to hear a story about a woman. You want to hear a tale of lust and beastly breeding aplenty.

I'll not give you one of those tonight.

How about, I tell you a story of love and loss and how I found out about the ultimate fate of man. You've noticed I don't smile overmuch.

There are reasons why.

You've taken it for granted that I am one of the barbarians from the foot of The Mountains of the Olde Gods.

I do wear the same style of dress as they and I talk in a similar fashion. It is by design. It has served my purposes to present myself as one of those murderers of women and children.

But, I am not.

I am a man without a clan, without a family.

My father was a farmer, a hard man.

202

I was a disobedient son. So he sold me and my sister to a roaming band of barbarians from the foot of The Mountains of the Olde Gods.

I understand why my father got rid of me. I never wanted to do my chores and was more trouble than I was worth, but he sold my sister Beth, purely because the foul smelling chieftain offered a good amount of gold for her.

Beth was always obedient and cheerful, a good daughter. Her reward was being thrown to a group of ugly mean spirited pigs as their plaything at the age of twelve. They used her for about a month then sold her to another band of cut throats. The last time I saw her face was through the bars of a cage mounted on the back of a wagon as they drove away.

But this story is not about her. I just have to let you know how I got to where this story actually begins.

I was made into a pit fighter.

It was the most profitable way they could use a strong, fast, rough, youth, who had seen but seventeen summers. I was born for the pit fighting arenas.

My owners couldn't have forced me to work if they had wanted to. As for making me into one of their boy sex toys, well if someone shoved a dick at me I would have bit it off and beat them with it.

I wanted to fight anything that moved. This way, they made money off my bad temper.

My owners carefully taught me how to use their weapons. I say carefully, because they knew I would turn on them the first chance I got. There were no illusions of friendship here. I was property to be used until I was no longer useful.

Chained up, they took me from camp to camp, from village to village. I was matched against the meanest, toughest guys in every town.

People paid to watch.

The winner received the pot. I should say, the winners owners, received the pot.

I got nothing.

I never lost. If I had, I wouldn't be alive. The fights were always to the death. I made my four owners a lot of money.

But, the story of my pit fights, are another tale in itself. Like my sister, that's not what this story is about.

Now, we come to the beginning.

*

When moving between villages, between fights, I was always chained to the bed of a horse drawn wagon. There was enough chain so I could stretch out and lie down or stand up and stretch.

My four owners, the ugly stinking bastards, had to have me ready whenever we showed up at any township. If I went into battle stiff or slow from not being able to move around at least a little bit my life would be over and their golden goose would be dead.

The end of my chain was fastened to the bed of the wagon by a large bolt. For the past few months I laid in the center of the wagon as we bounced along and pretending to be napping, I worked at the bolt with one hand just trying to wiggle it back and forth.

On this day, I got it to move.

At first, it moved so little I thought I was imagining it. But as I reclined there, curled up in a ball in the middle of the wagon to hide my straining right hand, I was able to force the bolt sideways, just a tiny bit.

Then I forced it back the other way. It gave a little each way I strained against it.

It seemed like I went on like that for hours, faking sleep and forcing the bolt back and forth, when the wagon stopped.

I thought for a moment one of them had seen what I was doing. But when I opened my eyes, the one who was the acknowledged leader, a grim faced guy named Carn, had his hand in the air in a gesture commanding silence as he peered intently upward into the trees a little to the right of us.

The wagon road we were on was shrouded by tall pine trees and stillness hung heavy in the air. Nothing seemed to move. It was as though with the stopping of the wagon, time stopped.

All four of my owners were frozen looking up at the same spot. Three of them rode horses. One of them was guiding the reins of the wagon I was in.

I followed their gaze to the spot that they looked at. For one long moment I perceived nothing. Then, I saw it.

Standing against the trunk high in the branches of an enormous ancient oak was a huge beautiful graceful bird. Its feathers were grayish, almost the same color as the bark of the tree and it was trying to blend itself in with its surroundings.

Carn reached over his shoulder, un-slung his bow and pulled an arrow that was hanging in the pouch on his horse's side. Like a signal, the tree others did the same and notched arrows in their bows.

The huge bird, that was easily the size of a grown woman, leaped away from the tree and took to the air. With the spreading of her wings we all saw that this was a woman, a beautiful woman who had wings that grew from her back, a woman who could fly.

A collective gasp of awe came from all of us. But that didn't stop the four from releasing their arrows at this flying beauty.

Two arrows missed completely, being lost somewhere in the branches and leaves.

One struck her in her well formed right thigh. The other sank deep into the woman's right wing.

She screamed a heart rending cry and with one useless wing beating the air in vain she plunged through the branches to the hard Earth.

My four owners shouted in triumph and leaped to the ground. Jumping and slapping each other on the back, drunk with their victory, arguing as to whose arrow had struck home first. They ran to where the woman with wings crashed down.

This was the first time since I was bought that I was unguarded. I wasn't going to waste a second.

I stood up in the wagon and grabbed my chain in both hands. I bent at the knees and straining with every bit of strength I had, I stood straight up and ripped backward.

The metal the bolt was screwed into creaked then squeaked and for one awful moment, I thought my back was going to break. Then the bolt came loose.

With the sudden release of pressure I staggered and fell backward out of the wagon. I only lay on the ground for a moment before regaining my feet.

Looking in the direction that my four owners had run, I knew I could take one of their horses and ride away. I also knew that they would track me and I would have to be looking over my shoulder the rest of my life. So I saved them the trouble of coming after me.

Using the tree trunks as cover I crept up on the four being as quiet as I could. As it turned out, it wouldn't have mattered if I would have came stomping up to them. They were too interested in what they were doing to be thinking about me.

The woman with wings was on her back. Her good wing was folded underneath her. Her injured wing was splayed out to the side. She was badly hurt. Blood was pumping out of her wounds.

That didn't matter to my four owners.

One, a cruel haggle-toothed guy named Brock, was holding her arms down to the ground from over her head. Carn was cutting her cloth garments from her with his knife.

Her eyes reeled back and forth wildly. She was muttering, "No! No! No!" Tears streamed down her cheeks.

The other two were standing back loosening their own belts to rape the winged woman.

It was the perfect time for me to attack.

I leaped from behind a tree just as one of the two loosening his trousers let them fall to the ground.

The length of heavy chain manacled around my wrists was around four feet long. I crushed the skull of the guy with his trousers around his ankles with the first swing of my chain. The other man turned his head just in time for me to bash his face in with a back swing.

The two working on the woman saw me now. A punch from Carn knocked her unconscious. Carn got to his feet.

The man holding the woman's arms let go and leaped to his feet. He ripped out his sword and charged me.

Maybe Brock hadn't been watching my pit fights or he was extremely stupid, either way, I wanted him to charge.

Brock slashed straight down in an overhand stroke. I sidestepped his blade and whipped my chain around his neck. Jerking him to me, I turned my back and using his own weight for momentum tossed Brock over my shoulder into the air. As he was flying I jerked backward with the chain.

All I was hoping for was to break his neck. The maneuver worked better than planned.

His head popped clean off.

Headless he landed standing up on his feet.

Blood flew.

Brock's headless body turned and with blood spewing straight up from its stump, it took off at a run and tackled Carn.

Carn was getting to his knees as I stood in front of him. He held out his hand to command me to halt.

"Listen boy," he said. ""I'll split all the money with you. And hell, we can both fuck this big bird here. Look at them titties boy. Bet you never had nothing like them in your mouth, have you. I'll share. We can be friends, boy." He had this big grin on his face like he was offering me something valuable.

"Sure we can," I told Carn and smiled back. Then I swung my chain around my head and bashed his brains in. I hated that son of a bitch so much I kept slamming him with the chain until his face looked like stew meat.

*

After I was done with Carn, I fell to the ground in exhausted relief. I was a free man for the first time in my life. First, I was owned by my father and all us kids were just farm animals to him. Then, these four bastards owned me.

For the first time in my life, I owned myself. What brought me back to where I was and out of my daydreaming about the wonders of freedom, was when the woman with wings moaned.

*

She was still breathing and blood oozed from her wounds. I looked down at her. There was not much I could do for her even if I wanted to and actually, I didn't really have a reason to want to help her.

Yeah, she was good looking but I wasn't like those other guys. I couldn't just stick my dick in something because it was a warm piece of meat. A woman I fucked had to at least be able to do something back to me or it just wasn't any fun. This woman looked to be past doing anything other than just bleeding and dying.

So, I started gathering up the weapons from the four that I figured I could use. They didn't need them anymore. There were a few hunting knives, four swords, four bows and a bunch of arrows. Figuring I could sell it all I loaded it in the back of the wagon.

I was going to head south with everything. At the first town with a blacksmith I'd use the money I got from the pouches of the four and get these manacles taken off of my wrists. Then I'd sell the extra weapons and head for parts unknown. Life was going to be my adventure. And I wasn't going to be taking any dying woman with wings with me. I didn't have the

208

time to take care of her. I didn't want to be weighted down with burdens of any kind.

Then the whispers began.

"Don't leave her," came from the left of me. It sounded almost like the breeze.

"Help her. Help her." Came from my right, as soft as the rustling of leaves.

"Save your soul," a voice from overhead chanted to me. "Save your soul. Change yourself." The singing whispers continued.

I looked around in confusion. I saw no one, just trees and bushes and leaves and I realized all of it was speaking to me.

"Help her," the forest spoke to me. "Mother Earth calls on your kindness. Learn kindness."

All things in the woods seemed to have focused its attention on me.

I looked again at the broken winged woman lying at my feet.

Beauty is fragile. Magic is fragile. On that day I had been touched by the magic of the Earth.

I could not refuse.

*

After bandaging her wounds as well as I could, I gave the winged woman water from one of the flasks the four had been carrying. She coughed and grimaced from the pain she was in. Then she smiled and when she looked in my eyes I saw that her eyes were like a cat's, with its slitted pupils. Her eyes also had a cat's glowing night-shine. It was in the middle of the day but her eyes glowed a soft pale blue.

The winged woman was too weak to be able to talk, which was alright with me. What was I going to say to her anyway?

After I managed to stop her bleeding, I picked the winged woman up and loaded her into the back of the wagon along with all the weapons and supplies.

She lay back and instantly fell into an exhausted sleep. I was afraid she died on me so I leaned close to her to see if she were still breathing and the scent of her filled my mind with a feeling of being pleasantly drunk from sweet wine.

Yes, she is still breathing, I said to myself as I watched her breasts gently rise and fall. That sight was intoxicating in itself. I covered her with one of the blankets I took from one of my owners.

I looked at her and voiced the question, "Now, what am I going to do with you?"

As if in answer, a buzzing came to my ears and something flew past my head so close I moved to the side without thinking.

A high pitched voice spoke to me from in front. "We will guide you," It told me.

"Yes, we will be your guide." Another voice agreed, high pitched, but different from the first.

The second voice came from my right. I looked and hovering in the air a few feet away from my head was a firefly about the size of my fist. As my eyes refocused, I realized it wasn't a firefly I was looking at, but a small man with firefly wings hovered beside me. He darted away, out of my reach.

"We will be your guide," he repeated. "Until, she is well enough to guide you to her home."

"Follow us," The other said and hovered in front of me also staying out of reach.

I'd never seen any creatures like these before. I'd never heard of anything like these small winged people, or come to think of it, the winged woman either.

"What are you?" I asked them.

The two firefly people hovered, side by side in front of me. I saw that one was a man, the other was a woman. They looked at each other and smiled.

"We have no name for what we are," The man said.

"We need no name for what we are," The woman said.

"Your people have called us Sprites," The man said.

"And Fairies," the woman added.

"Follow us," The man said.

Because I had no better destination that called to me, I drove the wagon with the horses tied behind it and the winged woman laying in the back, down a narrow trail deep into the forest toward the Mountains of The Olde Gods, to a place where it is said, no man is allowed to go.

*

The trail I guided the wagon over was just big enough for the cart to pass between the trees on both sides. Sometimes I had to drive the wagon directly over the top of bushes and brush. The going was slow. The terrain was harsh.

Suddenly, all of that changed.

It was like we crossed over a border from one world to another.

Where I came from was dark, cold and misty. Living in that forest was hard. Where we passed into the sun was shining, the breeze was warm and pleasant upon my skin.

The animals, birds and insects of the forest where I came from, fled at my approach. Here, they walked and flew beside the wagon unafraid. This forest was alive with sound as all the creatures spoke among themselves with no fear of man.

At first when I entered this realm, I thought the trail came to an abrupt end. But as I approached the trees that blocked the way, they glided to the side and made way for our passage.

This was an enchanting place. Everything was wonderfully alive. I followed the Sprites, if that's what they were, forward into the realm of The Olde Gods.

211

I cannot measure the amount of time I drove into that living forest. In that place, time does not exist. It may have been one hour. It may have been one year. I do not know.

I only know that a hand was laid upon my shoulder and when I looked, the winged woman was climbing forward to sit beside me.

The Sprites vanished into the trees.

The winged woman's wounds were not completely healed, but they looked like they caused her no great pain.

She looked into my face and her softly glowing blue eyes seemed to glimpse into the deepest part of my mind and heart. She smiled and something inside of me melted. The wall of ice I had built around my heart cracked and fell away.

It was as simple as that.

Before I met her, I was a heartless killer. I enjoyed the kill, the domination just before the taking of life. It was all that made me feel I was truly strong. But after looking in her eyes I did not need to feel strong anymore. I realized true strength is gained with the control of the power we have; Not just the blind wielding of that power.

Power needs to be used to build, create and protect to truly be strength.

The winged woman and I spoke that day without words. She spoke to me inside my mind and heard me, when I answered the same way.

Her kind never ages. Her race was old when man's first civilizations were being built. In the most ancient of times, her kind were named as Pegasis or winged horses, in myths because one of them carried a starving man to a city and swore that man to silence about their existence.

Before the more recent fall of man's civilization of two millennia past, they were seen as angels.

During the time of man's flourish, they hid in caves in the mountains and in the most remote spots they could find. Mankind was a destroyer. They knew if their existence became known, they would have been exterminated.

When night came I made us a fire and we sat and stared into each other's eyes. She allowed me to hold her in my arms. She was warm and soft and I could do nothing but be gentle with her.

That first night in her forest, in front of our small camp fire she gave herself to me and as I penetrated into her our minds merged into one.

Visions leaped out of her memory into my mind. Although I did not understand a great deal of what I saw, I did understand that the visions were of the past of mankind.

In times past, the race of man spread over all the lands of the Earth like a disease. He took all the green fields and plowed them under. He burned and cut down great forests and replaced them with jungles of stone. Where man went, he made the waters undrinkable and the air unhealthy to breath. Man placed himself above all other creatures and became the worst of all.

But the greatest evil that man committed, he committed against himself. Enormous groups of men, things he called armies, were sent against each other to kill and take what the others had. Any one of these armies numbered more than all the people who existed upon the Earth at the time when I met the winged woman. In the end it was that need to take and dominate everything that destroyed their world.

Mankind fought a battle against his own kind with weapons unimaginably terrible and nearly ended the life of Mother Earth herself.

*

The next day, I did not speak to my nameless winged woman about the visions that went through my mind as we made love the night before. I was in love with her on a level that no other man could ever understand.

Her kind was pure, faultless.

We rode on through the peaceful forest and I knew a happiness that knew no reasons or wants. She was happy with me. I could see that in her eyes. Her happiness filled me with warmth.

Many days we traveled.

Many nights we made love. Each night I learned more about the past of man until the night came when in the darkening twilight we caught sight of the spires of her city.

As we sat beside our campfire that night, for the first time, I asked my nameless lady what the meaning of my visions had been.

Her eyes grew sad. When she reached into my mind and told me her answer I felt the pain that she felt. Tears ran down her face.

"Your kind, are at an end," She told me. The words echoed inside my mind. "Mother Earth has turned her eyes away from man. Man caused Mother Earth too much pain. Each creature is given a special gift at the time of its beginning. Man was given the gift of seeing what is not, but can be. Mother Earth has taken this gift back. Some of what man created in the past still exists but nothing new will be seen. Man will never again build stone monuments to himself.

"Because of this, your kind will dwindle and die."

When we made love that night, with the lights of her crystal city shining down from the cliffs that seemed so close now, I had no visions of man's past. I knew with no future, the past held no meaning.

Instead, a vision came to me that was a certainty, a feeling, something I knew.

My winged woman loved me and so loving me, she was dooming herself to a life of loneliness. I saw knowledge of her people she had kept from me. If she took me to her people, she would be branded as a traitor and exiled.

Men were the destroyers. We were not allowed here. Our kind had lost the chance to ever live in the peaceful garden.

When she lay in a deep sleep, like a thief who had stolen something precious, and I had stolen her love, I took a horse and snuck away into the night.

As badly as it pained me, I would not sentence my winged lady to an eternal life separated from her own kind. And if I had taken her with me, where could we have gone? We would have had to have lived alone, where she would see me grow old and die, while she stayed young.

No. I would not put her through that.

She is the only woman I will ever love and because of that, I will never seek to see her face again.

*

Roasting Rabbits

Slickman had a grin on his face.

Bub wore a solemn expression. "If you laugh," He said. "I will beat you without mercy about the head and shoulders."

"Oh, I'll not laugh." Slickman told him, "Unless you begin bawling like a massive barbarian baby."

Bub's face reddened. "I should have hit you with a bigger rock." He said. "I told you, I am not a barbarian."

"Calm down," Slickman said. "Drink some more wine. The night is not done with tales of women just yet."

*

The Sea Sorcerer of Craven's
Saucy Slut
(A Slickman Tale)

Since you have told me something about your childhood, I'll tell you something about mine.

I'll make it short and sweet.

215

I never had a childhood. I don't know who my mother or my father was. The only memories I have of when I was growing up are I was always hungry and would do anything to get a mouthful of food.

I lived on the streets of the city of Poorland, sleeping in doorways or abandoned buildings. Foraging for food was what I lived for.

I got my name because I have fast hands ... *slick* hands. I can steal a man's money right out from under his nose and he'll never see me do it.

I'm the best thief there is, and I'm not half bad with a sword or knife.

None of this has anything to do with the story about a woman that I'm going to tell, but so what.

Drink up and sit back.

Here it comes.

*

After I relieved a wealthy Poorland merchant of some of his most prized possessions and had a pocket full of gold, I figured it would be a good idea to leave the city for a while. I was the only thief in that city good enough to be able to sneak into and get out of Demetrio the Merchant's estate without being caught. So it was just a matter of time before he sent some hired strong arms to beat knots all over me and take back what I took.

Besides, I was tired of Poorland anyway and hungered for new sights.

That was how I came to be riding into the coastal village of Craven.

Craven is a harbor village. On the coast, just to the south of Craven, overlooking Pathetic Ocean is steep treacherous cliffs.

Next to the cliffs is a long sandy beach where merchant ships dock. Just inland from that beach is the village of Craven.

Only a few hundred, if that many, people live in or around Craven. Most people steer clear of the coastal settlements because of hurricanes and storms that batter most of the coast of Pathetic Ocean almost constantly.

But Craven was different. For some reason, storms stayed away. Hurricanes blew past.

Craven did get winds, but nothing very strong. It did get rains, but never enough to cause flooding.

I came to Craven looking for a woman. Not any woman in particular, just some nice young innocent girl who would spread her legs and howl like a pack of hungry wolves as I fed her the bone.

That's all I wanted.

I had a pocket full of gold and a hard dick in search of adventure.

Craven was a dreary place. There were two houses of lodging, one tavern and one large whore house.

I rented a room at Craven Inn and headed on over to the whore house, a place named Julia Robert's Lip Smackin' Good Head House.

I could guess what they specialized in.

Julia Robert's Lip Smackin' Good Head House was a long flat wooden building. Inside, there was a large waiting room, a long hallway lead off that with dozens of doors for rooms for fucking on both sides of the hallway.

It was after dark. Torches were lit outside so customers could find their way in and candles were burning in the hallway so they could find their way to the right room.

The waiting room had a powerful smell to it like rotting fish. The putrid fish here didn't smell like they came from the ocean. The girls in here probably didn't bath too regular. Oh well, I'd just have to hold my nose closed with one hand and squeeze titties with the other. Maybe if the girl did me extra good, I'd make her a present of a bar of soap. Don't let anyone tell you I won't treat a woman right if she deserves it.

217

In the waiting room sitting on a chair there was only a mean looking old guy who seemed like he'd spent too many hard winters out on the sea.

I came in the door and asked the old codger, "Where's all your women? Bring them out. I'll fuck them all. I have a powerful need to plant some seed."

Without a blink of his eye the old salt said, "We're fully booked up. There's not a strumpet that's not a pumping in Craven tonight. Two fishing ships are in and all the sailors are dropping anchor."

"I've got money," I told the old fart and dug gold coin out of my pocket and showed it to him.

The old guy's eyes brightened at the sight of the gold piece. He licked his lips. "Why, I'll do you myself," He said starting to stand.

"Sit back down you ancient sausage swallower," I told him. "I only take my pleasures with the fairer sex."

"I can be mighty fair," He came back with and batted his eyes at me to try and look cute.

"This is not an argument you're going to win," I told him.

"No, I suppose not," He agreed.

"Women ?" I inquired again.

"Well," The ancient pole polisher said slowly. "Old Gerty is the only woman who's not taken tonight."

"Tell me about her," I said. Tapping Stinger at my side I added, "If you're not truthful or this is some kind of ruse to part me from my money without me getting what I came for, I'll come back out here and split your old skull for you."

"All right," he said. "Since you're asking, I'll be telling. Usually, I just tell the fellows to just go on up, go in and close the door so it stays dark. Gerty gives the absolute best head in existence. Bar none, she is the best. Only because you insist on knowing, I'll tell you her secret.

"Gerty had a husband once, a long time ago, who stabbed her left eye out. She killed him in his sleep for it. But that don't make no difference now. Gerty's special head technique is that she has a glass eye she can pop out. And let me tell you, that hole her left eye used to be, that is the sweetest hole I ever did stick my dick in."

"You are a sick old bastard!" I told that sick old bastard.

"You asked for the truth," He said. "I've done it myself many a times and it's good. Except she does shake like she's got the St. Vitas Dance and snot and drool flies from her nose and mouth when you get to really pumping on her eyehole. It must be that bumping into her brain that hakes her shake like that. It hasn't never bothered me none. In fact, it kind of adds a bit of excitement when she starts jerking all around like she's done lost control of herself. At least she doesn't shit herself."

"Well there is at least that," I said. "I'll be passing on Gerty." I headed out the door.

The old rump rider was laughing as I exited. Just before the door banged shut behind me he yelled. "You'll be back. I'll have her keep an eye out for you."

*

The smell of sea salt was in the air as I trudged across town toward the tavern. Gulls screamed unseen in the sky. The distant rumble of the surf crashing on sea shells and sand was strangely soothing to my battered bandit's nerves.

The only tavern in Craven was named, *They Always Look Better After A Few.*

Never was there a truer statement, I thought and entered.

A few oil lamps burned on tables where cards and dice were being played by the few sailors not occupied with digging for treasure at Julia Robert's Lip Smackin' Good Head House.

219

I went to the bar and ordered a mug of strong dark ale from a rotund smiling bartender. He gave me my beer and I took a drink from it. It was some throat strangling rot.

"Where can I find me a woman in this town?" I asked the barman.

"Been to Julia's?" He asked.

"Yeah," I answered.

"There's none to be had around Craven tonight," he said. "The girls at Julia's are all that are available. If they're all occupied, there are no others to be had."

"Then, what are they all waiting around for?" I asked, motioning to the two tables full of sailors.

"Look closely," The barman answered. "They've got what they came for. You could say those are some sailors who really like their seamen."

And watching closely I did see one of the guys run his hand up another's leg. A few moments later another sailor leaned over and kissed the sailor next to him on the lips. After what I'd seen of Craven so far, this village was beginning to look like a mud-packers paradise.

"That's just great," I told the barman.

I drank a few large mugs of the rotten tasting ale and had to admit after the fourth one it didn't taste all that bad anymore. Through a drunken haze I talked to barman Bob and wasted time. I wasn't getting what I came for, so I figured I may as well get drunk. I did a good job of that.

*

When I could barely stand and was the only drinker left in They Always Look Better After A Few, I stumbled out the door.

I was going back to go back to my room at Craven Inn and pass out when I heard her call out to me from a patch of blackness between two closed merchant shops.

"Mister, please help." She called and with the background of screeching gulls at first I didn't realize anyone was trying to get my attention.

Somehow after I had already passed the alleyway, her words made it through the beer glaze I was gliding in. I realized she was talking to me.

"Mister, please, please help me!"

I stopped, then went back and looked into the dark between the shops. Even though my mind swam in a sea of suds I was no fool. My right hand stayed on the grip of Stinger, ready to draw and spill blood in an instant.

"Who's back there?" I asked from the flickering light of the torch lit street.

From out of the blackness stepped a vision of loveliness. "Only me good sir," The young innocent maid I had been dreaming of said to me. "Could you help me good sir? I've escaped from Damgaard the Sea Sorcerer and need a place to hide until morning when I will get a horse and ride away from this accursed village."

I looked this woman up and down in the flickering torchlight. She wore the garments of a dancing girl, which is to say, she didn't wear much at all.

All of the curves on this woman were of the right proportions and in the right places. She had the kind of straight coal black hair I've always loved running my fingers through and milky white flawless skin. As I studied her, I could see she studied me also. The flash of her eyes told me she liked what she saw.

"I'll hide you in my room," I told the woman. "Of course to properly protect you, I'll need to keep a very close eye on you."

She smiled a sly smile when I said this and slid up against me. "Most definitely good sir," She said, "The closer the better."

*

221

To say this woman was enthusiastic would be like saying a fish likes to swim or a bird likes to fly. This woman seemed to be made for one mission only, and it was my good fortune that it was the same mission I had been on the entire night.

I'm not sure who tore whose clothes off. But we did some quick tugging and tearing until we wore what we came into this world wearing. We attacked each other like wild animals, except no animals ever made as much noise as we did and they never did as many different things to each other as we did.

After our fourth grappling and groping we took a breather. With her lying in my arms I asked. "Just what is your name anyway, and what is this business you were saying about this sorcerer?"

She laughed and snuggled close to me. "I am Angelina. The Sea Sorcerer Damgaard has been holding me prisoner inside his cave in the cliffs to the south of Craven. I don't know how long he has kept me. My mind is foggy as to how he captured me also. He has been keeping me drugged so he could use my body any time he wanted. Tonight, He took overlong with his incantations and invocations to the sea gods and his potions wore off me before he administered new ones. As soon as my mind cleared, I fled and was lucky enough to meet you.

"We should dress now and leave." Angelina said. "If he finds me, he will take me back. I would hate to think what he would do to you."

It was my turn to laugh then. "Girl," I said. "Whether he's a sorcerer or not, he can't see through walls and even if he could, I'll send him to his ancestors with Stinger."

That was when the door burst inward. It was shattered and turned to splinters and flung in pieces against the far wall.

A huge shaggy thing, so large it had to stoop over to pass under the top of the door lurched into the room. It was covered entirely by foul smelling black matted fur.

Angelina screamed and her voice ripped the night air.

I bounded naked out of bed, all the wrong parts swinging free, and sprang toward where my clothes and weapons lay scattered on the floor.

The thing was not a beast. The only noise it made was a deep throated raspy breathing.

It back-handed me as I made a grab for stinger. I was knocked flying through the air and bounced off the stone wall.

Flickering firefly spots danced in front of my eyes as the thing turned to Angelina.

It opened its mouth and the speech that issued from that throat sounded like a scholarly old man's voice. "You cannot leave me Angelina." It said. "You cannot. You know what that would mean. Why do you try?"

"I hate you!" Angelina shouted.

"And I hate myself for loving you," the voice from the thing's throat answered.

I regained my feet and charged again to where Stinger lay. This time, the shaggy thing grabbed me by the arm, picked me up over its head and pitched me full force over a table and into another stone wall.

All was blackness.

*

I came to with a ringing in my ears and a serious pain in my head and back. My beer buzz was completely gone. Guess a real good bouncing on the bed and a bouncing off the walls will do that for you.

It was still pitch black outside so I'm not sure how long I was unconscious. No one came to investigate what Angelina's screams or my crashing around the room had been about. Not sure I blame them either. If I would have been on the other side of the wall I bounced off, I probably would have just rolled over and went back to sleep thanking the Gods for good solid stone.

Or maybe it was just that after all the noise Angelina and I was making when we were banging like beasts, they thought her screams and

223

the crashing around was me just giving her the ultimate orgasm. If that was the reason and the guy next door had a woman with him he probably nudged her and said, "Come on honey, it's my turn now."

Whatever it was, no one came out.

The thought occurred to me that I could just go get my horse from the stable at the rear of Craven Inn and ride on out. I didn't want to pay for the busted door or the busted furniture and mainly I didn't want to explain what happened.

Just leaving might have been the best idea.

But to tell you the truth, something happened to me when Angelina was grinning up at me during the throws of one of her orgasms. She had a crazed wild look in her bulging eyes, a lusty insaneness about her.

Was it love, that look had awakened in me?

Are you fucking crazy? I don't think so! I just wasn't done fucking that woman yet. Maybe after the fifth time I would be. Maybe after the fiftieth time, I don't know.

I only know I wanted to find out.

*

After I'd dressed and donned my weapons, Stinger and my three throwing daggers on my belt, I got my horse and rode to the spot just south of Craven, where the cliffs came down and met Pathetic Ocean.

Wading out to knee deep in the cold water I peered up at the cliff face. If it had not been for a lantern hanging in the mouth of the cave, I never would have seen Damgaard's cave at all in the gloom of the night.

The cave was out over the crashing waves at least thirty yards and the climb up would be at least one hundred feet.

There were no other openings in the cliff face as far as I could see. The thought did occur to me that there must be some other entrance or else Angelina could never have made it out. But I wasn't going to search the surrounding countryside for holes in the ground.

Most men would look up at this sheer wall of jagged rock with crashing waves beneath and say, "That's it, I give up!" But not me, I'm an experienced night time wall climber and the walls I'm accustomed to climbing were built specifically to keep me from scaling them. While this cliff face would be difficult, it was nowhere near insurmountable.

I started up the wall, climbing more by feel and instinct than anything else. Night climbing is not much harder than day climbing actually. Usually, you're too close to what you're grasping at to see very much anyway.

Hand over hand I went. Toes and fingers searching out the smallest crevices, testing it to make sure it could sustain my weight. Then, pulling and pushing myself up to the side. There were patches of slimy moss growing on the rocks. A few times I grabbed onto hand holds that almost sent me sliding down the cliff face to be bashed against jagged stones by the crashing surf.

The going was dangerous and tiring. At least half a dozen times I nearly pitched to my death. But some day, something is going to kill me anyway. So I thought, why give up now. Besides, where I was already, it was just as hard to climb back down as it was to go forward.

Finally the lantern was just above my head. I pulled myself up and into the yawning cave opening and stood up.

*

The cave led backward into the rocky Earth in a pitch black tunnel. The hanging lantern was the only light. I took it down and started walking into the dark passageway.

The sound of the surf behind me was like the rhythmic breathing of one of the great Sea Gods. As I went into blackness so thick it was like oil in front of me, the sound of the waves faded away and I began to feel a soft breeze blowing past me into the interior of the earth. There must be an outlet I knew, otherwise there would be no place for the air that rushed past me to go.

I started to hear strange chanting ahead. At first I thought it was just the echoes of the surf being twisted by the walls of the cave into the sound of voices. But, moving forward, the chanting became more distinct and I knew it was not any echo of a natural sound.

This was the echo of one man chanting incantations and magic spells. This man was beseeching the Gods to keep the winds at bay and protect his village and for this he promised a sacrifice of a lamb.

I came around a bend in the tunnel and caught sight of the chanter.

The chamber I stepped into was enormous. At least seventy feet across, this bubble inside solid rock had a ceiling that was lost in shadows. All the walls were lined with book shelves filled with arcane tomes of all types.

The lone light inside the chamber was a bonfire that cast dancing shadows backward away from the three who stood in front of its flames.

By the fire stood the black shaggy thing that tossed me about my room like a child's rag doll. He held Angelina in front of him, pinning her arms to her sides.

Beside them stood the chanter, The Sorcerer garbed in dark purple robes with the symbols of the moon, stars and planets embroidered into it. He waved a knife in the air over his head and sang out to the ancient gods of the ocean. In front of him lay a softly mewing lamb.

The Sorcerer Damgaard was an old man with a long white beard and a shining wrinkled bald head. But for all of his ancientness, he radiated raw power like a volcano.

The Sorcerer's entreaties to the higher powers were reaching a crescendo, getting louder, beseeching, and demanding.

Their backs were to me.

With Stinger clutched tightly in my right fist I crept up behind them.

They didn't see me until the ugly black thing was almost within my blade's reach.

Catching sight of me out of the corner of his eye, Damgaard uttered a strangled cry.

Big And Furry hurled Angelina to the side and turned to me. It bellowed out a blood curdling cry that made the hair on my neck stand straight up. He reached out an enormous hand clutching at me.

I'd had enough for one night of being in the friendly embraces of that fiend. When he thrust his hand out, I ripped Stinger to the side and the beast's hand flew free from his wrist.

Blood spewed from the stump spraying the air and I was glad to see it. At least it proved this thing was a creature of blood and bone and could be killed.

It screamed and hurled itself at me swinging a death blow with its one good arm.

I leaped to the side and as the beast passed, slashed a disemboweling stroke across its stomach. The things steaming guts fell with a plop to the stone floor.

Rushing in as it fell I stabbed the creature through the chest, only to have Stinger, stuck in bone, ripped from my grasp by the weight of the thing.

Now I turned to the Sorcerer Damgaard.

"You ruined the ceremony!" Damgaard shouted at me. "I'll have to start from the beginning or the storm will come and wash Craven away."

I started for him. "I'm going to rip the head from your shoulders with my bare hands," I told Damgaard.

"I think not," he answered and with a flick of his left wrist flung something at me that looked like twinkling starlight.

Everything tilted crazily. I didn't know what was up or down. The points of twinkling starlight grew and all else faded until I was alone, floating in a white nothingness. White was everywhere.

Nothing else was there, only white. Up, down, everywhere, there was only the unblemished purer than the purest snow…..white.

227

I might have screamed then. I'm not sure if I did or not. To be stuck in an endless nothingness is a frightening place to be. Even being tortured to death is better than that. The torture would eventually end. But this….who knows?

Damgaard's voice spoke to me. "You came for her," He said. "The faithless slut, I brought her back from her grave in the ocean. Angelina was a whore who a sea captain had drowned for murdering the sailors who paid for her body. The ocean is my element. When Angelina was placed in my home, I saw her punishment. Being a foolish old man, I was in love from the first sight of Angelina with the beauty of her and the pleasure her body promised. But, in life she was a constant schemer. Even death has not changed that. I had hoped it would."

"You lie," I shouted and flung one of my throwing daggers at the spot where it seemed Damgaard's voice came from.

It struck home with a thunk and I fell forward onto my hands and knees as the world around me reappeared.

Damgaard sank to the floor. He sat wheezing and gasping out his last breath. He motioned toward Angelina, who was now getting to her feet.

"Take her," He said and laughed spraying a mist of red into the air. "Too bad you'll not have as much time with her as I have. Then, you would know torment."

He fell back and moved no more.

I took Angelina in my arms.

"There is a back way out," she told me and led us to a door I'd not seen before.

This route was lit by torches the entire way. The tunnel arced upward and while walking Angelina fell against me in weakness.

"I'm okay." She said. "The fall when the creature shoved me, I just feel a little dizzy."

So, supporting her weight on my shoulder, we made our way up through the tunnel. At first she only leaned on me as we moved along, but after a while, Angelina's strength seemed to give out entirely and I picked her up and carried her.

The tunnel came to an end at a sloping hole in the ground that I came climbing out of.

The sun was just starting to rise as I laid Angelina on the grass. By the new morning light her face was as pale as chalk and when I touched her skin it was cold. As I watched Angelina, her skin turned a soft blue and plumped up as though filling with a liquid from within.

Angelina's eyes flashed open. They were bloodshot, a harsh red. She reached for me. "No! No! Gods please don't!" Angelina screamed. "The things they did to me. They deserved what they got!"

Her arms flailed the air and pushed at something unseen and I realized she was trying to swim even though she lay on her back in the grass. Angelina looked like someone who was trying to swim with rocks tied to her. As she fought the air shimmered around her. Phantom fish-things appeared and swam in the air. They took bites from her skin. The fish darted and nipped and snatched chunks from her face and body.

I swiped at the things attacking her but my hand went through them as though they were not there.

Angelina's skin was eaten away and there was nothing I could do about it. The skin was chewed from her face until I saw the raw meat beneath. That was chewed off until the skull and bones was all that remained. Then Angelina's bones began dissolving. They turned into a filmy liquid that dissipated into the air. Then the thick shimmering air and the phantom fish things went away as though they and Angelina had never been.

*

A large wind kicked up almost immediately. Storm clouds came rolling in. I collected my horse from the beach at the bottom of the cliffs and rode away from Craven.

I had a feeling bad weather was on the way.

*

Roasting Rabbits

They were silent for a time chewing on their roasted rabbit and drinking large gulps of harsh tasting wine.

Finally Bub said, "You loved her."

Slickman laughed a noisy laugh perhaps a bit too loud for the perceived joke and slapped his knee.

"No, I guess you are not a barbarian are you. You my friend were born to be a poetry spouting pretty boy. The kind the barbarians love bending over and…"

"That's enough!" Bub roared, his face beginning to flush. "There is a limit to the insults I will take!"

"Okay-okay, calm down," Slickman said still smiling. "I won't pick on you anymore. Can't take a joke, can you."

Bub gave him another murderous look.

"About Angelina," Slickman said. "It wasn't love, but I sure would like to have lain with that woman some more. The things she could do, we'd only begun scratching the surface."

They went silent again, staring into the fire.

"But you did love your woman?" Slickman asked.

"With everything that I am," Bub answered and remained staring into the fire.

"Just why is it you are traveling to the east anyway?" Slickman asked.

If it was possible, Bub's face looked even more grim and intense than it had before. "I am searching for my sister, Beth. I have no one in this world. I seek her because she was without blame and was cast into a horrible life. I would free her from that and give her a life less harsh."

He looked into Slickman's eyes. "Why do you travel to the east?" He asked.

Slickman took a bite of rabbit, chewed and washed it down with a swallow of wine.

He shrugged his shoulders and said, "Why not?"

***

So they travelled to the east, one with honorable motives, and the other with no motives at all.

Such are the ways of wandering rogues.

3.

The Protectors

For the previous five days the biting cold had been relentless. This morning snow began falling. Huge flakes like the feathers of fallen angels floated to the Earth as Slickman and Bub urged their mounts forward upon a trail they were not sure even existed any more.

Their breaths came out as puffs of grey steam in the winter air.

They needed shelter for the coming bitter night. Building a fire out in the open on snow covered ground would not be an easy task. Keeping it burning till dawn would be near impossible.

As the grey of evening deepened into the black of night these two cold traveling rogues entered the boundaries of a thick pine forest. They rode into the woodlands for an hour barely seeing the trees and branches in front of them.

"We should stop," Slickman said as the last rays of the mist shrouded sun died away leaving a dense gloom. "We can cut branches from these pines even in the dark and make a lean-to that we can build a fire under. That will hold in enough heat so we can make it to morning before we set out again."

Bub grunted his approval and reined his horse to a stop as did Slickman. As soon as their mounts halted they caught sight of the eyes watching from the forest around them.

The eyes were red and glowing.

There appeared to be dozens of the animals. In the thickening gloom it was impossible to see how many of these things had been stalking them. But when Slickman and Bub stopped traveling forward they were suddenly surrounded.

The harsh sound of snarls and rumbling growls filled the air on all sides. The glowing eyes were at least four feet up from the ground. The intensity of the growls told that the unseen creatures were large and hungry.

The glow from these eyes was not just the simple night shine seen from a predator's eyes reflecting a campfire or a full moon. There was no light for these eyes to reflect. This eye-glow, whatever it was, was something supernatural.

Both Slickman and Bub's horses snorted and jerked their snouts back and forth nervously.

Bub, who had kept to a sullen silence for the last few frozen hours, spoke now.

"I do not think this is a good spot for us to be stopping tonight."

With that he kicked his mount into a full run.

Slickman did the same and they hurtled forward on the backs of their horses knocking branches out of the way with their faces.

Six long galloping strides were all that Bub's mount was able to put down before a pair of snarling shaggy beasts flew out of the darkness at its legs taking horse and rider to the ground.

Bub was thrown from the saddle to the frozen earth. He slid on his face in the snow and came to his feet with his sword clutched in his right fist.

Slickman's horse collided with Bub's and stopped so suddenly that Slickman flew over his mount's head and bounced hard to the ground.

Slickman rolled to a standing position and ripped Stinger from its scabbard.

The shaggy snarling things came at them. In the twilight of a fog shrouded, snow stinging gloom Slickman and Bub fought a grim battle against things that seemed to know no pain or fear, only rage and hunger.

233

The red eyes charged them in the thick blackness and were met with the slash of cold steel. The swords would bite home and blood would fly in Slickman and Bub's faces but the creatures cut did not cry out in pain.

These things of the frozen night came at Slickman and Bub in teeth-snapping, claw-ripping waves. The sheer weight of the attack drove the pair backward away from their fallen mounts. After a mere ten seconds of fighting in this blind nightmare they knew their horses were lost.

They could hear their mounts screams of pain as they were disemboweled and devoured alive.

Forced into a retreat until their backs met a solid vertical snow covered wall Slickman took a bite to his left thigh. Teeth pierced his pant leg and gouged deep into the muscle.

He hacked the head of the thing clean off with a single stroke from Stinger. The jaws of the creature remained locked closed even with the head separated from its body.

Slickman reached down and grasped a shaggy wolf-like head, although much larger, attached his leg. He ripped the teeth loose taking a piece of his own meat in the process. He hurled that head at another pair of charging crimson eyes.

Bub was slashed across the face above the eyes by a leaping snarling beast from hell. He grabbed the hurtling thing by the throat in his beefy left hand and tightened his grip until bones snapped beneath his fingers. He felt, but didn't see, his own blood run into his eyes from his wound.

So what? Bub thought as he one-handed strangled and broke the creature's neck that he held up from the ground. *I've never been a pretty boy anyway. Another scar might help my looks.*

Their backs were to a solid flat wall and they were surrounded. The snarling red eyed things paced back and forth in front of them taking turns leaping forward out of the darkness to rip and snap at the freezing rogues.

In the dim twilight a battle was fought that could have only one end result. There were simply too many of the beasts for Slickman and Bub to fight all of them off.

They knew in the end they would go down beneath the teeth and claws of these forest night creatures.

Bub took another claw slash, this time to his left arm. The wound was deep, possibly to the bone. He laughed and cleaved the snarling beast in half with a down stroke.

"Come on you shaggy bastards," he yelled at them. "Pray to whatever cold gods you have for when I fall tonight I'm taking all of you with me."

Slickman was knocked from his feet when one of the beasts somehow struck him in the back of the legs. The thing pounced on him and reacting instinctively he jerked a dagger from his belt with his left hand, stabbed the thing three times and threw it away from him.

He spit in the face of the next one that charged him as from his knees he slashed straight across the glowing red eyes.

"Bring it to me," Slickman shouted at the red eyes around him. "You out number us now but I'll continue this fight in Hell. I'll cleave you in the next world so that for all eternity you'll have to be dragging yourselves through the slime pits with only one leg."

They fought a bloody losing battle and accepted that this night was their last when on both sides of them, coming out of the wall, four glowing men appeared.

The men wore loose fitting white garments that looked to be designed for fast movement.

These men held no weapons yet they met the charge of the beast things and repelled it with quick precise punches and kicks.

235

The ethereal glow the four unarmed warriors gave off was as bright as any campfire, bright enough so that now Slickman and Bub could finally see the nature of their attackers.

Their first impressions of wolves had been correct but these things were more than just large wolves. The heads were wolf-like with slavering, dripping jagged teethed mouths. The shoulders were man-like and thickly muscled although covered with a heavy coat of fur. The arms were as long as an apes and indeed in claws with daggered talons.

These creatures stood on rear legs and charged hunched over slashing as they came.

The unarmed glowing warriors fought silently. The only sound they made was the smack of the punishing blows they landed. Their skill at unarmed combat was awesome to behold.

One of the warriors appeared to be the leader. Catching a moment of respite from the fray he pointed to the wall behind Slickman and Bub.

Glancing over their shoulders they saw in the glow given off by the warriors a large wooden door.

Slickman and Bub did not have to be invited twice.

Grasping the handle Slickman wrenched the door open amid the screech of rusted hinges. They stepped inside once again into pitch blackness.

The door slammed shut behind them.

*

Slickman and Bub were both bleeding and winded so they took a few moments in the complete darkness to rest and regain their strength. When they were sufficiently recovered Bub told Slickman, "We should go back out and lend them support. They came to our aid. We should not abandon them to the mercies of those beasts."

They could still hear the sounds of the ongoing battle through the door.

Slickman laughed a grim laugh.

236

"After being out of that wind for a few minutes I'm right as rain now. There's nothing I'd rather be doing, other than riding a harlot in Hilary's House of Hairy Holes than fighting a battle to the death. Swing that door open and let's have at them!"

Bub felt around and located the door knob. He gave it a mighty twist but the handle would not turn. He sheathed his sword and grasped the knob in both hands. Bub applied all the muscle in his brawny arms to the task of twisting the knob.

There was a clank of metal inside the wood door as the knob turned only a millimeter before coming to a dead stop.

"It's locked and won't budge," Bub said.

"Aint' that a crotch-kicker," Slickman exclaimed. "The one time in my life when I decide to do something noble and the Gods of Portals are against me."

"I didn't know there were Gods for doors," Bub said.

"Well, me neither. But there must be because they're not letting us out."

Bub banged on the door a few more times with his fist. The sound that came back at them told the two that this door was thick and solid.

"We're not getting out this way," Bub said.

Slickman told him, "Try ramming it with your head. You might have more success that way."

"How about if I rammed it with your skull," Bub said. "What little brains you have you never put to any good use."

"But I'm not the one with a thick barbarian skull," Slickman told him and there came to Bub a clicking like two stones being sharply smacked together.

A spark jumped and landed on a wadded up piece of paper on the floor. Slickman fanned the single flame and in a moment had a small fire burning.

"While you were busy throwing yourself against an immovable object I was busy getting out my flint and feeling about for kindling. There's a lot of this paper and broken furniture pieces lying around us."

As the fire was fed more fuel Bub saw that what Slickman said was true. The flickering flames showed them that this was a large room with three doorways leading off into darkness.

The sounds of battle coming through the heavy wooden door lessened then after a few more moments quit entirely.

"Well it's obvious," Slickman said. "Either our friends have vanquished the beasts killing them all or forced them to retreat into the brush or the beasts are having a feast on their flesh. Either way, there is nothing we can do about it."

"I don't like the looks of those," Bub said indicating the three doorways that lead off into darkness. "If it was the beasts who won outside, they might find a way in. If we stay where we are we could find ourselves trapped again."

"There's nothing else to do then," Slickman spoke. "We explore those dark hallways and find a place that is defendable, then wait it out there until morning."

Bub found a large broken wooden table leg and held one end of it in the fire until it was burning. Slickman did the same.

As soon as their torches were burning brightly Slickman asked, "Do you have any preferences as to which of these three hallways we explore first?"

"The left one," Bub answered.

"Any reason why?"

"No," Bub said and with his torch held in front of him set off down the black corridor.

*

By the dim flickering light of their torches Slickman and Bub could see the grey puffs of stream from their breath in front of them as they moved forward into the gloom. They hadn't gone more than ten steps down the pitch black aisle before they started hearing sounds.

At first the sounds were more like people talking in the distance. It was like whispers. The words were too soft to understand but people were talking.

As they moved further down the corridor and came to a doorway on the left hand side they distinctly heard laughter coming from within the room beside them.

Slickman and Bub passed a glance and without a word decided instantly they were going into that room.

They entered.

The floors and walls were done in porcelain tiles. Different small areas were separated with small walls that were raised about two feet off the floor.

There was a row of porcelain wash basins against one wall and a small room was off set that had short metal rods sticking out from the walls above head height.

But this was not where the soft whispers came from.

Through a doorway that looked across this chamber laughter echoed and a faint glow sneaked out from inside.

Again, without a word, the men moved forward and went through that doorway.

Inside snow blew in through a large jagged hole in the ceiling. The laughter came from all around them echoing off the walls. But they could see no one.

In front of Slickman and Bub was a large rectangular pit. The walls of the pit were shiny and flat. The bottom of the end of the pit nearest them was lost in shadows but the bottom at the far end was visible.

This end was clearly much deeper than the far end.

At the far end there were steps that lead down into the pit and sitting on those steps, glowing in the darkness was a small girl child.

With the strange spectral laughter ringing about them and bizarre splashing noises echoing from the walls Slickman and Bub walked to the far end of the pit and knelt down next to the girl.

The child was weeping into her hands. She was wearing only the barest of clothes and Slickman wondered why she was not shivering in the bitter cold.

"What is the matter little one?" Bub asked her.

She answered. "I want to go home. They keep splashing me and won't leave me alone." The child made a motion pointing into the middle of the pit.

Slickman reached out his hand to the girl saying, "We'll take you where you need to go." He was reaching to help the child up off the steps.

She reached out to the offered hand and when their fingers touched his hand went through hers.

Cold raced up Slickman's arm and the little girl winked out of existence in front of him.

One moment she was there, and then she was not.

Now they saw the source of the laughter and the splashing noises.

In front of Slickman and Bub, inside the pit stretched sparkling, glistening spectral waters. The pit was full of it.

Frolicking in these ghost waters were somewhere around twenty children. They swam and splashed and dove into the water from a board at the deep end of the pool. That board had not been there a moment earlier.

Slickman turned to Bub and asked, "Do you see this?"

Bub answered, "I'm not sure what I see. What is happening here cannot be happening."

Slickman and Bub walked down the porcelain tiled steps and entered the spectral waters. They could not feel the water but could see it shimmering all around them.

The two wanderers tried to talk to children that swam near but none heard a word they said. They tried to touch the children to get their attention but they touched nothing.

Slickman and Bub walked to the deep end of the ghostly pool and watched the phantom swimmers gliding above them. A feeling of calm overcame them and they sat on the bottom. The sound of children at play relaxed them as they watched.

"It must have been a good time when they were here," Bub said. "They had time to devote to just enjoying themselves."

"Yes," Slickman answered. "It must have been a very good time. I wonder what brought it to an end."

And just like that the spectral performance of children at play in a public swimming pool did come to an end. The ghostly laughing children, the shimmering spectral waters, all of it winked out of existence leaving them sitting on cold tiles with snowflakes floating slowly down on them through the rip in the ceiling.

Bub said, "You had to ask, didn't you?"

"It's my nature to ask," Slickman answered. "Don't tell me you weren't wondering yourself."

"No," Bub said. "I wasn't asking questions. I was just enjoying hearing children laugh."

They got up and retraced their steps back to the pitch black corridor. After but a few more steps the corridor came to an end at a brick wall.

Slickman and Bub walked back to the first room they had been in.

*

Gazing at the three pitch black doorways Slickman asked, "Which one now?"

From the corridor on the far right hand side issued a noise which vaguely sounded like a war cry.

"In there," Bub said. "If something is searching for us it is better if we find it on our terms."

They headed into that hallway.

Like the other corridor it was darker than the pits of Hades as soon as they passed the doorway.

Unlike the other corridor the source of the sounds was obvious the moment they came to the room they issued from.

On the right hand side a doorway opened into an area where luminescent warriors garbed in white stood in rows and practiced in unison different punches, kicks and blocks.

In front of this group of warriors being schooled in the finer aspects of their art was the man who had sent Slickman and Bub through the front door while he remained outside to battle the beasts.

The teacher saw the two men at the door and pointed to one of the warriors in the front row. He said, "Continue with the lesson."

The warrior took the teacher's place at the head of the class leading the others through their moves.

The Instructor came out into the hallway to stand with Slickman and Bub. He held out his hand in greeting.

Slickman and Bub looked at his hand without moving.

The Instructor smiled. "So you have already met some of the others who inhabit Skyhomish. The others are but wraiths, left over images of the world that has passed away. For reasons of their own the Gods have made this dead city a land of ghosts."

"If they are ghosts," Slickman asked. "Then what are you?"

"We … all of us," the Instructor indicated the warriors inside the room. "We all took an oath to protect this city from evil in any form. When the end came our souls remained here. We become flesh when we are needed. Until morning we will remain flesh.

"When the sun rises we return to nothingness."

Bub shook the man's hand then it felt as solid as his own.

242

"What is it like on the other side of the veil?" He asked.

"When I am here," The man answered. "I have no memories of the other side. Perhaps there is nothing. But if that were true none of us would be able to return at all. Perhaps it is so wondrous that my mind in this state cannot grasp what that other place is."

"Riddles inside of riddles," Slickman said.

"Yes," the Instructor answered. "All of existence is a riddle and there is one thing I should tell you."

"What's that?" Bub asked.

"Both of your destiny's lie to the East. I feel as though you should go in that direction to find what ultimately awaits you."

"What about the beasts outside?" Slickman asked.

"In the morning with the rising sun the door will unlock and they will be gone. Continue on to the East and what you ultimately seek will find you."

"And what is it that we ultimately seek?" Bub asked.

Slickman butted in with a quick reply, "It's our destiny you barbarian idiot. Didn't you just hear the man?"

"Speak when spoken to," Bub told him. "That way your mouth might not overload your ass. I was about to ask, what kind of destiny awaits us?"

The Instructor answered, "The same kind that awaits all men. You will either fulfill your purpose or you will not.

"Go now and rest. Your journey will be long and strange." He turned and went back to teaching his students.

Slickman and Bub retraced their steps to the doorway they had originally entered through.

Their fire was built larger. A bottle of wine sat beside it as well as a large platter of vegetables and cooked meats.

They ate ravenously and thanked the Gods for their good fortune but in the back of Slickman's mind he wondered if they were only pigs being fattened for the slaughter.

***

Finally: how Slickman and Bub got to Inagi.

They seemed done with their tales for the moment and after all three of us had taken large chugs of Splotch I had a question I could not help but ask.

"So, since you seemed to have told me everything else, how about answering the question I originally asked. How did you get down here?"

Slickman and Bub both looked at each other simultaneously. They seemed to do that a lot. It always looked strange to me since these two men who were just about on the opposite ends of the spectrum as far as builds were concerned, in some ways acted just like brothers.

Slickman opened his mouth to speak and as he did Bub interrupted him. "You've flapped your lips enough," he said. "I'll take the lead in this short tale."

"You might as well, since it's no tale at all," Slickman told him. "This is the perfect story for you to be able to do a good job telling."

Bub started speaking just like Slickman had never said anything at all.

*

The morning we left Skyhomish the sky was full of low hanging heavy white clouds. Just like the man had instructed us we headed as much as we could directly toward the east. It was bitterly cold but that was no different than we'd expected.

We walked maybe for an hour when we came to the eastern border of the forest and moved out onto a wide low open field. In the distance ahead of us we could vaguely see the outline of a mountain. Halfway up, the mountain faded out into a white haze.

244

The snow came. It fell suddenly and without warning. Thick stinging globs of wet snow smashed into our faces stinging our skin and blinding us. It was a blizzard and we were stuck out in it and there was nothing we could do. By then we'd went too far to even consider going back and finding the building we'd left and taking shelter there. We'd never find it in this blinding storm. I wasn't even sure we'd even find the city or the forest that the city hid inside.

We marched forward into the blinding white because there was nothing else to do.

The cold was unbearable but when you have no choice you bear what is thrown at you. We kept going, trudging forward just putting one foot in front of the other. We kept moving because to stop meant freezing to death.

Blinding white was above us as the snow fell out of a bleached colorless sky.

Blinding white was below us as the frozen ground filled deeper and deeper with the icy snow.

Blinding white was ahead of us as the mountain and all landmarks disappeared into a blurry pale nothing.

We marched on, stumbling forward because there was nothing else to do.

The snow froze our feet into blocks of ice so we couldn't feel the ground. It froze our faces. We couldn't even feel the snow's killing sting.

Then all at once we were not cold any more.

Warm air hit us like it was coming from a blacksmith's kiln.

Dry grit was hitting us in the face. This grit stuck to us, stuck to our faces and clothes.

At first I thought I had simply gotten so cold that my face and body had frozen so much that I stopped feeling anything at all and that this heat was phantom heat caused from my skin freezing and dying from frost bite.

But no, that wasn't it. As the feeling returned to my skin the grit, like tiny pebbles continued hitting me in the face. I took some in my hand and rubbed it between my fingers and it was sand.

It was then that I grabbed Slickman by the arm to stop him from stumbling forward and saw that he was staring straight in front of us.

Before us in the blurred distance was the outline of a city. That city ended up being the one over our heads. As we walked on further the storm blew away swirling off into nothing. It was only then that we could see we had been walking in a sand storm. The storm moved away almost like a living thing that was no longer interested in us.

Up above was that strange sun that everybody here calls Ra. The dammed thing never sets does it? And oddly enough, behind us was a bizarre looking mountain.

We shook that sand off us and came here.

That's the story of that. That's how we got to be here.

*

"You didn't fall down a hole?" I asked.

Slickman laughed. "Didn't the man just tell you that we walked out of a snowstorm and then into a sandstorm? We know it doesn't make any sense but whatever does?"

"Riddles inside of riddles," I answered.

"And all of existence is a riddle, is what the man in Skyhomish told us," Bub said. "We're here for a reason. What, we don't yet know."

"Drink up then," Slickman said. "My reason for being here is to get good and roaring drunk."

Leading the Revolt!

29.

Purpose

After we'd drunk our fill and stars began blinking in front of our eyes the conversation turned to fate. By then my words were slurring and the thoughts swam slowly from one side of my brain to the other like an ant caught in molasses.

"So, if you came down here or over here or out here or where ever Inagi is to fulfill your destiny, then what the hell is your destiny?" I asked.

Bub was in the middle of a big gulp when I spoke. He kept right on gulping.

Slickman answered, "I don't know and I don't really give a rat's cunt what my destiny is. I do what the hell I want to do and that's what I'm gonna do until I don't do it no more."

Bub slammed his mug down on the table making our mugs jump. His eyes were red. He looked at Slickman. He raised one finger in the air indicating he had something profound to say and belched so loud it was like a lion's roar.

Slickman slid himself back from the table fanning the air in front of his face.

"Uhhh," he exclaimed. "May the Ass of Atlanta shit in your hand so you rub it in your hair and from the way you smell he already has? You could at least have turned to the side. If that ain't butt-breath then I don't know what it is."

"You know butt-breath well," Bub told him. "You speak with it constantly."

I knew I had to stop this or we'd never move forward. I asked Bub, "Slickman doesn't seem to give a shit about his fate. What about you? What do you think it is that you need to accomplish before the end of your life?"

Bub thought for a moment. Since all three of us were now sitting in that inebriated alcohol encased fog where thoughts move slow and original ideas move slower. He seemed to take until just about forever to open his mouth and give an answer.

"The one purpose I had adopted for myself was to find my sister if she still lived and give her a better life than she had been handed by our father. Now, in this strange place that everyone calls Inagi I get the feeling Elizabeth is forever out of reach. I'm not sure what my purpose is now. We took on the task of freeing slaves when they look like they want freed as just a way to pass time and keep the fighting skills sharp."

Slickman interrupted, "And because Rico told us we'd always be welcome as long as we kept bringing him new members to his underground city."

Bub went on. "I seem to have no real long term goal or purpose now. Do you have any suggestions?"

I opened my mouth to speak but Slickman beat me to it by simultaneously slapping me on the back and shouting, "Ah-hah! That's what all your questions about fate and purpose are about. You bastard you, you've got a cause you want to recruit us for." He was grinning the whole time he spoke.

"Shut up and let the man talk," Bub told him. "The more you speak the more we know about your ignorance.

"Actually Slickman is right," I told the two of them. "I do have a cause. I'm going to free the Amura from the Nords, then take them back with me and re-establish Kalina's village. Then and only then will I be worthy enough to take Kalina as my woman. Maybe after doing that for her people she'll accept me."

"Those are strong words," Bub said. "You'll need a force of fighting men to take on the Nords. One man can't do it alone."

Slickman broke in again. "The only way for you to gain a fighting force would be to free this whole city. Xibalba is a place where there are really only three different kinds of people. There are slaves, slave owners, and people like us who live underground outside the law. Here, if you can grab someone and slap chains on them, you own them until they get free."

"Then I'll free the entire city," I told the two of them.

"That could get complicated," Bub said.

*

Rico was the leader of the nameless city that existed underground and just beneath the surface of the society of Xibalba. There really was no organization to what Rico was the leader of.

He simply told people to do things and they did it. The cavern city beneath the streets of Xibalba had existed so long that no one knew how it came into existence. Literally thousands lived in hiding down in this huge cave. A city of that size even without a formal government needs some organizing to keep it running.

Rico was the man who kept things running as smoothly as possible. If someone needed something outside the regular society of Xibalba and they couldn't get it themselves they turned to Rico.

He was the man the new arrivals came to when they needed a place to set up a home in the cavern. He was the man people turned to if they needed a good or service performed and couldn't get it themselves. He was the man who people turned to for justice when the strong took advantage of the weak.

Rico was the unelected, unnamed ruler of the underground secret society of Xibalba. And by all accounts I have ever heard he did his job very well.

*

We drank until we were bleary-eyed and in back of the tavern there were sleeping pallets provided for the customers who were as drunk as we were. I have never seen this arrangement on the Outer-Earth in any drinking establishment but it seemed to make perfectly good sense. Really, if you are going to sell something that gets people wasted, give them a place to pass out.

It was there where we slept off our drunkenness.

When we awoke although, I had a roaring headache, I was ready to go.

Slickman and Bub told me that Rico could be found most days up top at the gladiator arena watching the battles to the death that go on continuously. He loved gambling on the fights.

We went back into the tavern and there drank down a foul smelling and unbelievably horrible tasting concoction designed to cure hangovers. I think it worked primarily through the threat of having to drink a second one if the first didn't work. Your mind couldn't take in the idea of having a repeat taste of that awful crud so it forced the pain to leave.

Since I was now a wanted criminal my two new friends found me a change of clothes that blended in well with what the majority of people in Xibalba wore. To the ruling class I wanted to be as invisible as possible.

Then we set out to find Rico.

30.
Kalina's Tale:
Ocean Voyage

While Derek Walker was getting acquainted with new drinking buddies Kalina, Jorn and Tony the Inner-Earth Tiger were drifting out into the vast deep waters of Inagi's largest ocean. The current caught their raft and they were carried swiftly to the dark blue waters where massive scaled monstrosities glided the ocean depths beneath them.

They did not have a sail for their small craft, but they did not need one. Their raft was pulled along by the ocean current just as surely as if it had been tied by a rope and dragged by a speed boat.

The beach where they cast off became a distant speck that eventually blurred into grey mist altogether. Their small craft moved further out drawn ever deeper into the vast waters until any trace of a shoreline vanished into the climbing misty sea.

The oceans of the Inner-Earth are fresh water so the three of them did not lack for anything to drink. But they did know hunger after a time, if such a thing as time exists in Inagi because there was no way to carry any food with them.

Their stomachs made loud growling noises that all three of them tried to quiet by filling up on drinking water. It only partially worked.

Ra beat down upon their unprotected bodies with his relentless heat. They sat and waited and drifted in the strong ocean current because that's all that he could do. It seemed as though they had found a world filled entirely with water and rolling waves.

After all three of them slept twice dark ominous steely grey clouds gathered ahead. Lightning crackled in the distance making loud electrical pops and flashes that lit up the darkening sky.

A dark sky under Inagi's never setting sun was a rare and frightening phenomenon. As lightning bolts crashed and boomed and large stinging cold rain drops pelted them the three ocean voyagers hugged and huddled together in the center of their raft for the simple support of knowing that this terrifying ordeal was being shared equally.

The ominous storm swarmed over them like a marauding army. All they could do was clutch onto each other and their raft as it was tossed about on powerful choppy seas.

Suddenly out of the ocean something arose from the waters. Extending straight up into the air eight feet above them on the end of a long slender snakelike neck a grayish green slimy scaled bowling ball-sized head with bulging black reptilian eyes and a yawning jagged toothed mouth grinned down at them.

Although they'd lived their entire lives in a world filled with prehistoric monsters neither Kalina nor Jorn had ever seen a creature like this. If Tony had he wasn't saying.

For the first time in her life Kalina screamed like the frightened woman that she was.

As the head waved back and forth in the storm winds assessing how to best snatch its next meal Jorn scrambled to grab the spear he'd brought.

The massive sea creature's head dipped and dove driving in with jaws extended, mouth wide open, teeth ready to snap shut, rip flesh and crush bones. The sea serpent's target was the one of them that had shown fear and weakness ... the woman.

Kalina had cringed away, while Jorn went for his weapon and Tony remained low with his claws stuck fast into the wood of the tossing raft to keep from sliding overboard.

With a screech of pure terror Kalina jumped to the side as the sea serpent lunged down at her. The teeth smashed into wood missing Kalina's bare leg by a mere two inches.

Before the sea serpent could withdraw his head Tony struck. Faster than seemed humanly possible and actually it was faster than any human had ever moved, the white and yellow striped tiger became a blur of motion. In one movement he came up, leaped and clamped his huge claws and teeth into the scaly head of the thing that attacked his human friend.

Tony, the Inner-Earth Tiger was lifted up into the air, his back legs kicking with running motions ripping at the neck, his teeth buried into the face of the sea serpent.

The head swung violently in the air jerking from side to side trying to shake the big cat loose. The claws in Tony's back feet cut through the scales in the thing's neck and blood flew scarlet sprayed wide by the storm winds. Then with a massive splash the sea serpent dove beneath the surface of the water heading back down toward the dark ocean depths from which it had come taking Tony down with it.

Jorn stared out at the spot where his friend had disappeared beneath the surface. He crouched on the raft with his spear in his two hands ready to fight off any other threat that may appear.

The rain water stung his eyes as he stared out into the choppy roiling ocean.

"Tony!" Jorn shouted. He only shouted once. He knew his friend was somewhere Tony could no longer hear him.

After a time he sat down upon his raft. He laid his spear upon the wood.

Kalina sat beside him.

Neither of them spoke a word.

They waited and watched. When it was obvious what they waited for was not going to happen Jorn laid his head upon Kalina's shoulder and wept.

31.

Scenic Tour

The storm passed.

When the clouds parted and moved away Kalina and Jorn could see a shiny white sand beach not very far in the distance ahead of them.

With the rising distant landscape visible on Inagi during clear weather the two voyagers were able to see that beyond the shoreline was a strip of lush green forest hugging the shore. Beyond the forest, even though it was graying out in the misty expanse appeared to be a wide open plain.

The woman and the young man did not speak. Their hearts were heavy with the loss of their friend. Even though it seemed as though they had known Tony but a short while their bond had quickly grown strong. There was emptiness to their world that seemed impossible to fill.

Jorn was particularly struck by his loss. He stared endlessly out into the blue water hoping against hope to see some sign of his lost friend, but received none.

They sat upon their raft and observed the approaching shoreline catching their breath, rebuilding their strength from the beating the harsh storm dealt out.

The white sandy beach grew larger and larger until they could see details like logs and boulders that lay on the beach. Then they were no longer approaching the beach but Kalina and Jorn were drifting sideways to the shoreline, parallel to the land.

For how long their raft moved like this they had no way of knowing. They watched the scenery drift past, changing by small degrees. Until in the distance ahead of them much farther along the shoreline they saw what appeared to be a massive wall of mountain that sprang right out of the ocean.

Even in the extreme distance the mountain arose strange and ominous. The top of the mountain looked to be covered in jagged, sharp needle-like peaks. It also appeared to be covered in a weird filmy grayish to white covering that seemed to blur the features of the mountain altogether into an indistinct fuzzy mass.

Something about this mountain set Kalina's nerves on edge and made her want to flee in the opposite direction.

They drifted along the shoreline and then as the land started to gradually rise to a higher elevation their raft started being pulled back out toward the deep waters once again. Whatever current had carried them all the way across the vast ocean now was in the process of possibly doubling back and carrying them back to where they came from.

Their empty growling stomachs told the pair of travelers this was a journey Kalina and Jorn could not survive. As it was the both of them were feeling the first pangs of starvation in the form of light headedness and general weakness.

"We have to swim to the shore from here," Kalina told Jorn.

His answer was to give a simple nod and to dive into the ocean.

Kalina followed his example.

*

It didn't take them long to reach the sandy beach. Solid ground felt good beneath their feet after spending what seemed like forever on the raft adrift in the ocean.

Jorn and Kalina would have liked to have sprawled out in the sand absorbing the healing heat from Ra overhead. But the time for them to be able to relax was not yet at hand. Obtaining food was the first order that their weakening bodies shouted and that was an order neither of them could ignore.

As they dragged themselves out of the waves breaking on the ivory beach Jorn saw several of Inagi's versions of sand crabs scurrying back and forth along the beach almost like they were playing tag.

"Wait here," he told Kalina as she crouched down upon sand. Without waiting for her to answer the young hunter grabbed a fist sized stone and went in pursuit of the crustaceans.

The sand crabs were not worthy foes in this fight for survival. In only a few minutes Jorn had chased down and crushed the shells of four of them. He carried these back to Kalina. The raw crab meat dinner tasted wonderful and filled the emptiness in their stomachs.

After their meal they could have rested then. They could have lain down merely enjoying the heat falling from above. But such was not the ways of Kalina and Jorn.

They had set out across the ocean and lost a friend along the way in the quest to find and free their people and to find Derek Walker. They could not rest until they accomplished these goals.

After their stomachs were filled Kalina and Jorn went to the edge of the beach where the lush forest met the sand.

Jorn spotted a large tree and after climbing it broke off a long straight thick branch. This he fashioned into a usable spear by rubbing the end of it into a sharp point using the same rock he'd bashed in the shells of the crabs with.

Kalina still had her stone knife tied in the sheath at her side. She busied herself with planning the next move in the search for Derek Walker and her captured people.

32.
Caught!

"Where do we go from here?" Jorn asked.

Kalina thought for a moment.

"Since the warriors who stole our people came across the Great Waters in huge floating things I would believe they live on the coast somewhere or they never would have had a reason to build the floating things to begin with."

She pointed toward the mountain.

"We cannot go far in that direction. The mountain comes right out into the Great Waters. It only makes sense to follow the coast up that way," Kalina said indicating the opposite direction away from the mountain.

Without ceremony Jorn picked up his newly made spear and the two of them began walking up the beach.

After they went quite a distance their stomachs began speaking to them again.

On this particular stretch of beach the sand crabs were well hidden and were not in the mood to come out to play. Jorn and Kalina moved into the forest that bordered the beach to hunt.

This stretch of jungle did not have the thick overgrown feel of the forests that bordered their village back in the land of Amura. The trees seemed smaller and younger and there was less undergrowth.

Jorn spotted a tree that had fruit that on the Outer-Earth we'd see as a cross between an apple and a banana. It was shaped like an apple but had meat inside tasting roughly like a banana.

He climbed the tree while Kalina looked for other things to eat closer to the ground.

Jorn picked and dropped to the ground six of the fruits. Kalina shouted that she'd just found a rabbit.

Jorn just shook his head at the ignorance of a medicine woman in the ways of hunting because he knew the instant Kalina raised her voice the rabbit would have bolted.

Kalina screamed, her voice ripping through the forest.

Jorn quickly scrambled down the tree. The fruit he'd dropped forgotten for the moment. He sprinted in the direction Kalina's voice came from.

Ten quick steps brought him sliding to a stop at the edge of a twenty foot deep pit with Kalina at the bottom and a dead rabbit beside her. Kalina was laying on the collapsed mat of leaves and sticks she had stepped on when going to pick up the rabbit.

She'd stepped into a trap.

Jorn looked down at her and saw that getting Kalina out of that deep hole was not going to be easy.

Kalina looked back up and opened her mouth to speak and other voices came from the side of the forest away from the beach.

Several men were speaking back and forth, coming straight toward her and Jorn.

In a hushed voice so that only Jorn could hear Kalina spoke, "Run. Hide."

Jorn knew there was no time to discuss anything.

He did as he was told.

33.
Take Me to Your Leader

Most of the common people of Xibalba wore drab looking robes that were originally white but had turned grey and dingy from never being washed. This was the kind of clothes me and my two new friends wore.

As an escaped slave I was most definitely a wanted man as were my liberators Slickman and Bub. Wearing these dirty non-descript long hooded robes we became instantly anonymous.

There was also something else about these robes that were really good. Weapons of any kind found on common citizens of Xibalba were strictly forbidden. This law was obviously aimed at preventing armed insurrections. There was no regular police force in the city. But soldiers from the ruler's army walked the city keeping order and enforcing whatever laws they felt like enforcing.

The one law they were most enthusiastic about was the weapons ban on everyone but the aristocracy or themselves. Upon spotting anyone possessing weapons the soldiers would confiscate the weapon and deal with that person any way they wanted to. Most times they executed the person on the spot.

Wearing dirty robes enabled us to walk the streets fully armed with a sword and a knife at our sides and do it undetected.

By the way, if you're wondering who the rulers of Xibalba are the city is what would be called on the Outer-Earth a Theocracy. A theocracy is a city ruled by its religious leaders.

In most of Inagi the Nyseks are feared with a superstitious dread. They are thought of as some sort of Strange Dark Gods that oversee everything and cause good or bad luck to come to everyone. In reality the only luck they seem to cause is bad luck. Everyone is scared to death of doing anything against a Nysek or it will bring calamity to you and everyone you care about.

It is also generally thought to be impossible to kill a Nysek. When you are chosen as one of their sacrifices then your doom is sealed and nothing can be done for you.

I had already proved that was wrong when I rescued Jorn.

In Xibalba not only was the city ruled by the representative of its religion, The Nysek Worship, but here a big fat Nysek sat on the throne doling out orders and accepting sacrifices at will.

The God-Ruler of Xibalba was referred to as The Dingir Xul. I don't know if he had a name. *Do any of these super-sized spiders have any names?* But whenever anyone mentioned his title everybody would bow their heads and look away in fear.

The Nyseks inspired mindless terror in just about all of the people of Inagi. The Dingir Xul being the biggest and meanest Nysek in Xibalba, everyone in his city trembled at the mere thought of him.

Everyone except for Slickman and But and me of course. There weren't any big-ass bugs anywhere that were going to scare us.

To live in fear, being ruled by big ugly spiders was an awful way to survive. This was the way that the people of Xibalba were existing.

All of this was explained to me as we made our way through the streets of Xibalba to see if Rico was at the Gladiator Arena.

Slickman and Bub had a small residence set up in the underground city. It was only a tent but in the underground that's all they needed. They were well stocked in swords and knives and loaned me whatever I wanted.

The streets of Xibalba were pretty much just drab and dreary. People went through the motions of living without any of the joyful enthusiasm you see in most big cities. I didn't hear any music as we walked across town through the various neighborhoods. I didn't hear any of the normal chatter and babble that accompanies bustling metropolitan areas.

There seemed to be a pall, a hush to everything almost like everybody was afraid to raise their voices and be heard.

I guess that's what living under a ruthless religious dictator does to people. The citizens of Xibalba, the ordinary people who lived on the surface were scared, plain and simple. They were afraid they might be noticed. To be noticed means that you have a voice, an opinion, that you are alive and are to be reckoned with. To be noticed by the rulers of Xibalba meant that you are a threat and all threats are instantly disposed of.

It was because of this general hush that we heard from a great distance the shouts of the crowd from the Gladiator Arena.

That seemed to be the one place where a raising of the voice was accepted. Fear as well as bloodlust are dominating emotions in the human species whether we like it or not.

*

The arena was huge. It reminded me of something out of an Old Roman 1950's Gladiator Epic. As we got closer I realized that there was no structure in this city that even approached the size and scope of this Coliseum.

The arena was constructed like a huge ten story high salad bowl with wood and brick beams lining the perimeter to provide support so that the walls of the bowl don't collapse outward.

There were wooden stairs and walkways placed at twenty foot intervals around the outside that lead up to different levels of seating for the audience of these Gladiator fights.

There was a wide lane circling completely around the Arena. People hurried to and fro on foot for whatever errands they were running.

There were no wagons or horses at all on that street. I was guessing this was the one road where only foot travel was allowed.

As we stepped out into the lane making our way across aiming at a walkway that lead to one of the lower levels of seating I asked Bub how we would know where to find Rico.

He answered, "While you were still sleeping off your Splotch I went asking the specific area that Rico likes to sit at. I was told he likes to be as close to the action as possible. That means he'll be likely to grab a seat as low to the arena floor as he can."

Slickman continued from there. "He should be fairly easy to spot. Rico always travels with a group of his men and they should be seated off by themselves. Other people know to leave him alone so they give him and his men a wide berth."

It was right then when the crowd inside the arena erupted in a loud ear-shattering shout, a roar that shook the ground and made the hairs on my arms tingle and seem to stand on end. I'd heard that kind of roar before when I'd been a prize fighter and knocked down an opponent.

Bub's face darkened.

He spoke and his voice was harsh, grim. "Someone just died."

"Yeah," Slickman said. "But it wasn't one of us. Let's make sure we don't meet the same end."

We crossed the street and entered the arena.

34.

Raw Bloodlust and Fear

As men died in the dirt of the arena floor there was a party going on all over the place among the audience watching the bloodshed from the stands. Wine, beer, splotch or whatever the hell it was, was being passed around among the raucous crowd. Most of the people in the stands were drunk and getting drunker by the moment.

There was yelling and screaming as pieces of meat and rough bread was munched on and prostitutes of both sexes and all races, even some four-armed green men and women performed all manner of sex acts out in the open for everyone to see. This seemed to be the place where all inhibitions and all the darker drives of the human race were being acted out at once.

Gluttony, drunkenness and wanton sex was performed in the stands while butchery took place on the arena floor for the entertainment of the mob.

At one end of the arena, one level removed from the killing floor was something that could be referred to as VIP seats. In a section guarded by at least ten spear-carrying soldiers sat a big black bulbous Nysek on a huge embroidered cushion. He was accompanied by a man standing beside him who appeared to be translating everything the Nysek said to two other richly garbed men who also sat on large cushions.

This looked to be the rulers of Xibalba out to take in the sites and enjoy watching their subjects get chopped up into little cutlets.

At the moment when we entered the arena there was a temporary lull in the action down in the red dirt of the killing floor as the bodies of three gladiators were dragged away by the legs by six adolescent slave girls. The thought ran through my mind, *"If they are willing to accept this as young as they are, what kind of life will they be willing to live as they get older?"*

I instantly answered the question myself when my inner voice spoke, *"They are slaves. They accept whatever life they are thrown into because they have no choice."* This deepened my resolve.

We made our way around the edge of the arena walking through the stands between the tiers of benches on a pathway specifically looking for a group of men seated off in a separate group away from everyone else.

Most of the audience was broken up into groups of twos or threes or fours so it wasn't very long before we spotted on the other side of the arena a group of twenty men sitting by themselves. They were eating, drinking, talking and cheering but they weren't as wildly out of control as the rest of the crowd.

In fact what they reminded me of was a military unit relaxing in a recreation room on their off time. These guys were going to have their fun but they weren't going to sacrifice the safety of their unit to do so.

We made our way around the auditorium as the crowd cheered, celebrated, fought and fornicated.

In the center of the arena floor the bodies of the slain gladiators had been dragged off and something new was being brought out. It looked like an eight foot round, with two foot tall sides, children's wading pool. The kind I'm talking about is made of plastic and is inflated to keep the water in the middle where the kiddies splash around.

This thing was colored black and couldn't have been made of plastic since there was no plastic to speak of anywhere in Inagi. Maybe it was made of animal skins. I really don't know what it was made out of.

This empty pool was placed in the center of the arena floor and a post was driven down through the center of it into the ground.

Just as I was beginning to wonder what the things purpose was, from the same gate they'd brought the weird little pool out of came racing several men on horses. These men had whips in their hands and made a line at one end of the arena floor.

With a shout from the Nysek's translator the horses and riders took off on a race circling around the pool cracking their whips and trying to knock the other riders to the dirt. It was less a race and more a running battle on horseback than anything else.

We pretty much ignored that and kept moving while the crowd went wild over the mayhem on horseback.

Bub pointed out Rico long before we got within shouting distance so I got a good look at him.

Since he was sitting down I couldn't tell how tall he was but Rico didn't look any larger that the men around him. He was average sized. But his body looked as hard as a rock. He was not wearing a robe but a short sleeved buckskin shirt. He had black hair and actually looked like he would be more at home in an Apache War Party than sitting in the middle of a run down city.

Rico saw us approaching before we met up with his group of men and waved us over.

Rico's men that were seated on his sides got up and found other seats. They knew he wanted to have words with us and moved out of the way.

This guy seems friendly enough. I thought as we passed among his men and took seats on the benches next to his.

While still watching the race and the beatings taking place Rico spoke. "I heard of your battle at the Green's Gate. Didn't I tell the two of you that we need to be subtle when we free slaves and bring in new citizens to my private city?"

"Yes you did," Slickman answered. "But this time we had no choice. They were about to kill him. He's a brave, good fighting man who was about to go down before far greater odds."

"I didn't ask for excuses," Rico said. "I ask for and receive loyalty and obedience."

Bub answered now by drawing his sword and laying it across his thighs so that Rico could see it and no one else. "Like you were already told, we will not leave a good man to be beaten to death. He was one against many. I would do the same again. If need be we would do the same again now."

Tension crackled in the air.

We heard but didn't see the soft scrape of white blades being drawn on all sides of us.

Well, maybe this guy isn't so friendly, I thought.

Me and Slickman drew our blades ready to spill blood, fight and if need be die out in the bright light beneath Ra as so many others in this arena had slaughtered and been slaughtered.

Then Rico laughed.

It was a goo laugh, loose like a joke shared among friends.

"And I would have done the same," he told all three of us. "The standing order for secrecy and stealth is to cut down on recklessness. But sometimes being bold is necessary."

All three of us and Rico's men let out our breaths and relaxed.

"Why are you here?" Rico asked and now this was my cue to speak.

"I want to propose a drastic change in the order of things in Xibalba," I said. "You have the men and the power to free the city and all the slaves here. You also can become ruler of Xibalba."

When my first statement was spoken I detected an agreement to what I proposed. It was an unconscious nodding of the head. But when I spoke of Rico becoming the ruler his face and eyes darkened.

"The Dingir Xul rules here," Rico spoke. "None can act directly against him or the wrath of the Gods falls down upon him. I fear no man but I do fear the Wrath of the Gods."

I looked to Slickman and Bub. They seemed just as perplexed as I was.

Rico went on. "The Gods cannot be killed as men may die. They are immortal. They are forever."

"You're talking about the Nyseks?" I asked.

"Of course," Rico answered. "There are no other Gods."

"I have killed Nyseks," I told him.

"That's blasphemy," Rico spoke. His voice almost came out like a whisper.

"It's the truth."

That was when the race, down to only two riders, was ended. One rider snapped his whip at the other's head and missed. His opponent did not.

The second rider's whip snaked out through the air with deadly accuracy. When it cracked it struck the other in the neck popping his head clean off his shoulders.

As blood shot up into the air the spectators leaped to their feet shouting. Rico did the same. The triumphant rider trampled the other rider into the dirt until the loser looked like a bundle of blood soaked rags.

As they dragged out the corpses from the race Rico turned to me.

His next words were astonishing.

"Prove to me what you say and I will throw the weight of all I control behind you. I have never heard of anyone claiming to have killed a Nysek. Either you are insane or telling the truth. If you tell the truth, then all of Inagi has been living a lie that needs to be corrected."

Rico was the kind of man who was a pragmatist. He needed to see something with his own two eyes to believe it to be so.

In just a few moments events would take place that would force me to prove what I claimed was no lie.

35.

The Kindness of Savage Gods

Slickman and Bub were relatively new to Xibalba and I had barely arrived in this city so there were many things, secrets, and the secret shame of the city that the three of us had no knowledge of.

We now learned the reason why that large, weird wading pool had been dragged out to the center of the killing field.

The big fat Nysek sitting on the huge cushion stood up on his eight legs. He stretched to his full height. Even all the way across the arena floor, seeing this big black shaggy spider the size of a large horse standing like that made the goose bumps spring up on my arms.

Spiders bring to the surface in most people a primitive fear that is unexplainable and uncanny. I am no different than most people. This spider produced in me a loathing basic to my nature.

When seeing any of these creatures I felt like turning and running in the other direction. Such a feeling struck me at that moment and I am sure everyone else in that audience felt the same.

The Nysek stood up on his eight legs then leaned back and waved his front two feelers in the air in a complicated pattern resembling a form of sign language. That's exactly what it was because next, the man beside the Nysek spoke for him.

"Because you have been good and loyal subjects," the man shouted. "The Dingir Xul has decided to allow you to witness the sacred ritual of the taking of the flesh. Behold, this is how a God feeds!"

Ten strong men came hurrying out of the open gate. Each of them carried a large wooden barrel over their straining backs. They went straight to the strange wading pool and dumped the contents of their barrels into the pool.

The liquid that flowed out of the barrels was thick and dark crimson. A breeze carried the smell of that viscous fluid to our nostrils. It was the stench of rotting meat.

The slaves had just filled that wading pool with what I had no doubt was human blood.

I looked around me and everyone, except for Slickman and Bub had their eyes turned down to their feet looking away from what was about to happen in front of them.

"What's going on?" I asked Rico since Slickman and Bub didn't seem to have a clue either.

With his eyes still cast downward and his voice cracking with emotion Rico spoke.

"This is our secret dishonor, Xibalba's and all of Inagi's secret shame. Watch and you will see the kindness of our Savage Gods."

As soon as the pool was filled the slaves went out the gate they'd entered through.

Now two strong men came marching back. Between them they dragged a struggling woman who was screaming and begging the entire way.

They forced her into the pool. As one held her she was bound to the pole sticking up in the center of the pool.

The Nysek on his throne-cushion waved his front two feelers in the air once more.

The man beside him pointed at one of the spear carrying guards and yelled the orders, "You, down there. Prepare the meal for our lord!"

Mindlessly the guard obeyed. He hurried down a short walkway and a gate directly in front of the Royal Seating was thrown open. The guard marched straight to the woman with his spear held out before him.

I leaned over toward Rico. My words came out harsh and strained. All of us knew what was coming and none of us liked it even one little bit. But of everyone in the arena only I, Slickman and Bub was acknowledging that something completely unacceptable was happening.

"You allow this to go on?" I asked Rico. "You can that be?"

"They are our Gods," he whispered back clearly ashamed of what was taking place. "They cannot be killed. They choose who lives and dies in Inagi."

"It would be better to be dead than to have to live with knowing you allow this to happen," I growled at Rico.

In the middle of the killing ground in the heart of the blood-filled wading pool, the guard stepped forward and with his spear slashed the leg of the woman bound to the pole. She screeched out a cry full of pain and fear.

"Fuck your Gods!" Slickman shouted standing up.

I was already moving, climbing over two rows of Rico's men that were between me and the arena floor. Leaping over the barrier I landed in the dirt. Ripping off the long robe I wore, I drew my sword.

A moment later I was joined by Slickman and Bub as we raced out to the pool of blood.

While running I glanced at the Royal Box but the Nysek, The Dingir Xul was not there. That wasn't my concern at that moment as I shouted at the guard menacing the woman, "Back off or die!"

He appeared strangely dazed and his eyes looked unfocused but he brought his spear up pointing it at me as I came at him.

That was all the invitation I needed.

I slapped the point of the spear to the side with my sword. Leaping forward I landed a left hook to his jaw that shattered bone and made teeth fly. As he fell to his knees, I ripped the spear from the guard's hands.

Sheathing my sword, I grabbed the guard by the hair of the head and slung him to the side out of the blood pool.

Bub was behind the girl. He cut her loose and carried her out of the pool.

"Blasphemy!" was shouted in the air by the man who'd been standing beside the Dingir Xul and shouting orders. He now shouted to the other guards who were slow to react to what was happening in front of them. "Kill the blasphemers!"

But event though there were nine guards set to come onto the killing ground to cut us into bite-sized nuggets for their God's snack I had a more pressing problem charging at me.

The Nysek; The Spider-God, The Dingir Xul charged, barreling in at me in what could only be described as a blood-rage. He was like a crazed eight-legged hungry as hell bull and now that I'd deprived him of his leisurely snack, he wanted to sink his teeth into me.

This thing moved so fast I had no time to react. He slammed into me with the force of an out of control Volkswagen. I flew from my feet landing on my back in the pool of blood. As the putrid greasy liquid closed over my face the Dingir Xul attacked.

He leaped up on my chest coming down with a force that threatened to shatter bones.

Somehow, for some reason I'm not sure of, maybe pure survival instinct, I kept a grip on the spear I'd ripped from the guard's hands. Now I flailed upward with my free hand and grabbed the first thing my fingers touched and squeezed with all the strength that I had.

I was under the thick soured blood so I couldn't see what I'd grabbed but it popped and squished in my fingers and thick goo flooded down over my arm.

The Dingir Xul squealed like a stomped on Sea Gull and rolled off me.

I came up out of the foul-smelling plasma gagging and spitting and saw the Dingir Xul rolling in the dirt beside the blood pool. One of his sets of eyes was destroyed. It was deflated, squeezed down to a dried-out prune looking thing from the glimmering orb it had been before. Evidently, all the eyes on one side of the head were actually one body part. When I'd popped one the fluid drained from all of them simultaneously.

The Dingir Xul was making mindless screeching noises that informed me that these creatures, The Gods of Inagi, most definitely felt pain.

It was rolling around so much in the dirt, kicking its legs in the air, flaying around in obvious distress that I almost could have felt sorry for the thing ... Almost.

Suddenly the Dingir Xul rolled over and came up on all eight of its legs. Standing at an odd angle to me the ugly, disfigured Nysek fixed me with a glare that was pure death itself. This thing didn't just want to kill and eat me. It wanted me to be alive during the entire process so I could feel every single bit and rip into my flesh.

The Dingir Xul wanted me to feel pain hundreds of times worse than what it had just felt and it wanted to be the deliverer of that pain.

How I knew this became obvious to me painfully fast. The Dingir Xul reached into my brain and put that image into the center of my mind.

I realized this when he leaped at me again because I'd never seen the Nysek move until he touched me the second time.

In this instance my automatic responses saved my life. While the Dingir Xul reached into my mind planting images that froze me, he had scuttled forward and leaped. My conscious mind saw the planted image. My unconscious mind, the primitive part that is all about survival and nothing else, saw what was really happening and made my arm raise the spear.

The Dingir Xul impaled himself on the tip of my weapon and had been moving so fast that he slid halfway up the shaft before he stopped.

My mind instantly cleared.

I flipped him over onto his back using the spear. Standing with my foot in the center of the huge spider I ripped the spear loose then stabbed down again into the enormous arachnid.

The legs jerked straight up into the air going stiff and quivering. He twitched once then all eight of his legs went slack.

I looked up from the dead thing below me in the pool of the blood of his victims.

"Your God is dead!" I shouted to everyone in the arena.

Everybody was staring at me now. Silence descended over the arena.

Slickman and Bub were facing off with the nine guards. The nine guards froze where they were uncertain of what to do next.

I looked over to Rico. He met my eyes.

"My men are now yours to command," Rico shouted across the killing field.

"It is time to free Xibalba," I shouted out to everyone.

That was followed by a deafening cheer from every corner of the arena.

36.
The Revolution

Even the guards were ready to join the revolt once they discovered the Nyseks were not the Gods they had thought them to be.

I wanted to question the man shouting the orders for the Nysek but never got the chance. As soon as he turned to flee the nine guards ready to fight to the death against Slickman and Bub, turned their attentions to him and gave chase.

Despite my shouts for them to only capture him the Dingir Xul's translator found himself impaled by more than six spears in short order.

Rico and his men met me in the middle of the arena.

"What would you have us do?" Rico asked.

"Spread the word far and wide that the Nyseks are only flesh and blood creatures like you and me," I told him. "Demonstrate it by attacking and killing them anywhere you find them. The first few times you might be able to surprise the Nyseks and it might be easy. After that they'll be ready. Expect them to fight like the cornered animals that they will be."

Rico grinned. "My men like a good fight."

"One other thing," I told him. "Tell all your men, never look into a Nysek's eyes. They can freeze you if you do that."

Rico turned to his men giving orders that they were to go and find every able bodied man in Xibalba to spread the word of what had happened here, then to start killing the Nyseks.

*

We found the citizens of Xibalba to be ready enthusiastic freedom fighters. As any leader of a revolution on the Outer-Earth could attest to a hungry beat-down population will turn on its oppressors in a heartbeat if they think they have even a glimmer of hope of taking over the reins of power and becoming part of the ruling class.

The Nyseks and their guards were attacked wherever they were found. Just as predicted, the first few Nysek assassinations were trouble-free. What appeared to be ordinary docile citizens walked past half-asleep guards, and then from beneath their robes they pulled knives, swords or clubs and with no warning attacked.

Taken by surprise those few assassinations went smoothly. But after the Nyseks were aware the revolution was underway the fight began and quickly got brutal.

*

As it turned out there were only three of the airships floating in the sky above Xibalba. There weren't enough of them to play an effective role in defending the city.

Fighting broke out in every street. Just making your way across the city became a battle for survival.

The entire city of Xibalba became one continuous riot where anything that was owned by the ruling class was attacked by swarms of people. Once the people found out they'd lived their entire lives under the lie of the Nyseks being Gods they wanted revenge and were hungry to take it.

While most people were short on possessing traditional weapons the objects they used in their everyday lives were now picked up and used to kill. Knives used for crafts and carving were turned to the task of killing and carving up guards and Nyseks. Blacksmith tools became bludgeons. Any heavy blunt object became a lethal weapon.

Rico's people flooded out of the underground helping take back and free the city they'd had to flee.

Even though Rico had said I could direct his men, he knew the city and I did not. I followed him on a running fight down streets seeking out and killing any guard that did not throw down their weapons. The Nyseks fled to a central temple.

The city fell quickly to its own citizens. That's how it is in revolutions. The attackers out-number defenders so much that they are overwhelmed.

After Rico lead a successful attack on the guard's barracks we turned our attentions on the only two remaining threats within Xibalba: The Temple of the Nyseks and Green Man Town.

When the fighting broke out the Green Men had simply closed their gates and retreated back into their private little city. They were known as fierce warriors and they really owed no loyalty to anyone other than themselves.

There would either have to be a peace negotiated with the Green Men or they would have to be driven from the city. Since the Green Men were a large and complicated problem it made sense to take care of the other problem first.

The Temple of the Nyseks would have to fall.

37.

The temple of the Nyseks

The Temple of the Nyseks was a huge glimmering pearl white shrine to the unquestioning loyalty and worship of the Spider Gods of Inagi.

Rising up out of the ground a full ten stories tall with an enormous sphere at its crown the temple reminded me of the Taj Mahal in its pure size and majesty. But that's where the similarity ended. Carved into the outside wall of the temple were repeated renderings of Nyseks attacking, tearing apart and eating humans.

Seeing this I was surprised that mind controlled or not, no one had fought back before now. But that was not a time for contemplating past inaction.

Docked to the top of the dome above the temple was one of Xibalba's air ships. Another looked to be approaching from a long distance off. I knew the one air ship meant the priests and Nyseks inside had an escape route. I didn't know what the approaching airship meant but knew it couldn't be anything good for us.

We had to act fast.

By the time we arrived with a force of one hundred to attack the temple they had slammed shut the door shut in their former worshipper's faces. The front door to the temple was a huge thick wooden double door easily ten feet across.

I ordered a group of four men to go and find a battering ram to knock the front door down.

It was precisely that moment when a man came running up to Rico. The man was out of breath and clearly was distressed.

"The Green Men have attacked," he gasped. "They've come out in ordered military formation and are taking over the part of the city around their gates. Anyone who doesn't submit immediately is put to the sword. We need help or all of us are going to die or be enslaved by the Green Men."

Evidently the Green Men had been waiting for an opportunity just like this one to strike and take control of Xibalba. Our revolt had provided them with that opportunity.

Rico now became the stern leader of men I knew him to be.

"I will leave you ten men," he said to me. "That should be more than enough to take this temple. Slickman and Bub, I need you with me. If I fall you are to take command of my forces. We'll meet again when the city is free."

He thrust his hand out and gave me a hearty handshake. Then Rico turned and gave orders for his force to follow him to meet the attacking Green Men.

The four men I sent for a battering ram came back driving a horse drawn wagon. The wagon was heavy duty, constructed for hauling clumsy weighty loads like building materials.

It was perfect for what we needed.

*

After unhooking the horse and letting him run free I had the four-wheeled cart positioned in front of the temple doors.

Jumping up on the wagon I shouted to anyone inside who could hear, "If you open the doors now and surrender all humans will be spared their lives. Otherwise we are going to knock these doors down and everyone inside will die."

From a top window a shout came back. "What you do is blasphemy. You will all die horrible deaths under the fangs of our lords the Nyseks. But you will not die quick. They will keep you alive and in pain so that you will know true terror."

It was the ravings of a madman.

I jumped down from the wagon and gave the order to knock the door down.

Twenty strong hands took hold of the sides and rear of the heavy wooden wagon. All of us pushed with everything we had and by the time the wagon met the door we were at a full run.

Driven by the strength of ten strong men the wagon smashed into the obstacle stopping us. With a loud crash the wood of the door splintered and flew inward.

Whipping my sword out I went to leap over the battered wagon and ruined doors and someone grabbed me on the shoulder from behind.

I spun around ready to fight to the death if need be.

It was Jorn that stood before me.

38.
The Temple Fight

I pulled Jorn to me and gave him a bear hug but there was no time for extended greetings when a battle lay ahead just on the other side of the Nysek Temple's threshold.

"What are you doing here?"

"They have Kalina," Jorn answered. "She's there." He pointed to the second airship that was swiftly approaching the temple dome.

I went a little insane then.

Leaping up on top of the wagon I ran its full length and jumped over the doors we had just battered down.

My one single-minded thought was to get to the roof as quickly as possible anyway that I could.

As I landed on the rubble strewn marble floor I was already scanning the room for a direct way upward. Across a broad entrance chamber was exactly what I sought, a wide set of marble steps that lead to the next floor where it branched off in two directions. Both of those branches of stairways were upward spiral staircases.

On the marble floor between me and the marble steps waited two hissing Nyseks.

They both leaned back waving their front feelers at me in some strange complicated patterns no doubt meant to hypnotize me into immobility. Since I was a man on a mission and that mission was to save the woman that I loved their attempt at freezing me had the exact opposite effect.

I leaped forward and slicing left to right sheered off the foremost Nysek's feelers.

His blood spewed green and sticky into the air. He screeched out a cry that made the hair stand stiff up on my neck. I stifled his cry with a thrust of my blade straight into the center of his head.

A blur of movement from in front told me the other Nysek was moving. On instinct I ripped the sword upward parting the first huge spider's skull and skewered the second Nysek as it dropped out of the air from overhead.

I didn't take time to wonder at these creatures' incredible leaping ability before ripping the blade loose and splitting the Nysek open from head to tail ending his life in a squeal.

Shoving the thing to the side I charged up the marble steps.

Three priests were on the right hand spiral stairway trying to block anyone from going up. So I figured that's got to be the way to the roof.

"Get the hell out of my way!" I yelled. "Don't you see you don't mean anything to the Nyseks other than as food or slaves?"

The first priest was a bald-headed, pot bellied, fat-faced guy who held out a jeweled scepter and threw the curse at me, "Get thee to Nebiroth foul demon!"

I didn't know what or where Nibiroth was but that didn't matter to me. *This idiot's trying to protect huge spiders that eat people and he called me a demon,* I thought as I wrenched the scepter from his hands and knocked him over the railing to the floor below.

With a cry of, "Our lords will protect us," the two other priests fled up the spiral staircase with me in pursuit.

I reached the top of the stairs just as the door was being slammed shut. Diving forward I was barely able to thrust my sword blade in the doorway and prevent it shutting.

My sword blade shattered but the door was not able to be latched from the other side as I kicked it wide open.

The two priests were climbing into the docked airship as I sheathed what was left of my sword stepping out onto the temple roof.

39.

Into the Sky

Seeing an airship up close for the first time I found it was exactly what it looked to be from the ground. It was a huge gondola that had three platforms set up at regular intervals, one at each end and one in the middle, with fires burning on those platforms.

Above the fires were three separate bound together silk bags held to the gondola by thick silken ropes. The bags were being inflated by the hot air produced in a controlled manner by the fires in the platforms. The fire came from what looked to be huge glass oil lamps.

I was guessing the fire could be increased or decreased by the turning of a crank at the top of a huge man-sized glass oil barrel. The crank either extended or withdrew a three foot wide burning wick. The more the wick was cranked out, the bigger the fire became.

The airship was tethered to the roof of the temple by a grappling hook and another of those silk ropes. The craft was tugging on the anchor line as cranks were turned and the fire was increased.

As I came out onto the roof the other airship was maybe one hundred feet away and was approaching fast. It was too far to even think of jumping but close enough for me to still be able to see that Kalina was tied and bound to a central pole rising out of the middle of the airship.

My heart went out to Kalina as that airship slowed its approach to the temple. These people had no radio or any other way to pass messages from a distance. Although they could see from overhead that the city was in chaos, they had no way of knowing exactly what was going on or how bad it was for their side.

But just how dire the situation was for them was being demonstrated by the attempt at escape of the airship docked on this roof.

As the temple's airship rose up higher someone leaned out over the rail and gave the mooring rope a sharp shake. That was a well practiced movement. All it took was one try and the mooring hook shook loose. The airship was free.

For me the choice was clear as the temple's airship followed by the dangling mooring rope rose up in the air removing any opportunity I had of rescuing Kalina.

I only had one chance and only a few seconds to act.

Darting out of the doorway I chased the dangling grappling hook and as it rose over the open space of the street below I leaped out and grabbed onto the rope with both hands.

For one very, very long moment it seemed like my fingers would give out and slip loose from the perilous grip I had. But with Kalina depending upon the strength in my hands my grip upon the grappling hook became like steel.

I climbed that rope like a man possessed and actually if anyone has ever been possessed of any spirit higher than himself, at that moment, I was. The spirit that I was possessed of was the undying love that a man can have for his woman. When a man is possessed of that spirit and his woman is in danger then nothing is considered impossible for him to save her, and he will do anything to make sure his woman is safe.

I climbed hand over hand up that slick silk rope until I was able to shove one foot into the bend of the grappling hook and push upward to stand straight up. As I was climbing I could hear the wooden, dull clunks of a wood crank being turned as the teeth of the wheel clicked past.

The rope I was on was being drawn upward as I climbed.

I was almost at the rail when from above I heard, "Something's got hold of this. Are we snagged on the roof?"

A face was thrust out over the rail just above my head and peered down at me.

At the same moment the face appeared I had just grasped the rail with my left hand to pull myself up. Now I lunged upward and caught the man leaning out by the hair.

Jerking with all I was worth I slung him toward me over the rail. He fell screaming to the city streets far below.

Pulling myself up and into the boat I fell onto the deck of the airship.

There were two Nyseks sitting on cushions positioned between the fires. Five white robed priests were attending the flames. I guess some people just can't get their minds around the idea that blind loyalty is the same as signing yourself up to being a willing slave.

The priests and Nyseks must have all figured they were home free the instant their airship took flight because two of the slave-priests actually screamed in fright.

One of them grabbed up a spear and ran at me.

I jumped to the side as he lunged forward. He missed with his spear thrust. I grabbed the spear, jerked forward and kicked straight out catching him in the gut with my foot.

The priest stumbled back and went over the rail kicking, twisting and screeching.

The other airship was almost on top of us.

Down at my feet was a coil of rope with a grappling hook at one end and the other end tied to a notch in the rail.

Without thinking, hoping against hope to snag it on anything I grabbed the grappling hook and blindly pitched it at the approaching airship.

Then the other four slave-priests were rushing at me.

40.

Tangled

The four slave-priests were not seasoned warriors. They were delusion-filled holy-men accustomed to feeding frightened women and no doubt children to their Spider Gods as snacks. But four of anything rushing at you with weapons on their hands makes for some anxious moments.

All four of them had swords.

I had the spear that I'd taken off the guy I'd kicked over the side.

They came rushing in at me with their swords, two held very low in front of them, like they were practicing good safety in the kitchen and two up high like they were looking to chop wood.

I slashed left to right catching one short guy across the throat and the man next to him across the chest and through his right arm. The one slashed across the throat went down gurgling on his blood. The other guy screamed, dropped his sword and beat a swift retreat to the rear of the airship.

The two behind them seeing what happened to their friends didn't rush in so fast.

I didn't have time for a long tactical fight so whirling my spear up overhead then drawing my arm back I hurled the spear full force into the chest of one of the priests.

The spear skewered him like a piece of pork on a shish-ka-bob. He stumbled backward all the way to the middle of the boat, fell over one of the Nyseks still resting on his cushion, and smashed into the central glass oil barrel knocking it over.

There was a sudden, ***whoosh*** ... as the glass barrel shattered and the oil all caught fire at once.

The Nysek on the far side of the barrel was splashed and covered with flaming oil. He screeched and screamed and cooked. Let me tell you, if there is one smell that I may never get out of my nostrils to my dying day it is the smell of roasting Nysek.

It was awful. The smell was somewhere between brownies left in the oven and forgotten that burned to cinders and pan fried shit. There really was nothing else to compare it to and if I ever smell anything worse, I will know I have finally entered hell.

The stench made me want to vomit. But I didn't have time for that.

I grabbed the sword up from the guy whose throat I'd slashed and faced off with the remaining slave-priest.

He grinned and the light of insane religious fervor shown in his eyes. He raised his sword up over his head, spreading his arms looking upward to ... I have no idea who or what he looked up to.

"It is better to serve in our heaven," the slave-priest screamed at the top of his lungs. "Than to rule in their hell!"

Then he ran to the side of the ship and leaped overboard just one more religious nut-case who couldn't handle the truth when it stared him in the face.

My one remaining opponent on this airship, the last Nysek was up and off of his cushion. He was hissing and slowly advancing upon me. I guess he had finally figured out it was time for him to do his own fighting.

That was the moment the airship lurched to the side throwing me to the deck and up against the rail.

I grabbed the rail as flames increased tenfold by burning oil from the smashed glass barrel suddenly spread and filled all three hot air bags almost to the point of bursting. The airship was jerked upward by the increase in hot air and shot straight skyward toward the inner sun of Inagi, toward awaiting Ra.

What made the airship tilt sideways was a combination of two things. The fire had reached the side of the boat, burning through a rope tethering the ship to that side of one of the gas bags, and my grappling hook attached to the railing on the other side of the airship snagged the airship Kalina was held prisoner on.

So not only was I hanging sideways on an out of control airship hurtling straight upward toward a fiery doom in the flames of the Hollow Earth's Central Sun but I was dragging the woman I loved right along with me.

41.

Into the Fire

Both airships, mine and the one Kalina was imprisoned on, flew straight up into the sky. We ascended fast, faster than I would have thought possible.

Maybe the airships were lighter than I could have imagined. Maybe we were caught in an updraft, or maybe something unseen was drawing us upward. I didn't know and I do have to confess at that moment I wasn't contemplating the mysteries of physics that have to do with lighter than air flight.

I was only riding the ride that I'd bought a ticket on and was trying to figure a way to get me and the woman I love out of the amusement park.

The Nysek that was sharing the ride with me was now hanging on the side of the airship as the flames had spread to cover most of the deck.

The slave-priest that had run to the other end of the ship was long gone probably tossed over when the ship lurched to the side.

We flew upward and the city of Xibalba shrank beneath us. At first the buildings and streets had looked like a play city beneath us. But that shrank down to look like a grayish blotch with squiggly lines through it. Then that shrank to just look like a grey patch in the middle of some dull green surrounded by greener green bordered on one side by some of the bluest blue I'd ever seen.

We flew upward and as we flew I climbed to a better position so I could at least sit on the rail and not have to hang on for dear life.

I didn't see the Nysek anymore. I'd taken my eyes off him while I was climbing around. I'm not sure where he went. I hoped he wasn't climbing around the underside of the airship and was getting ready to come up and attack me. If he was, there wasn't anything I could do about it anyway.

Now that I had a few moments I took stock of the situation: I had lost the spear. My sword was gone. But I did have a dagger in my belt.

That was good to know.

The air was getting thicker as we went higher. Guess things worked different in Inagi than they do on the Outer-Earth.

Above was a globe of fire that we flew towards. Below us was the inside bowl of the Inner-Earth. In some strange way it almost felt as if we were falling as we went up.

I could see the curvature of the disc of Ra as we got closer. It reminded me of seeing the roundness of the Earth whenever I'd flown in an airplane. Except that this time there was a few differences.

The dome above on the Outer-Earth had been the blue sky or night time stars. Here it was green and blue smears. Also, the world below on the Outer-Earth had not been a flaming inferno.

That was really the one major difference that concerned me.

We flew upward and there was nothing I could do about it.

The flames grew larger and brighter and hotter and there was nothing I could do about that either. It really sucked not having control over anything going on. But that's just the way it was.

I had just about resigned myself to the fate of a flaming end and believe it or not, had started figuring that Kalina cooking up quickly was better than being fed to a spider when the Nysek reached around the edge of the bottom of the ship and tried to grab me. To be more accurate, the Nysek tried to skewer me on the pointy end of one of his long front legs.

I scuttled to the side, sliding along the rail I was sitting on. Then when I had secure seating again, jerked out the knife and slashed at the leg poking at me.

The Nysek had went to the underside of the ship and crept around. He now backed off when he found I was still armed because I'd gotten one good slash in on that poking leg.

Climbing downward more toward the deck of the ship, but still away from the flames I put as much distance between the Nysek and myself as was possible.

That was when we hit the wall of flame of Ra. Or rather, we passed through something that seemed to be burning.

There was one moment of blinding intense heat. The hair got singed off my arms and legs and some from the top of my head. Then we were through it, whatever it was.

We were flying upward even faster it seemed toward a massive strange-shaped pulsating silvery ball with all kinds of pockmarks and holes in its surface.

I saw things fly past us almost as if we were in a race. The things were weird. Things like rocks, kitchen utensils, and a steel sword, even a car went flying upward past us.

All of the stuff flying upward faster than us seemed to be made of metal.

I didn't have much time to consider what all that meant because with a smash and crunch we crashed into the side of the pulsating silver ball that was Ra.

I was knocked loose of the ship and slammed into something extremely hard. Darkness came down over me like a mortician's shroud.

*

Wandering through darkened echoing corridors I walked through a midnight world of unending black caves.

A voice spoke in the distance, chanting, whispering.

"John Carter, Mike Hammer, Conan, Matt Dillon, Lone Ranger, John Dark, Sam Spade, Philip Marlowe, Tarzan, Harry Callahan, Derek Walker ..." the chant-whisper was an unending listing of names, some of which I recognized. I sure recognized my own.

I walked on. I moved toward the sound of the chants, the sounds of the whispers.

Then all at once, there was a bright light before me, a glowing ball of white light that filled my vision, filled my eyes.

I covered my eyes but the white light burned through into me, into my brain, into my consciousness.

"All of them are you and you are all of them," a gentle voice spoke that bore all the way to the center of my mind.

"Mankind in all the different worlds, in all the infinite universes needs to be shown the path ... to greatness.'

I awoke to kind myself lying face down on a cold steel floor.

42.

Death Itself

I sat up on the cold steel floor.

Behind me was an open doorway leading outward. In the distance the smokeless flames burned keeping a never-ending vigilant life-force flowing out toward Inagi. For all I knew this was the same energy that caused life to flourish on the Outer-Earth as well. But that force seeping out through the very ground itself to the Outer-Earth would be weaker than it was here.

Maybe that was the reason why I had never seen any old people since I came to Inagi. Old people were unknown here. Maybe they didn't exist at all where the life-force was this strong. Maybe life didn't just wear out where it was close to its source.

That was something I may never know for certain.

In front of me was a steel corridor that looked to have many passages, too many to count, leading off to both sides.

I stood and went to the doorway and looked out.

Almost level with the opening I stood at was the smashed remains of the airship I'd ridden on. It was flattened and crushed to the side of this huge silver sphere. The silk hot air bags were flat and lay crumpled against the side of Ra like unmade bed sheets.

Evidently I'd been lucky enough to be thrown clear, right inside this doorway.

The Nysek hadn't been so lucky.

Three of his legs stuck out from under the bottom of the ship where it had smashed into the steel wall.

A little down from that that I saw the airship Kalina had been on. It was also smashed to the side of this massive silver globe.

Other objects were stuck to the side of this huge pulsating silver sphere. I saw bits of machinery, weapons, a motorcycle in the distance, even a small silvery airplane. All of the things stuck to the side of Ra seemed to be metal.

That is, all of the objects except for our two airships.

One of the objects affixed to the side of the globe was close enough for me to kneel down and grab hold of. Since that object looked just like a Roman short sword it was something I definitely wanted and had a use for.

I kneeled at the edge of the door and leaned out over the open space. Reaching down I grasped the handle of the sword attempting to pull it to me.

The thing wouldn't budge. It felt like it was welded in place.

Looking closely I saw why I would never be able to free that sword. Wherever it touched the silvery sphere that part of the sword seemed to have dissolved and become a part of the metal it was touching.

It was strange but true.

Ra, this silver sphere was absorbing all the metal it came in contact with. It was drawing to itself and absorbing all the metal that came into Inagi.

The question sprang to my mind; our ships are not made of metal, what is holding them in place?

These were riddles inside of riddles with no easy answers.

There was no sign of Kalina or anyone else on board the other airship. More than likely everyone on board had been knocked loose when it had crashed. Kalina had probably been thrown loose also. All of them were more than likely still falling to the ground far below.

But while there is life, there is still hope.

Until I saw Kalina's crushed, lifeless body I was never going to give up looking for her.

There was an opening into the silver sphere right beside that ruined airship. I would search this world made of steel until I found that opening and made sure there was no chance at all that Kalina was here.

I moved into the steel corridor, my footsteps making dull shuffling noises as I walked.

The corridor was well lit but I could see no source for the illumination. The light seemed to come from everywhere. Twenty paces up, was one of those side passages. Looking into that side corridor it appeared to be going down.

I took that passageway and the corridor did have a downward slant. It descended and curved around one way, then another, then back again upon itself several times until I wasn't sure what direction I was heading in, in relation to where I'd started.

I was just about to go back and retrace my steps when I came to a side passage that led down a very short corridor into what seemed to be an open room. For the pure need of seeing something different than these shiny, steel walls I traversed that passage and stepped into the open chamber.

The room was an extremely large, fifty feet across, hexagon. There were six doors leading off into hallways identical to the one I'd just come out of. The walls of the chamber were made of the same cold steel as the corridors I just walked.

But that's where the similarities to those hallways ended.

In the center of this room was a strange glowing, pulsating crystal chandelier. This hanging, throbbing crystal almost appeared to be organic. It had the look of a crystal that had naturally formed in a cave far below ground.

For some strange reason that I could not fathom I had the compulsion to touch that pulsating crystal. It was like the feel of the crystal promised warmth and comfort like a mother's breast or the soft skin of a woman.

I wanted to touch that crystal, to feel it, to know it, and be known by it.

But as it turned out I was already known by whatever controlled this world.

The crystal had been giving off a cold white glow when I'd entered the chamber.

I stepped forward, reaching my hand up knowing the crystal was too high for me to touch but just wanting to feel closer.

The thing's white glow changed to a soft pleasant warm yellowish orange. The light reached out and touched me, bathed me in a wonderfully refreshing, replenishing, healing glow.

My mind was filled with a great intoxicating feeling of well being. I felt, for the very first time a sensation of being one with the universe, as though I was a part of the family of all things.

Images danced all around me floating in the air, images, and mini-movies of heroic deeds done by all types of people. Black, white, male, female, from Earth, from other planets, it didn't matter. These images showed people putting their lives at risk, their every existence in jeopardy to save someone else.

This display of heroism was awesome to behold. It was uplifting and beautiful.

Without thinking I spoke the only question I could voice at that moment.

"Are you God?"

I don't really believe I expected to be answered. It's the kind of question that many people ask when they stare up at the vastness of space on a clear starry night.

But I was answered.

It was the same voice that spoke to me when I'd been knocked unconscious. It was the same voice that had whispered to me several times in my life and most times been ignored.

The gentle voice spoke to me. "Each of mankind has within them what I am. I am one of many. I am you and you are me. Of the millions of universes all are one."

A scream ripped through the air and all the images of heroic deeds being played out around me vanished.

The scream was a woman's voice.

It was Kalina's voice.

The source of the scream was the doorway directly to my left.

I turned and raced down that corridor. After running perhaps fifty paces the hallway took a sharp turn to the left.

Sliding around the corner I came to a long straight hallway. The corridor ended at the open air outside of Ra with the smokeless flames burning in the distance.

At the end of the hallway was a big furry gray-haired Nysek and two of the slave-priests. At their feet lying unconscious was Kalina.

The two slave-priests were chanting something as they hovered over Kalina. One of them had out a long dagger that he waved in elaborate patterns in the air.

The Nysek standing on all of his eight legs swayed from side to side with the rhythm of the chants.

I ripped my knife out once again and shouted at the three, "Stop what you're doing now! Harm her and I'll rip you to pieces."

They paused and I charged.

I covered the distance between them and me in maybe three seconds that felt like an hour.

The first slave-priest was the one waving the knife in the air. I stepped into him and knocked him sprawling with a left hook that would have downed an ox.

The next slave-priest had drawn a short bone sword. He took a swipe at me.

I stepped back then faked a lunge with my knife.

The slave-priest went to block the thrust that never happened by raising his sword up too high.

I kicked him so hard in the nuts it actually raised him up off the floor. His eyes bulged out and he made a noise like he was trying to shit an entire set of old Encyclopedia Britannica's, Year Books and all.

I stepped forward and ended his pain with two thrusts of my knife.

The shaggy gray Nysek hissed at me then leaped.

He knocked me from my feet and climbed on top of my chest. I actually saw the teeth snap together as this massive arachnid readied to end my existence.

I jammed my knife into his mouth and twisted it around in a circle like I was trying to stir some seriously thick cake mix. The Nysek didn't like that one bit.

He jumped backward, screeched and turned away.

That was my invitation to hop onto his back. I did and discovered why I never even liked watching the rodeo. Trying to hold onto something bucking and jumping up and down like its gone crazy is not pleasant and easy to do.

After almost flying off twice I slammed the knife down into the Nysek's back.

It stiffened, froze and fell over.

I rolled off and stood up.

Kalina moaned. She was unbound and slowly sat up.

Relief flooded over me.

I extended my arms and a sharp stabbing pain hit me from behind. I looked down and the point of a short sword was extending forward out of my chest like I was growing some strange new horn from the center of my body.

Extreme pain emanated from that blade sticking all the way through me. I went to grasp it, to push it backward out of my body and couldn't even lift my arms.

My knees buckled. I collapsed to the cold steel floor.

Darkness washed over me as I heard Kalina's scream once more.

43.

A Little Assistance

I fell forward into a black pit without a bottom, forward into the dark nothingness of forever sleep. There was no up. There was no down. There was only falling, endless ... pitch blackness, falling.

"You will not be allowed to die," the gentle soothing voice spoke to me as I sank into the blackness. "Your time of rest has not yet come."

I opened my eyes and Kalina was like a mad-woman. She waded into the slave-priest who'd left his sword jammed inside me like an escapee from the most demented Kung-Fu fantasy that any martial arts nut-case had ever dreamed up.

The slave-priest never stood a chance.

With a scream the would have shattered all the windows in a skyscraper she hit, kicked, elbowed, kneed, bit and generally just beat the living shit out of the slave-priest. Kalina overwhelmed the guy with pure ferocious aggression.

She drove him around the hallway with her kicks and punches until his back was to the open air of Inagi. Then Kalina kicked him with what looked like a classic Jean Claude Van Dam spinning thrust kick in the gut, and knocked the slave-priest out the doorway careening to his doom miles below us to the hard dirt of Inagi.

While that was going on, and it was really fun to just lay back and watch someone else kick-ass for a change, I saw the blade sticking out of my chest slowly recede backward. I was lying on my side so the blade slid out and fell to the floor at my back.

As soon as the slave-priest was sent on his long fast journey home Kalina ran to me with open arms.

I sat straight up as Kalina reached me.

I took her in my arms and crushed her to me in a passionate embrace. After covering her face with kisses that she eagerly returned Kalina drew back.

"But you are dead," she spoke slowly with wide open amazed eyes. "I saw the blade come out the front of you, through your chest."

We both looked down then and saw the wound, the slice in my skin, had sealed back up like a zipper drawn shut. Blood covered my chest from where it had spurted from the wound. The blood seemed to be absorbed back inside my skin, like my flesh had become a highly absorbent sponge. As for the wound itself, it faded from a slice in the skin, to a pinkish raw looking raised spot. Then that flattened and faded out to nothing.

Within what I would estimate was twenty seconds my chest looked like it had never had a sword run through it from behind.

"You are a very special man," Kalina breathed.

"I didn't do anything," I answered.

The voice, the gentle strong voice spoke again. This time Kalina heard it as well.

"The two of you have your destiny to fulfill," it told us. "Go now. This world needs you."

"But how," Kalina asked, "Our airships are destroyed?"

"One is restored," the voice spoke and despite many other questions we asked, the voice of Ra would give no more answers.

*

The airship outside the doorway was as it had been before it crashed into the silver sphere. In fact, it was in better shape than it originally had been.

I took Kalina's hand and lead her to the airship and although neither of us knew how to guide this craft it seemed to know where to go.

We sailed off down to Inagi in search of our friends and new adventures.

A Word from the Chronicler of This Tale:

The people of Inagi call me Lincar. Some call me The Man from the Mountain.

*

Indeed, it seems as though the airship that Derek Walker and Kalina rode upon knew exactly where to go. It sailed the skies of the Inner-Earth until it came to rest just outside the cave I make as my home in the side of a secluded cliff.

I am a chronicler. I always have been. I love to hear and tell a good tale.

So when two travelers arrived on my doorstep I insisted that they share their tale with me. It is a requirement I make of all my visitors.

And what a story it was!

I have now shared this tale with you.

But there is more to come, much more.

There is the tale of Jorn in the city ravaged by revolution and torn by war from within its own walls.

There is the tale of the freeing of the rest of the people of Amura from slavery by the Nords.

And there is the tale of a friend thought lost forever ... found.

Derek Walker and his mate Kalina have promised to come back and visit me carrying these new tales.

When I know them, so shall you.

Finis!
For Now
Lincar